THE BODY IN THE CANOLA

At that moment, the sound of vehicles coming up the driveway reached them and they both stood up. Two plumes of dust indicated the progress up the driveway. A moment later, Kate heard car doors slamming and the sound of voices rose above the stalks of canola.

They waited until Friesen and Olinchuk emerged from the field and joined them. The minute their gazes fell on the dead girl, Friesen took a sharp breath in and stopped. His face paled and he looked down at his feet.

Olinchuk, by comparison, swept the entire area with his gaze, finally narrowing down on the girl. He examined her from head to toe, and Kate was willing to bet that he would be able to recreate the scene in a drawing if called upon.

BOOKS BY THE AUTHOR

Mendenhall Mysteries series:
The Shoeless Kid
The Tuxedoed Man
The Weeping Woman
The Untethered Woman
The Forsaken Man
The Wronged Woman

The A'lle Chronicles series:
Backli's Ford
Epidemic

Standalone novels:
Ghosts of Morocco
Identity Withheld
Jilimar
Kirwan's Son
Obeah
On Her Trail
Shelter

THE**WRONGED**WOMAN

Marcelle Dubé

FALCON
RIDGE
PUBLISHING

THE WRONGED WOMAN

Falcon Ridge Publishing
The Wronged Woman (Book 6 of the Mendenhall Mystery series)
Copyright © 2021 by Marcelle Dubé
Cover image copyright © Andrii Medvediuk via Shutterstock
Cover copyright © 2021 Marcelle Dubé and Falcon Ridge Publishing

ISBN: 978-1-987937-30-5

Falcon Ridge Publishing
marcelle.dube@gmail.com

For Éric, Josée, Michèle, and Diane,
who know me well but love me anyway.

THE**WRONGED**WOMAN

Book 6 of the Mendenhall Mystery Series

by

Marcelle Dubé

CHAPTER 1

Kate stood in front of her office window, hands clasped behind her back, staring past the detachment parking lot to the Church of the Nazarene across the street. It was a little cool for August but the sunlight felt warm on her face and the leaves hadn't started turning yet. It had rained last night, leaving everything smelling fresh and clean.

It looked so peaceful. So calm.

So temporary.

A rap on the doorjamb brought her back. She turned to see Rob McKell, her deputy chief, standing in the doorway. His short-sleeved uniform shirt looked a size too big for him still, but otherwise, he looked fully recovered from the sniper attack that almost took his life nearly a year ago.

"You know you can't hide in here," he said conversationally.

"I'm not hiding," she objected, heading for her desk. "I'm still on duty until they get here."

His left eyebrow rose eloquently.

"Shouldn't you be home to meet them?"

"Rose will call me when they leave Winnipeg," said Kate. "That gives me plenty of time to head home."

Her sister Rose and Rose's husband John, Kate's mother and her beau Fred, and Kate's brother Charlie were landing in Winnipeg in less than an hour. There they were renting a camper and driving to Mendenhall. Kate's nephew, Sean, was already here.

Mom and Fred would be staying with Kate, and Rose and John would be staying with Kate's niece, Amanda. Sean and Charlie would camp out in Kate's driveway.

Somewhere, deep inside, a tendril of panic began to unfurl.

There would be noise. There would a stressed-out Rose to manage, an elderly mother to protect, a brother she hadn't seen in four years to get reacquainted with... and Sean, well, she hardly knew the boy. The last time she'd seen him, he'd been seventeen and graduating from high school.

And then there was Alfred Stilwell, Mom's beau. Kate still didn't know how she felt about that.

A week of them all in Mendenhall, culminating with Amanda and Trepalli's wedding.

She wasn't sure she would survive.

"Trepalli's family is already here," said Rob helpfully, settling onto one of the hardback chairs she set out for visitors. "They want a tour of the detachment."

Oh, Lord.

It wasn't just her family—Amanda's family—it was Trepalli's family, too. And there were a lot more of them.

She wanted to see her family, she did. But she didn't know if she could handle seeing them all at once, on top of dealing with Trepalli's family, too.

"I don't see why they didn't just elope," she muttered before she could stop herself.

Rob's grin got even wider.

"It a wedding," he said. "Dancing and food, and everyone will cry at the vows. Just watch. It'll be fun."

She gave him The Look. "You sound just like Bert."

Bert, her "boyfriend," if a 55-year-old woman could be said to have a boyfriend, was safely in Winnipeg, where he was the deputy chief of the Winnipeg Police Services. He would come in tonight for the dinner, then scurry back to Winnipeg until the wedding, leaving her to deal with the chaos.

"Bert's a smart man," said Rob solemnly.

"You know, Rob, not everybody likes weddings as much as you do."

It came out sharper than she had intended but Rob just grinned again. He'd been married three times and divorced three times. He'd been seeing that geologist, Jillian, for a while now and it wouldn't surprise Kate to hear that they were going to get married, too.

But maybe he was learning caution.

"The monthly reports are filed," said Rob, aptly judging that she'd had enough teasing. "I got a call from the dealership and the new SUV is arriving in Winnipeg today. They say it'll be retrofitted by next week."

Well, now. That was good news. She was surprised the mayor and council had agreed to it, but even they had to see that the squad cars were getting old. Some of them spent more time in the shop than on patrol.

"I'll be leaving now," said Rob, getting up. "I shouldn't be gone more than a few hours. I'll see you tomorrow."

Kate nodded and stood up, too. Today was the monthly meeting of southern Manitoba deputy chiefs. Brandon was hosting this month. The meeting always started with lunch before getting down to business. There often wasn't anything important on the agenda but Kate saw the value in meeting face to face. It was a good way to build relationships, relationships that came in handy sometimes.

"All right," she said, following him into the duty room. As Rob went to his office to grab his bomber jacket and keys, she nodded at Charlotte, her admin assistant seated at her desk by the only window in the duty room.

A plastic hair band pushed the girl's glossy brown curls away from her face. An unaccustomed frown warned Kate not to disturb her. Charlotte was smart, capable, and hard-working. She was also one of the most evenly pleasant people Kate had ever worked with—unless she was working on the financial reports.

Kate turned away and looked at Martins, who was sitting at the duty desk, an elevated platform that overlooked the outside door and hallway through a large pass-through. He was focused on the computer, his shoulders slightly hunched. Kate peered at the screen and almost sighed. He was updating the detachment's web page.

"What's there to update?" she asked.

Martins straightened and turned around to look at her. As always, she had to suppress a smile when she saw his face. Nick Martins had spent a lot of time outdoors this summer, judging by the crazy jumble of freckles on his face and arms. His brown eyes stood out as the only still point on his face. Then he smiled, revealing white teeth.

"Oh, you know," he said airily. "Taking off the out-of-date notices. Thanking people for their tips in finding Simon Grenner. Asking them to be on the lookout for a stolen car."

Kate wanted to grumble that the damned website was a time sink, but it wasn't as if they were fighting off a crime wave. Every morning for the past two months she had come in and read the log entries from the night before. It took about thirty seconds. Except for a few drunk driving charges and some fights at the local bars, it had been an exceptionally quiet summer.

Even with Trepalli on leave, the remaining constables on day shift—Friesen, Olinchuk and Paterson—were ample to deal with patrols and problems.

"All right," said Rob, coming out of his office. "I've got my phone. Call me if you need me."

"See you tomorrow," said Martins, back to the web page.

Charlotte didn't even look up. Kate wasn't sure she had even heard. Rob wiggled his eyebrows at Kate and she waved him off. Moments later, his green Honda CRV drove past the screen door as she headed into the break room.

The phone rang as she poured herself a cup of coffee. She may as well head home, she thought glumly. Get the family settled. She might have a chance to swing by the detachment before heading for Marco and Amanda's place.

The tone of Nick Martins' voice changed and she tilted her head toward the open door of the break room.

"Are you sure?"

Abandoning her coffee on the counter, she headed back into the hallway.

"I'm sending someone right now," Martins said. "Don't touch anything."

He hung up and looked at her as she stopped in front of the desk.

"Dead body," he said. "In a canola field. The Hurst farm off the Three Fifty."

"Foul play?"

He shrugged. "The caller was pretty rattled. She didn't say anything more than there was a body in her field."

She nodded. "Have Samantha meet me there and call the ambulance. No sirens." She headed for her office to grab her jacket and cap. If the person really was dead, the ambulance could transport the body to the morgue at the hospital.

"What about your family?" asked Charlotte.

Kate stopped in her tracks. Crap. Her family. She glanced at her watch. Nearly noon. They hadn't called yet. And it would take a good hour to get to Mendenhall from Winnipeg.

"There's time," she decided. Besides, it wasn't as if she had a choice. Dead bodies trumped family.

CHAPTER 2

It took Kate a good twenty minutes to get to the Hurst farm. It was still within Mendenhall jurisdiction, but just. A small sign on a post at the end of the driveway said "Hurst Farm" and she turned in, pulling the sun visor down to cut the glare.

Clouds of dust rose up in her wake and she closed the air intake on the Edge. Better to be warm than to choke.

The farm seemed to concentrate on crops, not animals. Fields of sunflowers and canola as far as the eye could see bordered the long driveway.

In the distance, a white farmhouse with green trim poked above the sunflower field. Behind it was a trio of tall metal silos, clearly for storing grain.

A hundred yards ahead, a woman emerged from the waist-high field of canola onto the driveway. She wore jeans, work boots, a short-sleeved, red gingham shirt, and a wide-brimmed floppy hat. She took the hat off and waved Kate down.

Kate pulled off to the side and cut the engine. She placed her ball cap on her head and got out, trying not to choke on the cloud of dust.

"Ma'am," she said. "You're the one who called?"

The woman nodded. "Jane Hurst."

"Chief Kate Williams," said Kate. She judged the woman to be in her mid-forties but it was hard to tell. Her squint lines showed up white on her deeply tanned face. A red bandanna was stuffed into her back pocket. She had curly blonde hair liberally threaded with gray and had pulled it away from her face into a ponytail.

"This way," said Hurst, turning away and heading into the field. She was tall, at least five feet ten, and Kate had to hustle. She climbed down the shallow ditch and up into the field proper, following Hurst between two rows of bright yellow canola.

Within seconds, she had to control an urge to cover her nose and mouth. What was that smell? Not decomp—that smell was burned into her memory. More like dirty socks. Or gym shoes.

Maybe she made a sound because Hurst glanced over her shoulder. Unsmiling, she said, "That's the canola. It gets ripe when it gets ripe."

Holy...

Then there was a change in the field ahead—a flattening of the rows of canola. The woman stepped aside and Kate caught sight of the body.

It was that of a woman. Naked. Thin—her ribs showed prominently—but not skinny. Long, wavy dark hair, so dark it almost looked black except for the reddish highlights gleaming in the sun. Lying on her side as if she had fallen asleep there. Her hair partly covered her face.

Kate took a tentative sniff, but if there was decomp, it was slight. The canola smell covered it.

She looked up at Jane Hurst. "Did you touch her?"

"No," said the woman.

Just in case, Kate dropped to one knee and felt for a pulse on the wrist of the arm that was draped over her belly.

"How did you come across her?"

Hurst took a deep breath and stuck her hands in her jean pockets.

"We're about to start combining. I always walk the field before we do, just to make sure there's nothing lying around that could damage the machine. That's what I was doing this morning when I found her."

Kate nodded and stood up. No pulse. Body was cold to the touch. And blood had settled where her body touched the ground.

"Do you know her?"

Hurst hesitated, then swallowed.

"I don't know. I didn't want to look too close."

Kate blinked in surprise but didn't look at Hurst. She looked tough as nails, but death was scary, no matter who you were.

Especially when there was something hinky about it.

"All right," said Kate. "Can I ask you to go back to the road and wait for my constable? She should be here any minute. So will the ambulance. You can just direct them here. After that, if you wouldn't mind waiting at the house, I'll come and see you when I'm done here."

Hurst nodded and turned to leave.

"Just a sec," said Kate. When Hurst glanced back at her, Kate asked, "How did you get here? From which direction?"

Hurst pointed southeast and Kate let her go. She would need to get her kit out of the car, but for now, her cell phone camera would do.

Before anything else, she stood still and surveilled the field in all directions. She could see the path she and Hurst had taken but only because of their footprints in the moist soil. As she scanned three hundred and sixty degrees, she finally made out the path to the southeast that Hurst had taken when she stumbled on the body. As far as Kate could see, there was no other path.

Which meant nothing. It had rained in the night. If the young woman had traveled though the field of her own accord—barefoot—before the rain, she would have traveled on dry soil.

But if someone had dragged her or carried her, that would have left marks, even in dry soil.

She was just finishing taking photos of the girl when she heard a car drive up the driveway. From her vantage point, she couldn't see who it was. She quickly pulled up her contacts list and punched the number for Samantha. It rang twice before being picked up.

"I'm here," said Samantha. "Ambulance is about fifteen minutes away. They were dealing with minor injuries in a kids' playground. And since there was no urgency..."

Kate nodded at the sky.

"Bring your kit," she told Samantha. "And grab mine, too."

"Will do," said Samantha and hung up.

Kate returned to her work, taking photos of the area around the girl and working her way out in concentric circles. She found nothing suspicious, not even damaged stalks.

She saw her tall constable rise from the field like an apparition and had a moment of guilt when she saw her readjust her hold on the heavy plastic kits. Still, it was better than making her go back for them.

"Chief," said Samantha, emerging from the field into the small clearing created by the body. She carried a roll of bright yellow crime scene tape on one wrist. She stopped at the edge of the flattened canola stalks and blinked, taking it all in.

Her green eyes were shadowed by the brim of her cap so that Kate couldn't read her expression. She had threaded her luxuriant brown ponytail through the hole at the back of the cap. Her mouth tightened as she examined the young woman on the ground. Finally she deposited the plastic kits at her feet and opened one.

"Do we know who she is?" she asked quietly.

"No," said Kate. "We need to search the terrain around her."

Samantha stood up and looked around the canola field. She held a small gardening claw.

"I know," said Kate at the other's unspoken comment. "I'm calling in Friesen and Olinchuk."

While Samantha examined the body, Kate pulled her phone out and called the detachment. When the wind cut out momentarily, the sun beat down on her head, reminding her that it was still summer. She was glad she had left her jacket in the car.

"Hi, Chief," answered Martins. "What do you have?"

Kate filled him in and asked him to send Friesen and Olinchuk to help search the field. "And call around to see if anyone nearby has a missing woman in their jurisdiction. She's young—under twenty-five, I would guess. Maybe five feet three. Long dark hair."

"Eyes?" asked Martins.

Kate glanced back at the body. "I'll get back to you on that."

"Got it," said Martins. "Anything else?"

"All for now. Send Friesen and Olinchuk."

"Will do."

"Wait!" said Kate, suddenly remembering.

"What?"

"Contact Doc Kijawa," she said.

"Will do," he said again and hung up.

Kate tucked her phone in her pants pocket and headed for her own kit.

Faith Kijawa had a medical practice in Mendenhall but she was also a medical examiner for the province. She would need to see the body.

Usually, a medical examiner wanted to see the body on-site, but in smaller jurisdictions, when they were also full-time physicians, that wasn't always practical.

And Kate couldn't wait.

She pulled out a pair of gloves and her own gardening claw and joined Samantha at the body. Moving slowly, on hands and knees, they worked their way from the body to where the stalks of canola still stood straight. They raked every inch of the ground surrounding the body but found nothing.

Finally Kate sat back on her heels.

"All right. Help me roll her onto her back."

Samantha nodded and set her claw down.

At that moment, the sound of vehicles coming up the driveway reached them and they both stood up. Two plumes of dust indicated the progress up the driveway. A moment later, Kate heard car doors slamming and the sound of voices rose above the stalks of canola.

They waited until Friesen and Olinchuk emerged from the field and joined them. The minute their gazes fell on the dead girl, Friesen took a sharp breath in and stopped. His face paled and he looked down at his feet.

Olinchuk, by comparison, swept the entire area with his gaze, finally narrowing down on the girl. He examined her from head to toe, and Kate was willing to bet that he would be able to recreate the scene in a drawing if called upon.

After giving them a chance to take it in, Kate spoke up.

"Jane Hurst, the homeowner, found the body. She was checking the field before combining. She came from that direction." She pointed southeast. "I need the three of you to section off the field and walk it. Hurst didn't report finding anything unusual, but we still have to check. As soon as the body is removed, I'll circumnavigate the field to see if I can find the entry point."

Because the girl got here somehow.

"The ambulance followed us in," said Friesen. His face had recovered its natural ruddy hue. He turned toward the road and she saw that he had tucked his cap in his back pocket. "They're waiting for us to let them know to come in."

Kate's phone rang and she pulled it out of her pants pocket. It was Doc Kijawa.

"Chief Williams," she said into it.

Olinchuk, Friesen, and Samantha huddled together, whispering so as not to disturb her.

"Hello, Chief," said the familiar voice of Dr. Kijawa. A native of South Africa, she had moved to Canada decades earlier but still retained her charming accent. "I understand you have an unnatural death?"

"We don't know if it's unnatural," said Kate. "She's naked, in the middle of a canola field, without a mark on her that I can see."

"But the circumstances are unusual," said the doc, almost to herself. "I can't get away right now. Document the scene and have her transported to the morgue."

A small part of Kate bristled at the doctor's orders, then she let it go. At five feet ten and weighing two hundred and twenty pounds, Doc Kijawa was a force of nature and accustomed to being in charge.

Kate might have done the same thing herself if the situation were reversed.

"Ambulance is already here," she said calmly. "The body will be there in half an hour."

"Very well," said the doctor and hung up.

Kate grinned at her phone and slipped it back in her pocket. Doc Kijawa wasn't strong on social graces.

"All right," she said, turning back to her constables. "Ben, let the paramedics know they can take her now."

Friesen nodded and headed toward the driveway. Immediately the small clearing felt less claustrophobic.

"Let's turn her over," said Kate.

Samantha and Olinchuk knelt at the girl's shoulder and hip and pulled. The girl flipped heavily onto her back, the arm across her belly remaining rigidly in place. Kate knelt by her head and brushed the dark hair away from her face.

She had strikingly dark eyebrows but that could be in contrast to the pallor of her skin. Her eyes were closed and her face looked relaxed. She had full lips and high cheekbones.

She might have been sleeping, if not for the ligature marks around her neck. Deeply indented, with circular marks at regular intervals at top and bottom, two inches apart, with dark bruising in between the two parallel marks. As if the blood had collected in the middle.

Kate pulled back one eyelid to reveal green eyes clouded over. She moved closer and thought she detected telltale red dots in the whites of the eyes. Petechial hemorrhaging. Maybe. But added to the bruising, it meant probable homicide. Definitely unnatural. There were fly eggs in the corners of her eyes. Probably in her mouth, too.

"Chief."

Something in Samantha's voice made Kate sit back on her heels and look around at her constable.

Samantha was holding up one of the girl's hands.

"There's something under her fingernails."

Good.

"Let's bag her hands and feet," said Kate. "Carefully."

Samantha stood up to go to her kit.

"There's something in her hand," said Olinchuk, his voice even lower than usual.

Kate automatically scanned down the girl's thin body to where her other hand had been trapped beneath her body. Sure enough, her hand was clenched around something flat that protruded from her fist.

Kate took the girl's fist in her hand and forced her fingers open. A piece of paper slipped from the girl's palm and fluttered to the ground. Kate plucked it up before a stray breeze could take it.

It wasn't a piece of paper. It was a crumpled business card. Kate unfolded it and flipped it over to read it. Samantha and Olinchuk leaned over, too.

After a moment, they all looked up and stared at each other.

The business card belonged to Marco Trepalli.

CHAPTER 3

While Samantha, Friesen, and Olinchuk walked the canola field, Kate followed the driveway toward the road, walking slowly as she examined the edges of the field. The EMTs had taken the body away and Kate had placed the business card in a baggie before tucking it into her pocket.

What was the girl doing with Trepalli's business card? Everyone at the detachment had one, even Charlotte. It was another tool and as common as dust. But not everyone's card showed up at a body dump.

That poor girl. What kind of trouble had she found to end up naked in a farmer's field?

The sun beat down on Kate's head and she was glad for the billed cap that kept it out of her eyes. A cool breeze promised a cool night to come. She scanned as she walked, looking for a break in the canola stalks. Whoever had brought the girl here hadn't levitated over the stalks. They had to have driven here with the body and then carried her into the field. Except for where the field was flattened from the weight of the body, Kate had seen no disturbance. The girl hadn't been killed in the field.

She hadn't seen any damage to the girl's heels, so she hadn't been dragged.

It took a lot of nerve to fling a naked body over your shoulder and trudge through a field within sight of the farmhouse. At a distance, sure, but anyone standing on the porch would have seen a figure walking through the field.

It had to have been done at night. And maybe it had taken two people to carry the body.

Maybe Jane Hurst wasn't as shocked as she seemed to be. But tall as she was, Kate doubted she would have the strength to carry a dead body into the middle of the field. She would have needed help. Maybe a husband, or a son.

But why strip the girl naked?

And why leave Trepalli's business card in her hand?

With a sigh, Kate pulled her phone out of her pocket and called Martins. She hadn't had lunch but it didn't matter. The smell of the canola had ruined her appetite.

"Chief?" said Martins at the other end of the line.

"Looks like murder," she said glumly, avoiding a pothole that still had some water at the bottom. "Strangulation, maybe. The body's on its way to the morgue. I don't know when Doc Kijawa will get to it."

"It's past two," said Martins. "She probably has appointments all afternoon. We may not know until tonight."

Kate nodded as she scanned the edge of the field. No breaks that she could see. She was almost at the secondary road.

"I need you to call Trepalli and get him to meet me at the morgue at..." She glanced at the time on her phone. Two fifteen. "About four o'clock."

There was a pause at the other end. Finally Martins said, "Okay. He's going to wonder why."

"Tell him he seems to have a connection to the woman and I need him to help identify her."

"Holy..." Nick Martins swallowed visibly. "All right, Chief. Will do. Do you need me to call in backup?"

"No. I've got Samantha, Ben, and Mike searching the field and I'm walking the perimeter. If we don't find anything, I'll send Ben and Mike back on patrol and Samantha and I will interview the farmer. I'll keep you posted."

They hung up and Kate turned right at the road. She walked the shoulder, ignoring the odd pickup truck that slowed down as it passed her. This was farming country. There wasn't much traffic.

A water-filled ditch separated the road from the field and she just knew she was going to have to cross it at one point. But as it turned out, a narrow access road allowed her to cross the ditch and turn right. She hadn't noticed the access road when she drove up, but it made sense. The combine or tractor or whatever needed to be able to travel between fields. The sunflower field to her left lifted the pall that had settled over her.

She had thought that moving to Mendenhall would mean she would never have to deal with murder again, but this was the third murder she had investigated in the past two years.

Geez.

As she turned away from the cheerful sunflowers, she saw what she had been looking for. A break in the regular spacing of the canola stalks, about a hundred yards away. Far enough that a car wouldn't be easily spotted from the road and too far from the farmhouse to be visible, especially at night.

She made a mental note to ask Hurst if she had any dogs. She hadn't seen or heard any when she got here.

She took out her phone and took a picture of what she was seeing, then walked closer, filming as she approached. She hoped her phone's battery would hold out.

When she reached the break, she stepped off the access road and into the field. Immediately she was swallowed up by the tall stalks that brushed her shoulders and reached her eyes. She tried to breathe through her mouth.

Dear Lord, how could anything made from this stuff be used for food?

She was only five feet three and the stalks of canola were almost taller than her. The killer would have to be taller than her to see where he was going. Where they were going?

She stood still for a moment, studying the way ahead. The path was very clear—stalks of canola were broken or bent in a straight line. It was narrow, but wide enough to accommodate someone carrying a body.

Kate kept walking and filming, aware of the canola catching on her shirt and pants. The damned stuff even caught in her hair. They had found no stray vegetation on the girl, not even in her hair.

She had been wrapped in something.

After five minutes, she arrived at the mini-clearing where the body had been left. She took a moment to orient herself. There to the right was the driveway and the beaten path they had all taken. Straight ahead was the faint path Hurst had taken when walking her field.

"Find anything?"

Kate jumped and turned to find Samantha, no more than ten feet away. Only her shoulders and head stuck up over the field. She grinned unrepentantly at Kate.

Kate turned off the recording.

"Found where the presumed killer entered the field," she said. She pointed. "There's an access road. If they came at night, nobody would have seen them."

Samantha nodded, serious now.

"We're going to be here for a while," she said. "It's a big field."

Kate looked around and saw Olinchuk and Friesen slowly walking in different sections of the field, heads down. Against the deep blue sky and garish yellow field, they looked almost like a surrealist painting. She sighed.

"I'll help you finish your section," she said. "When Ben and Mike are done, they can go back out on patrol. I want you to come with me when I interview Jane Hurst."

Samantha nodded. The sun had brought out freckles over her cheekbones and the bridge of her nose, making her look younger than her early forties.

"I've done this part," she said, holding her arms out in a pie shape.

Kate nodded. She was going to be in this stinking field for a while yet.

CHAPTER 4

Kate and Samantha were walking down the driveway when Kate's phone rang. She pulled it out and answered. "Yes, Nick?"

"Chief, your family is here."

Kate stopped walking.

"What do you mean, 'here'?" She'd been waiting for Rose to call her from Winnipeg for the past couple of hours.

"They're at the detachment, ma'am."

"All of them?" said Kate, her voice rising in alarm.

There was a pause. Finally Martins said, "Five of them, ma'am." Then his voice dropped. "Your parents look tired."

Her parents? He must think Fred was her father.

"I can't get away right now," she said, and hated the faint note of panic in her voice. "We're about to interview Jane Hurst."

"Amanda will be here in a minute," soothed Martins. "She said she'd take care of it."

Kate glanced around at the farmhouse, the field with Olinchuk and Friesen bobbing in it, the slightly alarmed look on Samantha's face.

"Have her call me," she said finally and slipped the phone back in her pocket.

"What's the matter?" asked Samantha.

"My family," muttered Kate. "They're here." Trust Rose not to stick to the plan. "All right," she said, "let's do this." Because she still had to meet Trepalli at the morgue in an hour.

Why, why, why didn't they elope?

As they approached the wide porch, Jane Hurst met them at the door. Clearly she'd been watching. She led them deeper into the house, past a wide wooden staircase covered in a burgundy, green, and blue runner. As they walked through, Kate couldn't help but notice the wide-planked pine floor that covered the hall-way and sitting room. It looked battered and ancient and beauti-ful. The sitting room furniture wasn't new but it was well kept and comfortable looking.

The only thing old in the kitchen, on the other hand, was the cast iron cook stove in the corner. The rest of the room was a mar-vel of granite on the island, butcher block on the counters, and stainless steel fridge and stove. Somewhere, presumably, there was a dining room.

"Do you use it?" asked Samantha, nodding at the wood stove.

"Only in winter," said Hurst. "In summer it gets too hot."

She seemed to have regained some of her composure and waved them to the stools at the island while she poured boiling water into a teapot. She'd already set out mugs and a plate of homemade cookies. They looked like chocolate chip. Kate's stomach rumbled.

The smell of bergamot filled the room as the tea began to steep. Kate didn't particularly like tea, but she loved the smell of Earl Grey.

They sat down and watched as she set a small pot of milk next to the mugs and pulled down a sugar container from a cabinet behind her. She set out small plates, napkins, and small spoons. Finally, she poured the fragrant tea into the mugs and pushed them toward Kate and Samantha.

"Thank you," said Kate.

Hurst remained standing across from them, her shape limned in the light from the window behind her. She rested her hands one over the other on top of the granite countertop. She was ready. Kate pulled out her phone and set the phone to record. She identified herself, Samantha, and Jane Hurst, the date, and the time. Then she nodded at Hurst.

"Tell me again how you came across the body," she said gently. She glanced at Samantha but her constable had already taken her notebook and pencil out. You couldn't be too sure with technology.

"We were planning to do the canola field today," began Hurst softly. Her head turned and she looked out the window over the sink at the field of canola waving gently in the breeze, with the blue sky over it. "Perfect weather for it," she continued absently.

"A couple of years ago, the combine ran over one of the kids' bicycles and we had to wait two weeks for repairs. To the combine, I mean. Since then, I always walk the fields to make sure nothing was left. That's what I was doing when I found her."

Kate pulled the phone toward her, found an appropriate picture of the dead girl's face, and turned the phone toward Hurst.

"Do you know her?"

Hurst's gaze slowly found the phone's screen and she swallowed, but didn't look away. A small frown grazed her forehead.

"She looks a little familiar, but I can't tell from where."

Kate nodded and turned the phone away from Hurst. It wasn't surprising that she couldn't place the dead girl's face. A face lost its muscle tone in death, and the natural skin hues changed. If you didn't know the person intimately, it would be hard to recognize them.

She asked the standard questions and learned that Hurst lived at the farmhouse with her husband, Elliott, and their two children, Tallulah, five, and Jamieson, three. They had two regular hired hands who came in when called. Two cats and two dogs.

"Where are the dogs?" asked Kate in surprise. "We didn't see them when we drove in." She looked to Samantha for confirmation and she nodded in agreement.

Hurst's face took on a pinched look.

"We think someone poisoned them," she said tightly. "My husband took them to the vet, but it's not looking good."

Holy... Two poisoned dogs and one dead body.

"When did this happen?" she asked softly.

Hurst took a deep breath. "We found them by the barn this morning. We'd heard them barking in the night, but we often get coyotes or other critters coming through and they stopped almost right away, so we didn't pay much attention." Her voice caught on the last word and her hands tightened on each other.

Kate swallowed hard. She was used to what people did to each other, but she could never get used to what they did to animals.

"Do you have any idea who could have done it?"

Hurst shook her head. "We've known our neighbors for years. We've never had any problems."

"Where are the kids?" asked Samantha suddenly.

Hurst looked directly at her. "My mom picked them up this morning so we could deal with the dogs. She took them to her place in Mendenhall. I called Frank and Giuseppe and told them not to come today."

"Frank and Giuseppe being your workers?" said Kate, just to get it on record.

Hurst nodded. "Yes, and before you ask, they've been with us for years."

Kate got the workers' particulars and asked a few more questions, but it was clear Hurst knew nothing more than what she had already told them.

Kate and Samantha thanked the woman for her time and headed out the door. In the distance, Olinchuk and Friesen were still walking the field. Samantha looked at them for a moment, then sighed.

"I guess I'd better go help them," she muttered. Then she looked at Kate. "Do you need me still?"

Kate shook her head. "Go. The sooner we finish with the field, the sooner these folks can get it back." Hopefully their traipsing through it wouldn't have damaged it even more.

She watched Samantha head into the field but her attention was on the interview she had just done.

Two poisoned dogs. To keep them from barking and alerting the farmers that someone was out in their field?

That implied that someone knew the area and the family. Knew enough to come prepared with poison. To use the out-of-sight access road. To plan how to dispose of the body.

Was it someone who had a grudge with the family? Or was the farm just handy?

Finally she got into her Edge and did a three-point turn on the driveway. Time to meet Trepalli at the morgue.

CHAPTER 5

Kate was late getting to the morgue. She parked in the hospital parking lot and looked around for Trepalli's silver Mustang but didn't spot it among all the other cars.

As she walked toward the hospital entrance, she called Martins.

"Chief," he answered.

"Any news on the missing persons front?" she asked. The front doors whisked open automatically and she went in, pausing for a moment until the inner doors whisked open, too. An older woman with a cane passed her in the lobby.

"Nothing," said Martins. "But everyone's on alert."

Good. If a missing person did get reported, the jurisdiction would alert Mendenhall right away. Until then, they would have to do things the hard way.

"I've just arrived at the hospital," she said, turning on her heel and heading back outside to her car as she remembered what she needed. "Is Trepalli on his way?"

"He should be there now."

"All right," she said, pulling her car keys out and unlocking the back. "I'll check in later."

"I'll let you know if anything changes," said Martins.

"Wait!" said Kate, suddenly remembering. Her poor mother. "Any word from Amanda?"

"She's got everything under control, Chief," said Martins. "She'll call you with an update when everyone is settled." He hung up and Kate stuck the phone back in her pocket.

Rose would be ticked off but Kate wasn't worried about her. At seventy-nine, Mom should be taken care of, not shunted off to her grandchild. Kate knew Amanda would take care of her grandmother, but dammit, Kate should have been there to greet them.

Then the memory of the young woman lying in the field floated through her mind and she sighed. Mom and Rose would be fine. Kate's job right now was to find out who that young woman was.

She lifted the back door of the Edge and pulled the heavy kit toward her. No need to bring the whole thing with her. Moments later, she had plucked the fingerprint kit from the large case and slammed the back door closed.

* * *

At the end of the brightly lit, very white hallway, about ten feet from the double doors of the morgue, Marco leaned against the wall, his arms crossed over his chest, staring down at his feet. He looked up when the elevator doors opened and waited until Kate got close enough he didn't have to raise his voice.

"What's going on?" he asked, straightening and uncrossing his arms.

He wore a white shirt with long sleeves rolled up to his elbows and pale jeans that looked like they'd seen a lot of wear. Of course, he could have bought them that way. She had never seen him in a white shirt and wondered if he wore it for his family. She had to admit that his tanned good looks stood out against the white.

"I need you to look at a body," she said baldly.

He nodded at the morgue doors. "I figured."

They both turned toward the double doors. It always struck Kate as incongruous that Dr. Kijawa had installed blue gingham curtains on the other side of the windows set in the doors.

She rang the doorbell on the right side of the door, and a moment later, the curtain twitched to reveal Dr. Kijawa's brilliant brown eye. The curtain swished shut and the door opened. Immediately smells of various, dubious origins swept past Kate and into the hallway. Trepalli let the door close behind them, trapping them inside with the smells.

The doc wore a light purple, short-sleeved shirt and a pair of plaid pants. Kate had expected her to be in scrubs, but a quick glance at the only autopsy table showed a body covered by a white sheet. She hadn't started yet.

"I just got here," said the doc, nodding at the still figure. "I still have to do the preliminary examination."

"I need to take her fingerprints," said Kate, holding up the black plastic container.

Dr. Kijawa nodded. "Very well," she said. "Let me examine her hands first."

They stood aside while the doctor lifted the sheet to pull out first the right hand, then the left. Next to her, Trepalli stood still and tense. Kate figured he hadn't spent much time in a morgue. Or seen many dead bodies, for that matter.

As the doc removed the paper bags covering the girl's hands to take scrapings from under each fingernail, Kate glanced around the small morgue. It was barely the size of two hospital rooms, with four refrigerated drawers at one end and a small desk at the other.

It still surprised Kate that Mendenhall had a morgue at all. When she first moved here, she had assumed that all bodies were sent to Winnipeg, or maybe Brandon, for autopsy. Not every test could be performed in her small town, of course, but it was very useful to be able to get preliminary information so quickly.

"Very well," said Dr. Kijawa, replacing the girl's left hand under the sheet. "You may take the fingerprints."

Kate nodded and moved closer. "First, I'd like my constable to take a look at her."

Dr. Kijawa's impassive face betrayed a faint hint of surprise, but she moved to the head of the table, and without comment, pulled the sheet down to the girl's shoulders.

Trepalli moved closer to get a better look and Kate watched his face carefully. He scanned the face, then frowned. He stared at her, eyes narrowed, and Kate could see him trying to get past the strangeness of death. Then his eyes widened in shock.

"Mio Dio," he whispered.

Kate had never heard him speak Italian before. She hadn't known he could.

"Do you know her?" she asked softly.

He nodded jerkily. "It's Kelly..." He paused, clearly searching his memory. "Kelly Lawson."

"All right," said Kate. She took him by the arm and steered him toward the door. "Wait for me in the hallway."

Without a word, he left, leaving Kate alone with the doc. And Kelly Lawson.

"I still need to take her fingerprints," she told the doctor.

As Kate worked on inking the woman's finger pads, Dr. Kijawa informed her that Lawson had been dead for approximately sixteen hours, give or take. She was incubating the fly eggs she had found on the woman to determine more closely when she died.

"She's still in rigor," continued the doc. "I'll know more after the autopsy."

Five minutes later, Kate left the morgue and gathered Trepalli on her way out.

"Let's get out of here," she said. They could talk just as easily outside as in the hallway with its lingering smell of death.

By mutual consent, they took the stairs up to the main floor and walked quickly through the emergency room waiting area. Only half a dozen people waiting today: a man cradling his arm, an older couple clinging to each other, a young woman whose hands were clamped on the chair arms, and a woman holding a toddler on her lap.

Kate's phone rang as they exited the hospital and when she pulled it out, she saw that it was Amanda. She stepped away from the doors and stopped. Marco waited a few feet away. His face was pale.

"Hi, Amanda," said Kate. "I'm with Marco."

"Hi, Aunt Kate. I'm just calling to let you know everything's fine. Grandma and Fred are settled at your place. Uncle Charlie and Sean are there, too. The camper is set up in your driveway, and Mom and Dad are with me at the house."

In the background, birds sang faintly and Kate imagined Amanda was standing on her back deck for privacy.

Kate closed her eyes.

"How bad is it?" she asked.

"I told you," said Amanda calmly. "Everything is fine. Their flight was delayed by a few hours, which is why they were late getting in. But everything else worked out fine."

Uh-huh.

"How's your grandmother?"

"Grandma is fine. She slept on the plane so now she's worried she won't sleep tonight." Amanda laughed. "And Fred keeps trying to get her to sit down and rest."

Since the attack on Mom almost a year ago, she'd been walking with a cane. Kate imagined it was exhausting, but Mom certainly never let it slow her down.

"What about your mom?" she asked her niece. Marco stood with his arms crossed over his chest, looking down at the sidewalk. A couple had to walk around him to get to the hospital entrance. He didn't seem to notice.

"Well, Mom's Mom," said Amanda cautiously. "She was disappointed that you weren't there, of course, but I explained and she's fine."

Translation: Rose was ticked off.

They had been so close while they were growing up, but now it seemed that everything Kate did ticked her sister off.

A breeze swept over her, carrying the smell of green growing things. Someone had recently watered the flower beds in front of the hospital.

"Anyway," continued Amanda. "Will you be able to make it to dinner?"

Kate considered what she had to do. She needed to debrief Trepalli to find out what he knew about Ms. Lawson, locate and notify next of kin, interview next of kin, discover where Ms. Lawson had lived, search her home, identify and interview friends and coworkers…

The list stretched out in front of her. Every item she added to it seemed to spin off new items.

Damn, damn, damn.

Marco looked up, his navy-blue eyes bright in the sunlight.

"Martins can start the ball rolling," he said calmly. "Samantha is a capable investigator, too. And Stan Albertson is on duty tonight."

Kate knew what he was telling her. Albertson's crew consisted of Tourmeline, Boychuk, Fallon, and Oppenheimer. John Tourmeline and Dan Boychuk, in particular, were experienced officers.

She blew out a breath. He was right. She had good people. They could start the work. She'd be back early in the morning to pick up the investigation.

"Yes, I'll be there," she said firmly. She glanced at the time on her phone. Four forty-five. "I'm on my way back to the detachment with Marco. After I'm done, I'll go home, change, grab the crew, and meet you all at the house."

Where the entire Trepalli clan would be waiting to meet the Williams-Coburn clan.

God help them all.

Then she remembered that Bert would be there, too, and cheered up.

"All right," said Amanda. "See you at six."

Kate put the phone away and sighed. She had a sudden urge to start running, as if something had been put into motion that she might not be able to escape.

* * *

By the time Kate and Trepalli reconvened in the detachment break room, Kate's stomach was complaining bitterly about missing lunch. Martins was on the phone when they walked in and Charlotte was gone for the day. Kate led the way to her office and waited for Trepalli to sit down on one of her visitor chairs before closing the door and squeezing behind him to get to her own chair.

"Why did you think I might know her?" asked Trepalli before she could sit. "How did she die? Where did you find her?"

Clearly his shock had worn off and he'd been thinking. Kate

studied him for a moment, taking in his freshly cut black hair, his brilliant blue eyes fringed with thick, dark lashes, his high cheekbones. The rolled-up sleeves of his white shirt revealed lean, muscled forearms. He was tall, with wide shoulders and narrow hips.

He'd been a player until he met Amanda a year and a half ago. Was Kelly Lawson someone he had dated?

"How did you know Ms. Lawson?" she asked.

Trepalli sat back. She was treating him like a witness and he didn't like it. But after a momentary struggle with his ego, he relaxed.

"I met her last year," he said, "not long after Amanda went back home."

It was a year ago, exactly. After Amanda was almost drowned by a madman. After she realized just how dangerous Marco's chosen profession really was. A month later, Marco drove all the way to Montreal and brought her back, over Rose's objections.

What had he done in that month?

"Did you go out with her?" she asked evenly. She wasn't sure how she would react to a "but we were on a break" excuse.

Not well.

But Marco was already shaking his head.

"No, ma'am. She came on to me, but I wasn't interested." He blushed and Kate was feeling a little uncomfortable herself. "But there was something about her that struck me."

"What do you mean?" she asked. Trepalli had very good instincts, and she had learned to trust them.

He shrugged.

"I don't know, really. She didn't fit. She didn't look like a woman who ever went to a bar. Do you know what I mean?" He didn't wait for Kate. "And she was alone," he continued. "Women hardly ever go to a bar alone."

Well, that wasn't much to go on.

"Did you talk?" she asked. "Did she tell you anything about herself?"

Trepalli sat quietly for a minute before finally shrugging again.

"Not really. I mean, we chatted, but about nothing. She was a dental hygienist, I think. I told her I was a police officer."

Kate nodded. "And you gave her one of your business cards."

Trepalli looked startled. "Yes. She joked that she'd like to have one, in case she ever needed help. How did you know?"

Kate dug through her pants pocket for the baggie with the card and pulled it out. She put it on the desk between them.

"This was found clenched in her fist."

Trepalli stared down at the crumpled card, his expression grim.

"How did she die?" he asked again.

"We're not sure," said Kate, "but it looks like strangulation. She was left naked in the middle of a canola field. The owner found her this morning."

"She lived in Brandon," he said slowly, looking up at Kate. "Where was she found?"

"On the Hurst farm," said Kate.

Surprise spread over Trepalli's face. "Jane and Elliott's place, off the Three Fifty?"

It was Kate's turn to be surprised.

Trepalli knew the people whose farm had been used to dump the body of a woman he also knew.

A shiver ran up her spine.

CHAPTER 6

The travel trailer was almost as big as her house.

Kate pulled up to her tiny two-bedroom, one-bathroom home and parked on the street. There was no way she would fit the Edge in the driveway behind that behemoth and the pickup truck that had pulled it.

She got out and quickly crossed the front lawn, noting the long shadows on the grass that needed cutting again. Before she got up the first step to the front stoop, the door opened and Mom stood framed in the opening, looking like a fuzzy angel in the softening light.

"Hello, sweetheart," she said, a warm smile crinkling up her brown eyes. Her white hair was swept up in the familiar loose bun, framing her face. She wore a pair of cream linen pants and a loose linen shirt that was a riot of color in a paisley pattern.

She looked wonderful.

"Mom," said Kate, gathering her mother in her arms. She was careful not to squeeze too hard. Mom would be eighty at her next birthday, though she barely looked seventy. To Kate's relief, Mom had put some weight back on after the terrible accident that had left her with a broken leg, cracked ribs, and a concussion.

"You look great," said Kate, stepping back a little to get a better view. And it was true. Clear skin, shining eyes, straight back.

For a moment, Kate wished that she could spend the next week alone with her mom, catching up, visiting the area, being with each other.

A movement caught her eye and she looked up to find Fred Stilwell smiling down at her. Fred was a tall, thin man with a lean face and a slightly hooked nose that always seemed vaguely sinister. His hooded brown eyes could skewer a person in place. Right now, however, they were crinkled up in a smile, too.

"Hello, Kate," he said.

"Fred," said Kate, smiling back.

"Come in, come in," said Mom, for all the world as if this were her house. She backed up, almost bumping into Fred. He put a hand on her elbow to support her and they both cleared the doorway, allowing Kate to enter.

The smell of coffee wafted over to her as she crossed the stoop.

"Where are the boys?" she asked, looking around the living room and peering into the kitchen.

"On the back deck," said Fred. "It's such a beautiful day."

Kate hung up her jacket and tossed her cap on the shelf above the rod.

"Any problems getting here?" she asked, bending over to unlace her work boots.

"No," said Mom, standing next to Fred. Kate smothered a smile. Mom was short and roundish and Fred was tall and thin. A walking cliché.

"The flight was delayed leaving Montreal," said Fred, "but otherwise everything went well."

Kate straightened and kicked her boots into the closet before closing the doors.

"I thought you were going to call me when you landed," she said reproachfully, following her mother into the kitchen. Mom went to the French press and poured coffee into a waiting cup. She added a bit of sugar, stirred, then handed the cup to Kate.

Kate grinned and sat down at the counter. A whiff of canola wafted up and Mom frowned slightly.

"Your sister wanted to surprise you," said Fred. "We got to the police station only to find that you were out on a call."

The door to the deck opened suddenly and there was Charlie, looking so much like Dad that tears sprang to Kate's eyes.

"I thought I heard my kid sister," he said gruffly, advancing on her. She stood up in time to be enveloped in a massive bear hug.

Charlie, only fourteen months older than her, always acted like it was his job to protect her, even though she was the police officer. Of course, when they were younger, his idea of protection had involved chasing away any boy who was ever interested in her. No wonder she never married.

"How are you?" she asked, her voice muffled against his chest. At almost six feet tall, he towered over her. She finally pushed him away so she could get a good look at him.

Well, age had been kind to him. The sun and open seas had weathered his skin, leaving paler squint lines. His gray hair was thick, unruly, and, as always, in dire need of a trim. Like Kate, he had blue eyes. To her surprise, he wore glasses.

"I'm good," he said, taking her in with one glance. "What the hell is that smell?"

Kate laughed. "It's canola."

The three of them stared at her uncomprehendingly.

"Hi, Aunt Kate."

Kate peered around Charlie to find her nephew Sean grinning at her.

Dear God. Seeing him still sent a jolt to her stomach, even though she had seen him yesterday when Amanda picked him up at the airport and took him to her home. He would give up Amanda and Marco's spare room to his parents and move into the travel trailer with Charlie today.

"Hi, Sean." She accepted a bristly kiss on her cheek.

When did he get old enough to have whiskers? In her mind, he was still sixteen, not twenty-four. She really had to visit her family more often.

"When did you grow up?" she asked plaintively.

"Enough chitchat," said Charlie. "I'm hungry."

Fred laughed, and Kate almost jumped at the booming sound

of it. She'd never heard him laugh like that. The only other time she had met him was when Mom was struck by a car and almost killed. Nobody had felt much like laughing.

"Give me a chance to shower," said Kate, heading for the bathroom. "Are you guys all ready?"

"Just about," said Mom, while the men all nodded. Kate spared a glance at Charlie's worn jeans and plaid shirt but didn't say anything. This pot wasn't going to call his kettle black.

Forty-five minutes later, she parked in front of Marco and Amanda's little house, with Charlie and Sean in the pickup just behind her. Several white cars were parked along the other side of the street.

She had always liked this street, with its post-World War II-era houses. Every one of them had been spruced up over the years. The yards were lovingly tended, and mature trees—mostly Manitoba maples, oaks, and willows—grew in every yard. As she looked down the street, a canopy of leafy branches almost met in the middle.

Amanda's green Tercel was in the driveway, and Marco's silver Mustang with its double black stripes was parked behind it. She wondered who had ended up in the low-slung car with him. She loved the looks of the car but practically needed a crane to haul herself out.

Just as she, Mom, and Fred were getting out, Bert drove up in his Honda and parked on the other side of the street. The sun was low in the sky and cast long shadows across the street as he got out. Kate watched him walk toward them, enjoying the easy way he moved. At 58, Bert was stocky but fit, and while only a few inches taller than her, he always seemed so much bigger. His red hair was fading to gray but his brown, copper-penny eyes were as bright as ever.

"Hello, Bert," said Mom. She tightened her shawl around her shoulders against the slight chill.

"Hetty!" said Bert, a delighted grin on his face. He hurried over and kissed both her cheeks. Then he looked her up and down. "You look wonderful!"

Kate exchanged an amused look with Fred as the red crept up Mom's cheeks.

"Thank you, dear," said Mom with a grin.

Fred and Bert shook hands, then Charlie and Sean arrived and Kate introduced Bert to them. She never knew how to introduce him—her boyfriend? Too teenagerish. Her lover? She would have to be French or Italian to get away with that.

In the end, she always just gave his name and let people figure it out for themselves. Charlie and Sean figured it out the moment Bert kissed her.

Then it was her turn to blush.

"Shall we go in?" said Fred, ever the gentleman.

The Town of Mendenhall had made Amanda and Marco install a wheelchair ramp since they were operating a business out of their home. Marco had built it himself with the help of Ben Friesen, his usual partner. They had painted it cream, the same color as the house, with green trim to match the house trim, and planted vines that now covered the railing.

Kate could see figures milling around through the big picture window of what used to be the living room.

Good Lord—how many of them were there?

She rang the doorbell before pushing the door open. Then she took a sharp breath. There were even more people than she had first thought.

"Geez," murmured Bert in her ear. "Just how big is Trepalli's family?"

Bert had grown up as an only child. He didn't even have cousins. She could see growing panic in his eyes.

"His grandparents are gone," she whispered back, "but he's got four brothers and sisters. And lots of uncles and aunts." And cousins.

Before Bert could do more than gulp, Rose descended on them.

"Katie!" she cried, wrapping her sister in a hug. "You made it!" Without giving Kate a chance to respond, Rose turned to Bert and gave him a quick hug and a peck on the cheek. "Hi, Bert!"

"Hi, Rose," said Bert with a lopsided grin.

Rose wore her hair longer than the last time Kate had seen her. Thick and wavy, it was brushed away from her face and helped soften her features. While she and Kate were essentially built the same—short and round—Rose kept herself thinner with assiduous dieting and a strict regimen of exercise. She wore a knee-length dress of some light fabric printed with a riot of flowers. Fitted, and with three-quarter length sleeves, it showed off her figure to advantage.

Kate barely resisted an urge to look down at her blue slacks and matching silk top.

And then Amanda was there, pulling everyone into the living room she and Marco had converted into a dining room for their part-time restaurant.

"Everyone!" Her raised voice cut through the hubbub of voices. A few more people emerged from the kitchen. Dear God. There had to be twenty people there.

Next to Kate, Bert sighed.

"This is my grandmother, Hetty Williams," continued Amanda, taking her grandmother by the hand. "And this is Fred Stilwell, her friend." She grinned up at Fred. "My aunt Kate and her friend, Bert Langdon." She gave Kate a quick hug. "And my uncle Charlie and my baby brother, Sean." She looked at the group staring back at her. "And these are Marco's family. This is Marco's mom and dad, Camilla and Henry." From the crowd, an older, well-dressed couple waved and smiled. "Now, the rest of you, please introduce yourselves and get to know each other."

And with that, Kate was thrown into the maelstrom.

* * *

An hour later, she escaped to the back deck. Although it was growing dark, the party lights weren't on yet. No one had chosen to eat on the deck, preferring to mix and mingle with each other near the buffet table. Amanda had outdone herself with the food, though she confided she'd had lots of help from Marco and her friend Julianne.

The front and back doors had been opened some time ago to let more air into the house, and while some people had spilled out onto the front porch, it seemed no one else had chosen the back deck. Kate had done a rough count several times and came up with a minimum of twenty-four people.

She stepped to the railing, looked up at the pale stars just beginning to peek out, and took her first deep breath of the evening.

"Feeling trapped?" said Bert.

Kate jumped and turned to find him lounging in the corner of the deck furthest from the door.

"You were hiding," Kate accused. No wonder she had lost track of him.

"Nonsense," he said. "I came out for a smoke."

A smile tugged at Kate's lips. He didn't smoke.

"You're in a pool of light," he pointed out. "Come here if you want camouflage."

The smile spread. She walked over to him and leaned into him. God, he smelled good. His arms crept around her and they stood quietly, closely, for a long minute.

"How's your mother?" she finally asked.

She felt more than heard his sigh.

"Not good. She doesn't recognize me anymore."

Kate's heart squeezed. Bert's mom had been in care for the last year, diagnosed with Alzheimer's. Kate couldn't remember how old she was, only that she was nearing her mid-nineties. She didn't want to ask Bert how old she was—that always seemed to imply that she'd had a good run and, really, maybe it was time for her to go now.

"I'm sorry," she whispered in his ear. And she was. His mother was older than hers, but she saw the inevitability of the road ahead and she didn't want to go there. "How are you?"

Bert shrugged, his cheek rubbing against hers.

"I'm okay," he said. "Or as okay as I can be."

They stood quietly, giving and receiving comfort. Finally he cleared his throat.

"I hear you've got a body." His voice rumbled in his chest.

Kate sighed. They were moving on.

The evening was warm, with just a hint of a cool breeze. The backyard was a deep pool of darkness. She had fully expected to see a forest of tents in the yard when she arrived, but according to Marco, he and Amanda had managed to find two houses to accommodate his family. Friends and customers of Amanda's Place who would be away for the week and were happy to let Marco's family stay in their homes in exchange for complimentary meals at the restaurant.

Many complimentary meals.

"Yes," she said, straightening up but staying within the circle of his arms. "A young woman in a canola field."

"Friend of Marco's?"

It never ceased to amaze Kate how quickly information spread in a small town, but all the way to Winnipeg?

"How do you know that?" she asked.

"Charlotte told me."

Geez. True, Bert was practically an honorary member of the Mendenhall Police Department—he was the deputy chief of the Winnipeg Police Services and she had worked with him on a number of cases; and as her boyfriend, he was here all the time—but still…

She would have a talk with the girl.

"Acquaintance," said Kate. "He met her once."

"But she had his business card."

Now she was getting pissed off. Charlotte had no call to be sharing this information with anyone outside the investigation. Kate pulled out of his arms.

"I should go check on my mother," she said.

Bert straightened and placed a warm hand on her arm.

"Are you upset?"

Someone stepped onto the deck from the kitchen and they both turned to see Marco Trepalli looking at them.

"Am I interrupting?"

"No," said Kate just as Bert said, "Yes."

"What's up?" asked Kate as the boy hesitated.

Trepalli glanced over his shoulder. Two older women and a young man had entered the kitchen and were tidying up. He approached Kate, clearly not wanting to be overheard.

"I just checked in with Albertson. They've found her next of kin. In Brandon. Her husband."

"Husband?" said Kate, one eyebrow rising.

Trepalli nodded. He was outlined against the bright light in the kitchen and she couldn't make out his expression. Had he known she was married?

"Albertson wants to know how you want to handle the notification."

Kate thought for a moment.

"Had he put in a missing person's report?" she asked slowly.

"No, ma'am," said Trepalli. "Martins checked all of southern Manitoba, including Winnipeg." He nodded toward Bert.

"Then tell Albertson that I want to do the notification myself. Tomorrow." The man hadn't reported his wife missing. He could wait another night to find out she was dead.

She would have to connect with the Brandon Police Service to avoid ruffled feathers. Besides, she might need their help.

Only as she was entering the kitchen did she realize they had discussed the case in front of Bert. She was no better than Charlotte.

CHAPTER 7

Kate woke up at five. She rarely needed to set the alarm but always did anyway. She was a belt-and-suspenders kind of gal. She was as quiet as she could be while taking her shower and getting dressed, but as she left her bedroom, the smell of bacon cooking announced she wasn't the only one up.

"I'm sorry," said Kate, entering the brightly lit kitchen. "I didn't mean to wake you."

"Nonsense," said Mom, waving to the counter where the French press waited, full of enticing coffee. "I haven't slept past four thirty in thirty years."

"Now there's something to look forward to," muttered Kate as she poured them each a cup. She pulled down the sugar container and added a bit of sugar to her cup, then grabbed the coffee creamer from the fridge to add to her mother's cup.

It was still dark outside but it would be getting lighter by the time she set out for Brandon.

She had stocked the fridge with everything she thought her family would like. Now as she replaced the creamer in the only spot available, she hoped they wouldn't leave her with all that food.

"Thank you, dear," said Mom as Kate set her cup down on the counter. "How did you sleep?"

"Fine, thanks," said Kate, though she'd had wild dreams of

stumbling about in a canola field and finding dead bodies every-where.

"Good," said Mom, her back to Kate as she cracked eggs into the fry pan. "Is everything all right with you and Bert?"

Kate stared at her mother's back, her coffee cup forgotten half-way to her mouth.

"Yes," she said finally. "Why do you ask?"

Mom glanced over her shoulder at Kate. "He didn't spend the night."

Kate shrugged. "He was never going to. He has to work this morning. Besides, his mother isn't doing well and he doesn't want to be away for too long."

Mom nodded and placed two slices of whole wheat bread in the toaster. She was no stranger to ageing and its ravages. Of all her friends in the St. Lambert neighborhood, only Mrs. Bernier was left. All the others had died or succumbed to Alzheimer's.

She wished again that she could spend time alone with Mom. It was easier when Kate went to St. Lambert. Fewer distractions. More time for just the two of them.

"I'm sorry I have to leave," she said.

Mom raised a hand to silence her, then took the fry pan off the burner and turned the heat off.

"Don't apologize, Katie," she said firmly. "Best to deal with this poor young woman's death and not have it taint the wedding. Although that may already be too late."

"What do you mean?" What did Kelly Lawson's death have to do with the upcoming wedding?

Mom divided the eggs onto two plates, added the bacon, then buttered the toast before sliding one plate over to Kate along with a fork. She brought her plate over to the other side of the peninsula and sat down on the stool next to Kate.

"I heard Marco and Amanda arguing about it last night," she finally said. "Is he going with you to... where is it you're going again?"

"Brandon," said Kate absently. "And no, he's not coming." Although he had really, really, really wanted to come. But Kate couldn't take the chance. Until they figured out what had happened to the young woman, and what Trepalli's connection to the case was, he had to stay away. "What were they saying?" she asked around a mouthful of toast.

"Don't talk with your mouth full, dear," said Mom reproachfully before popping a strip of bacon in her mouth. She chewed, then swallowed before answering. "I only caught bits of the argument but Amanda seemed angry that he had never told her about this woman." She looked at Kate. "Was he seeing her?"

Dear Lord. How had she come to be discussing the case with her mother? Kate put a forkful of egg in her mouth to stall. Basil and a little cheese—just the way she liked them. She sipped her coffee and set the cup down before finally turning to her mother.

"I can't discuss the case, Mom, but I can tell you that Marco has no reason to reproach himself." Probably.

Mom nodded and returned her attention to her plate. "He seems like a good man," she said. "It's just that Amanda is very dear to us and I wouldn't want her to end up with a man who is less than honorable."

Honorable. Kate chewed on her bacon and considered the word. Honor had always been important to her—doing the right thing for the right reason. She had lived by the principle in her professional life and in her personal life. Bert was an honorable man and she loved him for it. She had never given it any thought, but now that she did, she considered Marco Trepalli to be an honorable young man, too. She couldn't imagine him doing anything that would shame him.

Including taking up with a married woman.

"Mom," she said slowly, "you don't need to worry about Marco. Amanda made a good choice."

She hoped.

* * *

The streets of Mendenhall were practically deserted at five thirty on a Tuesday morning. Kate drove to the station, enjoying the solitude and the coolness of the morning. She cracked the window open and caught the fleeting scent of sweet hay. Not that she knew what sweet hay was, exactly, but the elusive, sweet scent was never more present than early in the morning.

When she arrived at the detachment, only Stan Albertson was around. He came out of the break room when she came in.

"Hi, Chief," he said with a smile. Even after almost twelve hours on duty, he still looked freshly shaved, his uniform crease-free. How was that possible? Did he keep an iron in his locker? A razor?

"Stan," said Kate, following him back into the break room where he finished making a fresh pot of coffee. "Anything to report?"

"Not really," said Stan, pouring the pot full of water into the container and setting the pot down on its hot plate. He turned on the coffee maker and it immediately started hissing. He crossed his arms over his chest and leaned a hip on the counter. "A couple of kids tried to break into the high school. God knows why. Oppenheimer took them back home and put the fear of God into them. Someone ran a stop sign right in front of Tourmeline so he had to give them a ticket. Someone thought they saw a wolf in their yard but it turned out to be a neighbor's dog. You know. Regular stuff."

Kate smiled wryly. Oh yes, indeed. Policing in Mendenhall. Then she remembered Kelly Lawson and the smile left her face.

"I want to do the notification to the husband before he sets off for work, so I need to leave soon." She knew Stan would be up to date with the case, thanks to the log. And Martins would have briefed him. "Who can you spare?"

Stan shrugged. "Anyone of them, really. Oppenheimer is from Brandon, if that helps."

Kate nodded but didn't say anything. Oppenheimer was a good police officer, but he never stopped talking. She hadn't had enough coffee yet to deal with him. Tourmeline would be good, but she knew he helped get his kids ready for school when he got off work.

"How about Boychuk?" she asked.

"I'll call him in," said Stan.

Five minutes later, Boychuk and Tourmeline walked into the detachment. They nodded at Kate, who was reading the duty log at the end of the counter and sipping coffee.

"Hey, Sarge," said Boychuk, running his hands through his already unruly brown hair. "What's up?" Tourmeline headed for one of the common computers at the desks in the middle of the room.

Dan Boychuk was the only person Kate knew who always looked like he had hat hair. As he stood in the duty room looking at Stan, Kate couldn't help but compare the neat, pressed and clean-shaven Albertson to Boychuk's rumpled uniform and bloodshot eyes. The man always had bags under his eyes. Kate wondered what he did with his free time to make him look so tired all the time.

It didn't matter. Boychuk might look half-asleep, but he had a keen mind and never missed a detail. His looks might even be an asset since they led people to routinely underestimate him.

Stan nodded toward Kate and Boychuk turned a questioning look on her.

"I need to go to Brandon," she said. "I expect to be back here by nine at the latest. You up for a bit of overtime?"

Boychuk stared at her for a moment, then nodded.

"Sure. We doing the notification?"

"Yes. We'll take my car. I can drop you off at your place after. Do you need to let your wife know?"

"I'll just text her," he said, pulling out his phone. "She and the kids are probably still sleeping."

He had two boys, eleven and twelve, old enough to get themselves fed and to school without too much effort.

It was all Kate could do sometimes to get herself out the door. She couldn't imagine having to wrangle kids, too.

Five minutes later, they were heading west on the Trans-Canada, chasing their shadow as the sun peeked over the horizon. Kate loved this time of day, when the golden light slowly erased the night. She always thought more clearly first thing in the morning. Unlike Rose, who had to be up for an hour, showered, and caffeinated before she felt semi-human.

Kate spared a little sympathy for Amanda and Marco, who would be dealing with Rose's truculence. Oh well, her husband John was there, too. He could handle her.

And she'd be back by nine, anyway. They wouldn't even know she'd been gone.

"BPS knows we're coming?" said Boychuk, startling her out of her thoughts.

"Yes," she said. "Albertson contacted them before we left."

She would still have to talk to Larksen, the chief of police there. A courtesy call, really, but necessary. She wouldn't want someone from another jurisdiction traipsing all over her territory without checking with her first.

"He doesn't have a record," said Boychuk, and for a moment, she thought he was referring to Chief Larksen. Then she realized he meant Calder Bragg, Lawson's husband.

"No," agreed Kate. Not that it meant anything. She'd learned over the years that not all crimes were known by the police.

"Is Trepalli a suspect in the Lawson death?" asked Boychuk suddenly.

Kate kept her gaze on the road but her hands tightened on the steering wheel. Was that what they were all thinking? That one of their own might have killed a woman?

"He's a person of interest until we find out more," she said calmly.

She saw Boychuk nod out of the corner of her eye.

"We can't interview him," he said slowly. "We need to ask someone else. Probably Brandon."

Kate swallowed her irritation. He was right. They couldn't interview one of their own. And she couldn't ask Winnipeg to interview him, because of her relationship with Bert. It would have to be Brandon.

"I'll ask their chief while we're down there," she said.

Boychuk nodded again. "What do we know about the husband?"

Glad to be off the subject of Trepalli, Kate relaxed.

"Calder Bragg. He's 31 and a machinist at Balderson Industries."

They both lapsed into silence as they approached Brandon. She wished she'd had more time to find out more about Bragg but she really wanted to catch him at home, before he left for work. He'd be alone and more vulnerable. If he was at work, he'd have his coworkers around for support.

Careful, she warned herself. Don't assume he's guilty because you don't want it to be Trepalli. But at the back of her mind, from the dim recesses of her memories as a rookie, she could hear her old training officer saying, "It's always the husband, it's always the husband, it's always the husband."

It wasn't true, of course, but it was true often enough that the husband, or boyfriend, was the first one police looked at when a woman was murdered.

It was depressing.

The Bragg and Lawson home was on Third Street, not far from Park Avenue. The block consisted of renovated post-war houses painted in neutral colors. Most of the lots had a large front lawn, neatly trimmed, and big trees. Only a few houses still had stucco, but even they had been freshly painted.

While the Bragg house had been recently painted, the paint only served to cover the blemishes in the stucco. The wood trim around the windows looked like it was rotting. The grass needed mowing.

"There's always one on every block," murmured Boychuk as Kate parked in front the little house.

That struck her as funny, considering how Boychuk always looked like he had been dragged through a knothole backward, but she managed to hide her smile. They walked up the narrow walkway to the front door. A shiny red truck was parked in the driveway. Boychuk whistled softly.

"Ford Lariat," he said. "New one. That'll put you back at least fifty thousand."

Huh. She glanced around the street. It still being early, there were cars or pickups parked in almost every driveway, or in front. None of them looked as fancy as this one.

Boychuk knocked on the solid wood door and they waited. Just as he was about to knock again, the door opened to reveal a man dressed in brown coveralls with a name patch stitched over the left breast. It read "CALDER."

"Yes?" he said, addressing Boychuk.

"Mr. Bragg?" said Kate, forcing his attention to her. "I'm Mendenhall Chief of Police Kate Williams and this is Officer Dan Boychuk. May we come in?"

The man's gaze swept up and down her uniform, pausing on the ball cap that Mendenhall used as opposed to the peaked cap of the Brandon Police Service. She could understand his confusion. Except for the hats, both jurisdictions' uniforms were similar.

"What's going on?" he asked, stepping back and opening the door for them.

Kate and Boychuk automatically removed their caps and tucked them under their arms before entering.

To her left, a pony wall separated the entrance from the living room. Across from the living room, Kate could see the end of a dining room table and a couple of chairs. The wall-to-wall carpeting in the living room looked a little worn but it was clean, and while the furniture was from an older day, it was neat and in good shape.

"Mr. Bragg," she said, returning her attention to him. He was a tall one, at least six feet one, and had thick blond hair that seemed to want to curl. It was still damp, as if he had come out of the shower recently. His blue, blue eyes were staring at her intently, as if willing her to get on with it. He had a good mouth and chin. She knew he was only thirty-one but she would have judged him to be closer to forty, thanks to the softening of his chin line and the thickening of his belly.

"Sir, does Kelly Lawson live here?"

He frowned.

"She did," he said stiffly. "Until I threw her out last week. Why?"

"Do you know where she went?" asked Kate.

Bragg's frown deepened.

"No. Ask her boyfriend."

Kate's eyebrows rose. "Boyfriend?"

A slow tide of red crept up his face. For the first time, Kate noticed that he was in his stocking feet.

"That's why we separated," he said, looking away. "I got tired of her lies."

"Can you tell us her boyfriend's name?" asked Kate.

"No," said Bragg shortly.

"Who are her friends?" asked Kate.

He shrugged. "We just moved here last year."

That wasn't an answer.

"Where does she work?"

"She's a dental hygienist," he said with a touch of impatience. "At Leaf Dental."

"When is the last time you saw her?" asked Boychuk. Kate glanced at him but he was staring intently at Bragg, who shrugged.

"Friday. I handed her her coat and purse and told her to get out. Is that why you're here? Is she accusing me of something?" He looked confused.

Boychuk slid a glance at her and she sighed silently.

"Mr. Bragg, is anyone else here?" She always asked, since the time she had informed a young woman her husband was dead and she promptly passed out.

"No," he said, his impatience clearly evident. "I'm alone."

"Do you mind if we sit down?" she asked.

"Ma'am," he said tersely, "please tell me why you're here."

She nodded. No more stalling. "I'm sorry to inform you that the body of your wife was found in Mendenhall yesterday morning."

Bragg just stared at her. His face went from red to colorless and he looked down at the floor. He spread his legs as if for better balance and crossed his arms over his chest. His powerful shoulders strained the thick cloth.

Everything about him spoke of containment, as if he were afraid of losing control.

"How?" he asked finally in a hoarse whisper. "How did she die?"

"We're not sure," she said gently. "We are waiting on the medical examiner's report."

He looked at her. "Where?"

Kate hesitated. There had been something under Kelly Lawson's fingernails. Maybe blood. That probably meant that someone had scratches. From what she could see, this guy didn't have any, but he wore coveralls. And she didn't have reason enough to ask him to disrobe. He might be completely innocent.

Or he might be her killer.

She had to be careful about how she shared information.

"She was found in Mendenhall," she said carefully. "For now, that's all I can say."

His arms uncrossed and his mouth opened slightly.

"Are you saying she was murdered?" His voice almost strangled on the word.

"Right now," she said soothingly, "all we can say is that the circumstances of her death are of concern. Is there anyone we could call for you?"

He looked stunned, as if her words were blocks of cement flung at him. He shook his head.

"No," he said. "No, there's no one."

Kate felt a pang of pity for the man. "May we have your phone number?" she asked softly. "In case we have more questions?"

He gave it to her and Boychuk jotted it down in his notebook.

Kate nodded finally. "We'll contact Victim Services on your behalf and they will follow up with you." She handed him her card.

He said nothing and they let themselves out the door, leaving him alone.

* * *

They drove in silence to Victoria Avenue, where the police station was located, and parked in visitor parking. The front lot was practically empty. It was still early, only seven twenty. Most civilian staff wouldn't arrive for a while.

Kate turned the engine off and listened to the engine clicking as it began to cool down. The sun was slowly easing its way up the sky, and drops of water glistened on the grass where an underground watering system had sprinkled water during the night.

"What did you think?" asked Boychuk finally. He was staring out the windshield and turning his cap in his hands between his knees.

Kate took a deep breath. The car smelled vaguely of breath mints.

"I don't know," she admitted. And she didn't. Everyone reacted differently to this kind of news. There was no right way to grieve. But something about Bragg's reaction kept catching at her and she couldn't pinpoint what.

"Me, neither," said Boychuk. He shrugged and looked up at the police station.

Kate looked at it, too. She really didn't want to be here. She didn't want to have to ask Chief Larksen to arrange for an interview with Marco, especially as they didn't have the results of the autopsy yet. But the bruising around Kelly Lawson's throat left no doubt: someone had assaulted her, whether or not it resulted in her death. And Trepalli's business card had been in her hand. Marco would have to be interviewed.

She felt old, suddenly. She was fifty-five. She could retire any time. Her house was paid for and she had no debts. She could live quite comfortably on her pension and her modest investments. She didn't have to keep dealing with this crap.

"Chief?" said Boychuk.

"I'm going to retire and start drinking," she muttered and opened the door.

CHAPTER 8

Ford Larksen was a tall, thin man whose green eyes always looked like they were made of flint. In his late fifties, Kate judged, or maybe his early sixties. He had thinning grey hair that he kept short.

This early in the morning, he was already in and working. He stood up as she was escorted into his office—a large space filled with filing cabinets, a big desk with a laptop on one corner, and a couple of comfortable, padded visitor chairs. His desk was clear except for a pile of file folders, a notepad, and a couple of pencils. A south-facing window filled the room with oblique light, revealing a wall full of photographs of groups of uniformed men and women.

His shirt sleeves were rolled up to his elbows, baring corded forearms covered in fine blond hair.

"Kate," he said, coming around the desk to shake her hand. He nodded to the constable who had escorted Kate in and the young woman left, closing the door behind her.

"Hello, Ford," said Kate. She always felt awkward addressing him by his given name, even though he was only a few years older than her. It had something to do with the sense of authority he exuded. He always reminded her of her high school English teacher, Mr. Jarvis.

"Have a seat," he told her, going back around the desk. He

waited until she sat down before seating himself. "Did you make your notification?"

Kate nodded. She placed her cap on her lap and tapped her fingers on the brim. "Calder Bragg. He was our victim's husband."

Ford rested his elbows on his chair's armrests and clasped his hands over his flat stomach.

"Do you have a cause of death yet?"

Kate shook her head. "Still waiting on autopsy results, but there were ligature bruises around her neck."

"Is the husband good for it?"

"I don't know yet," she said. "He says he and his wife split up a few days ago and he thinks she's been staying with her boyfriend, but he doesn't know who the boyfriend is." She shrugged. "I don't think he's telling us everything. We need to speak to him again. To her coworkers and friends."

Ford nodded. "I hear one of your constables is involved."

For Pete's sake. Did everyone know about this case?

"I see the gossip mill is running full tilt," she said sharply.

Ford's eyebrows rose fractionally.

"It's not true?"

She took a deep breath.

"He met her once. He's the one who identified her at the morgue." She wanted to say that she didn't think it was anything more than a coincidence, the kind of thing that was bound to happen in a small town. In two small towns. Instead she said, "I was hoping Brandon could interview him, to avoid any hint of impropriety." The words came out stiffly and she realized she was resentful. She didn't want to have to depend on anyone else. She trusted Trepalli. If he said he'd only met Lawson once and had no involvement with her, Kate believed him.

But a defence lawyer would tear the case to shreds with reasonable doubt. She had to run this by the book.

"Of course," said Ford. "We'll call him in. What's his name?"

So Kate gave him Marco's particulars and mentioned that he was on leave because he was getting married on Saturday. Ford shook his head.

"Poor timing," he murmured.

Yes, indeed. "His family is here from Ontario," she continued. Then, because she knew she had to do it, she said, "My family is here, too. He's marrying my niece."

Ford looked up from his notepad, frowning.

"Well, that could get tricky."

Kate sighed. "That's why someone else has to interview him. I'm hoping to avoid the minefield."

Ford sat back, still frowning.

"Should you even be investigating this case?"

And there it was. Should she be investigating Kelly Lawson's death? Was she risking accusations of bias? But Lawson had been found on her turf. And she didn't want to turn the case over to anyone else.

"That's why I'm asking you to interview Trepalli," she said calmly. "If you find anything questionable, we'll turn the case over to the RCMP."

Ford stared at her for a long moment. "You must have a lot of faith in this officer."

"I do," said Kate. She realized suddenly that it was true. It was her job to keep an open mind until all the facts were in, but she believed the boy. "But that doesn't mean I'll give him a pass if he's involved in her death." She proceeded to give him the details of the case, sparse as they were.

Then she stood up. "The ME estimates that Lawson died sometime between six and nine o'clock on Sunday evening." There. Now he knew everything she did. "We'll be in and out of Brandon for the next few days," she said, "interviewing coworkers and whoever else we can dig up. Are you all right with that?"

Ford stood up, too. "Of course. I'll attach one of my detectives to accompany your investigator."

She didn't like it, but Kate nodded. She would have done the same.

"Thanks. As long as it's understood that the case belongs to Mendenhall. Unless I have to hand it over." She would send McKell to do the interviews. No way was she sending one of her constables to be outranked by a Brandon detective who might just try to take over the interviews.

Suddenly, Ford grinned, completely transforming his face. Kate stared, trying to remember if she had ever seen him smile before. No. No, she definitely would have remembered how handsome it made him.

"I wouldn't give up my case, either," he said cheerfully. He came around the desk and placed a hand on her back as he escorted her to the door.

"Oh, just one thing," said Kate, suddenly remembering. She stopped and looked up at him. "The husband, Calder Bragg, has no record, but I wonder if your folks might have run across him more informally. Maybe nothing got written up but they would still remember him."

Ford nodded. Patrol officers knew their beat, their neighborhoods. They lived in the same town. Someone might remember an incident that hadn't risen to the level of action.

"I'll put the word out," promised Ford. "I'll let you know what I find."

* * *

She found Boychuk in the coffee room, chatting with a woman in uniform. Kate's first reaction was to bristle, but as she got closer, she realized they were talking about softball.

"All done?" said Boychuk, standing up.

"Yes. Time to go."

He grabbed his cap from the chair and nodded to the woman.

"Chief, this is Officer Jessica Melnyk. Jess, this is Chief Williams."

Melnyk nodded but didn't stand up. Only then did Kate notice the cast on her foot.

At her raised eyebrows, Melnyk sighed. "Softball accident. Now I'm stuck on desk duty."

Kate smiled her sympathy and she and Boychuk left.

"Did you contact Victim Services?" she asked as they got into the Edge.

"Done. The duty sergeant took care of it."

"Good."

They swung by the Tim Hortons on the highway on their way out of town and were back in Mendenhall by eight thirty.

She drove to his house and parked in front of it.

"Thanks for staying late," she told him.

He nodded. "No problem, Chief. I can stay on if you'd like."

Kate hesitated. Boychuk was on nights and he had one more shift tonight. He needed to get home and get some sleep. She understood his eagerness. She wanted nothing more than to go back to Brandon and take him with her to interview Bragg again, and Lawson's colleagues, and try to find this boyfriend of hers, but she had to pick her battles.

"Thanks," she said, "but DC McKell will take over the Brandon side of things for now." Even to her ear, she sounded disappointed. "I'll tell him you're up on the case if he needs you."

"Right. Well, see you on Saturday."

Kate watched him get out of the car and finally sighed. Saturday. The wedding was taking place in Marco and Amanda's backyard. The wedding itself would be limited to family and close friends—which to Amanda and Marco meant the whole detachment. Afterward, anybody could drop by—neighbors, officers from Brandon and Winnipeg, casual acquaintances... The on-duty Mendenhall officers would take turns dropping in during the afternoon.

In the meantime, there was all that bloody setting up to do.

In fact, the tent people were supposed to be arriving today. Or was that tomorrow?

In any case, she should be around to lend a hand. As if there weren't already enough hands to go around. But she could at least visit with her family.

With another sigh, she pulled away from the curb and drove to the detachment.

She remembered to grab her cooling coffee from the cup holder before closing and locking the door.

One patrol car was parked in the slot farthest from the door, as if ostracized. It was the one nobody wanted to drive because it kept breaking down.

Martins looked up from scribbling in the duty book when she walked in.

"Chief. How did it go?"

Kate shrugged as she entered the duty room.

"Fine, I guess. He didn't break down or anything." She looked around the empty duty room, turning the words over in her head. He didn't break down. Or anything.

That was it, wasn't it? Bragg didn't cry, or yell, or stagger back. He didn't even look surprised.

In fact, he didn't deny her words or even question them. In every other notification she had ever made, the person she was notifying inevitably responded with, "Are you sure?"

But not Bragg. No, his reaction was to distance himself from his wife and point the finger at her boyfriend.

"How're things here?" she asked, juggling the paper cup still half full of coffee while shrugging out of her bomber jacket. The detachment was warm, especially to someone just coming in from outside. She longed to open the window over Charlotte's desk. Speaking of which...

"Where's Charlotte?"

Martins closed the log book and replaced it at the end of the counter where any constable could stand out of the way of traffic and read it.

"Josh is on the road today," he said with a grin. "She'll be coming in a little later."

Kate nodded and headed for her office. "Could you let the DC know I want to see him when he comes in?"

"Will do."

In her office, she dropped the jacket and cap on a visitor chair and went back out to the break room, where she took the lid off the coffee cup and reheated the coffee in the microwave. She was just pulling it out gingerly—too hot, too hot!—when the exterior door opened and Rob McKell walked in. He glanced in the break room as he walked by, then backtracked.

"Morning," he said.

"Morning, Rob," said Kate, resorting to a tea towel to retrieve the cup. "I hope you don't have plans today."

One eyebrow rose and he entered the break room. At fifty-three, Deputy Chief Rob McKell was still in his prime, with the solidity of a mature man. Nearly six feet tall, his leanness gave the impression that he was even taller. He always kept his graying hair cropped short, not even trying to hide his receding hairline. He was very fit, especially now that he had recovered from the gunshot wound, though still too thin. She saw him every morning at Stan's Gym. She had started going there when her regular gym closed for renovations. She found Rob working out every morning, trying to regain his strength. They fell into working out together after she learned that he worked out harder when she was there.

"I heard about the body," he said, taking out his notebook. "You notified the husband?"

Kate nodded and blew on the hot coffee, trying to cool it down to drinking temperature. She wasn't surprised Rob had already heard about Kelly Lawson's death. Nothing much happened at the detachment without Rob finding out about it.

"I would like you to go to Brandon and interview her work colleagues. She worked as a dental hygienist at Leaf Dental. When you're done with that, go back to the husband's street and interview the neighbors. Hopefully, some of them will be home. If not, we may have to send someone back this evening to interview those you couldn't get."

Rob finished writing, then looked up at her. "I'll get Samantha to come with me."

Kate shook her head. "Brandon will be assigning one of their detectives to go with you."

His face told her exactly what he thought about that idea. She grinned reluctantly.

"I know. But it's their turf."

He flipped the cover of his notebook closed and stuffed it into his back pocket.

"Doesn't mean I have to like it," he muttered.

"Also," continued Kate as if she hadn't heard him. "Brandon will be interviewing Trepalli."

Rob opened his mouth as if to object, then closed it in a grimace. His blue eyes darkened with reproach.

"Speaking of which," she added, ignoring his distress, "I'd better call him and let him know."

Rob nodded sharply and turned on his heel, leaving Kate to sigh into her coffee. After a while, she went back to her office and closed the door. Setting the coffee down on her desk, she pulled out her cell phone and tapped on Trepalli's number.

She stood by the window, staring out at the church across the street and listened to ring after ring. Samantha Paterson pulled into the parking lot and came inside the detachment. When the ringing rolled over to voice mail, Kate hung up and tried Amanda's phone.

The girl picked up after the third ring.

"Hi, Aunt Kate!" She sounded cheerful but the background sounded like the circus was in town.

"What is all that noise?" asked Kate, half aghast, half amused.

"The tent folks are here," said Amanda. "We're helping them set up."

And I'm sure they appreciate it, thought Kate, listening to the cacophony.

"I'm looking for Marco," said Kate. "Is he there?"

"I sent him for more groceries," said Amanda. "His mom and aunt went with him." There was laughter in her voice.

"All right," said Kate. "Is my mother there?"

"Yes," said Amanda. "She's making tea right now. Do you want to talk to her?"

"No, I'll be there soon," said Kate. "In the meantime, if Marco comes back, have him call me."

"All right," said Amanda, her voice suddenly louder. She had gone inside. "Is everything all right?"

Kate hesitated. It really wasn't Kate's place to tell her.

Or maybe it was but she still wasn't going to do it.

"No, just a case he's involved in."

They hung up and Kate left the detachment for home, taking her coffee with her. The day was going to be lovely, judging by how warm it felt already. A few popcorn clouds graced the sky and there was barely a breeze.

She waved at the firefighters washing the fire engine and they waved back. She wondered idly if she could persuade them to wash her Edge.

Her phone rang just as she pulled in behind the travel trailer. With the pickup truck gone, there was just barely room for her Edge. She turned the engine off and grabbed the phone, expecting to see Trepalli's number. It was Bert.

"Hi," she said into the phone. She opened the car door and slid out, remembering to grab her coffee before closing the door. It was almost nine o'clock, and all along the street, driveways were empty except for a couple where either the dad or the mom stayed home with the kids.

"Hey," said Bert. Just the sound of his voice calmed her. "Just checking in. How's it going with the family?"

Kate shrugged, even though he couldn't see her. She unlocked the front door and went inside.

"Had a nice breakfast with Mom, but then I had to go to Brandon to do the next-of-kin notification. I just got back."

There was a long silence at the other end and Kate actually looked at the screen to see if they had been cut off.

"You're not avoiding them, are you?" he asked finally.

"No, I'm not," she said patiently. "I'm at home now to change into my civvies and go join them at Amanda and Marco's."

"Good," said Bert. "There's no telling how many more times you'll all be together."

It was Kate's turn to go silent as she stood in her small entry-way, staring into her kitchen. Then she sighed silently.

"Did you see your mom today?"

"Not yet," said Bert. "I'll swing by this afternoon. She doesn't know who I am anymore, but she thinks I'm a nice man because I bring her cupcakes."

Kate laughed softly. What else could she do?

"All right," continued Bert. "I'll let you get on with it. Just wanted to make sure you're okay."

"I am," said Kate firmly. "I'll call you tonight."

"Bye, love," said Bert and hung up.

Cheered by his call, Kate hurried to change before heading out again.

* * *

The black pickup was parked in front of the house, as were three white sedans that had to be rentals. Nobody in Mendenhall drove a car that clean.

She didn't even bother with the front door. Judging by the noise level in the backyard, an airplane was getting ready to take off. She made her way down the driveway past Amanda's Tercel and Marco's Mustang to find people scurrying all over the back lawn, more people attempting to erect a large event tent, and Mom and Fred sitting on the deck enjoying the show.

Kate made her way to the back steps and joined them at one of the small tables that Amanda had set up for her part-time restaurant.

"Hello, dear," said Mom with a smile. She wore a long-sleeved, loose tee-shirt and a pair of cropped linen pants along with sandals. She had one of Amanda's china tea cups and matching saucers in front of her while Fred nursed a mug of coffee in his big gnarled hands. He wore a pair of khakis and a white shirt with the sleeves rolled up to his elbows.

Kate dropped a kiss on top of Mom's head and nodded to Fred.

"Supervising?" she asked.

Fred grumbled something and looked away.

"They won't let him help," explained Mom, smiling sweetly.

Kate looked over the people swarming over the backyard and shuddered. She couldn't even tell individuals apart. And what was making all that noise?

"I think it's safer up here," said Kate, raising her voice to be heard.

Fred smiled reluctantly. "Ants on a cupcake," he said.

"There's coffee inside," said Mom and Kate nodded. She had no idea what had happened to the coffee she had taken home. Before going inside, she glanced around the yard one more time, hoping to pick out Marco, with no luck.

Just as she was entering the kitchen, however, the front door opened to reveal him, laden down with at least eight cloth bags full of groceries. Behind him were two older women, clearly his mother and aunt, both carrying two bags each. They were going to have to break out the downstairs refrigerators.

Trepalli entered the kitchen and carefully set one armful of groceries down on the table and then the other. Then he turned to help his mother and aunt. Only then did he notice Kate standing in the doorway.

"Chief!" he said with a smile. "You met my mom and my aunt last night." He pulled his mother closer. "Camilla Trepalli, and my aunt, Gaetana Verger. Mom, Aunt Tina, you remember Chief Williams."

All three women turned to look at him. Then Kate stepped forward to shake Camilla's hand. "It was a little crazy last night." She shook Gaetana's hand. "Call me Kate, please."

"And you can call me Tina," said the aunt. Both women were lovely, with dark, sweeping eyebrows and thick dark hair that Marco had clearly inherited. Both had brown eyes, so Kate presumed Marco had inherited his eye color from his dad.

"Do you mind if I take Marco away for a moment?" she asked with a smile.

Camilla shrugged. "We'll go tell Amanda we're back." She raised her eyebrows at Kate. "She's very particular about where the food goes."

Kate laughed. "Well, it didn't take you long! She was living with me for three weeks before I realized she would come along behind me and reorganize all my cupboards and refrigerator every time I went shopping."

The two women laughed and went outside.

Kate turned to Marco. "What is that noise?" she asked plaintively.

He grinned. "The tent people brought a generator for their tools." He glanced out the kitchen window. "I suspect it would go a lot faster if people stopped trying to help."

Kate suspected it, too.

"Did you get a call from Brandon?" she asked.

He frowned and slapped a hand on his butt. Then he looked around the kitchen.

"I left my phone here," he said, finally spotting it tucked in a corner, recharging. He wore jeans and a black tee-shirt with the name of a band on the front. "Why? Were you trying to reach me?" He retrieved his phone and unplugged it. He scrolled through a couple of screens, read something, and then looked at her, frowning.

"Brandon Police Service?"

Kate nodded. "Yes. I've asked them to interview you about Kelly Lawson."

"Kelly Lawson?" asked Amanda, walking into the kitchen with Camilla and Tina behind her.

Later it would occur to Kate that things would have gone much better if Marco hadn't blushed.

CHAPTER 9

When it became clear that Amanda was furious with Marco, everybody scattered. Charlie and Sean decided to take the pickup truck and go for a drive. Kate gathered Mom, Fred, Rose, and John and took them for an early lunch to Boston Pizza, the only restaurant in town with a real, honest-to-God patio that could accommodate all five of them on short notice. She hoped Marco's family would take the hint and leave, too.

Before she left, she reminded Marco to set up an interview with Brandon as soon as possible and let her know when it would be.

They found a spot on the patio that was partly in sunlight for Mom, Rose, and Fred—and partly in shade for her and John. It was a lovely day, but the breeze was a little cool. Still, Kate would rather be a little chilled than bake in the sun.

After everyone ordered, Rose settled back in her chair and looked at Kate.

"Tell me again how he's involved with this dead woman?"

Kate smiled tightly. "I see we're picking up where we left off." Rose had spent the drive from Amanda and Marco's house to the restaurant wondering what Marco had to do with Kelly Lawson and opining that it was suspicious, no matter how she looked at it.

As always, Rose wore makeup, something light that enhanced

her brown eyes and put color in her pale skin. Like Mom, she wore white cropped pants and a short-sleeved, flowing top in blues and greens. Her sandals had a two-inch heel but even so, she barely came up to Kate's five feet three. Her longer hair framed her face nicely.

But it was still dyed dark brown.

"Yes," said Rose, cocking her head. "We are. You say he's not involved with her, but now he has to be interviewed by another police department? Can you blame us for having questions?"

"Us?" said Kate sharply. "As far as I can tell, you're the only one beating this to death."

"Actually," said John slowly. "I have concerns, too." He looked at Kate, eyebrows raised.

John was usually patient with his wife's exaggerations, but if he was lending Rose active support, Kate would have to pay attention.

"I'm a little worried, too," said Mom quietly. Fred took her hand and they both stared at Kate. A gentle breeze teased tendrils of white hair from Mom's loose bun.

Kate looked from face to face. Even Fred looked concerned. Holy cow.

"I can't discuss an open case," she said seriously. "I can tell you that he freely divulged having met the victim, once, last year. You have nothing to worry about."

All four pairs of eyes still looked troubled but everyone remained silent as the waitress returned with their drink orders.

"Clearly you have a lot of trust in this young man," said John after the waitress had left. "But this is my daughter we're talking about. You say we have nothing to worry about, but why is he being interviewed by another police department?"

"Because no matter how tangential, he's a witness in this case," said Kate patiently. "And we can't interview one of our own. You always need an outside agency when the witness or suspect is one of your own. This way, if Marco is called to testify, the defence won't be able to say that we gave him a free pass."

"Is he a suspect?" asked Mom worriedly. "Why is Amanda

marrying a man who's involved in a murder?"

"Mom!" said Kate reproachfully. "That kind of talk can ruin a police officer's career."

Mom blushed but her chin jutted out in a familiar way.

"I'm sorry, Katie," she said, "but I'm serious. Is he involved in this young woman's death?"

"No!" said Kate, more forcefully than she had intended. They stared back at her in varying states of alarm. She took a deep breath. "This isn't Montreal, or even St. Lambert," she continued. "Mendenhall is a small town, and Brandon isn't much bigger. My officers live here or around here. They are bound to meet or know people who become involved in our investigations. Marco Trepalli is one of the finest young officers I've ever worked with. He may be the most honorable man I know. Do you honestly think I would let Amanda marry a man who could be a criminal?"

It upset her more than she had realized that her family—her own family—would distrust her judgment to that extent.

There was an awkward silence, then John picked up his glass of draft beer and took a sip.

"I trust you, Kate," he said gently. "We all do. It's just that we'd hate to see Amanda hurt."

At that moment the waitress returned, accompanied by another young woman, and they set plates out in front of everyone. The food looked great, but Kate had lost her appetite.

* * *

After a strained lunch, Mom announced that she'd like to take a nap, so Kate drove Mom and Fred back to her house before driving Rose and John back to Amanda and Marco's place.

During lunch, Marco had texted her that the interview would take place that afternoon at one o'clock. Kate had excused herself to go the bathroom, where she called Rob and asked him to meet Marco at the Brandon detachment. Rob wouldn't be allowed to sit in on the interview but he would be allowed to watch it from the viewing room.

As she parked across the street from Amanda and Marco's, she realized she was irritated that Charlie and Sean were still missing in action. Probably sitting somewhere drinking beer, she thought uncharitably.

The rental cars were still parked in front, but Marco's Mustang was gone and so was the noise from the generator. They followed the sounds of voices in the backyard and found that the tent had been set up. Kate stared at it for a long time, trying to figure out how they had managed to fit such a big structure in their small backyard. The tent had at least three center poles and had to be twenty by forty. There wasn't room for anything else in the back-yard, but already round tables and picnic tables were set up under it. The sides of the tent were rolled up and tied to the metal frame to allow for air circulation. If the weather turned suddenly, they could roll them down and be protected from the elements.

Amanda was in the tent, as were Camilla and Tina and their husbands, who were placing tables and chairs under the direction of the two older women. From inside the house came the sound of voices arguing and laughing. A couple of younger men, clearly from the Trepalli gene pool, pulled tables and chairs from a tall stack set precariously by one of the tent supports, supplying the father and uncle.

"Dear God," murmured Rose, clearly aghast.

Yes, thought Kate. Dear God.

At that moment, Amanda turned and Kate's heart squeezed in alarm. The girl's face was white and her eyes were bloodshot. She surreptitiously slid a tissue into her shorts pocket and pasted a smile on her face.

"Hi!" she said brightly. "How was lunch?"

At that moment, Kate felt about as low as she had ever felt in her life. They had all decamped, leaving her alone with the Trepalli clan with no support. Clearly, the Trepallis hadn't had the grace to leave her and Marco alone.

"Hi, sweetheart," said Rose. She walked over to her daughter and gathered her in a fierce hug. "I'm sorry," she whispered. "We thought it would be better to leave you and Marco alone. We didn't realize they would be staying."

John went up to Amanda and wrapped an arm around her

shoulders. "Sorry, honey. We thought we were doing the right thing."

"Nonsense," said Amanda firmly, though her eyes were suspiciously bright. "We were all busy with the tent and setting up the tables. There are still sandwiches inside if you're hungry."

Kate turned as Camilla approached her, her sister by her side. Both women had fixed smiles on their faces, and when they stopped a few feet away, both crossed their arms in mirror gestures. Both had their dark hair up in a casual chignon that managed to look sophisticated and revealed their angry faces.

Uh-oh.

"Hi," said Kate cheerfully. "You're doing a great job on the setup."

Camilla shrugged, as if that wasn't important right now.

"Do you think my son murdered this woman?" she demanded.

Oh, for Pete's sake! Had Marco told them about the case?

"No, of course not," she said cautiously. "But—"

"But what?" asked Tina angrily. "If you don't think he hurt her, why does he have to go to another police station and answer their questions?"

Rose stepped away from Amanda and came to stand next to Kate.

"She's just doing her job," she began reasonably.

"Really?" said Camilla, her dark eyes flashing dangerously. "I would have thought her job would be to stand by her police officers."

"Now hang on," said John sharply. At his tone, the two husbands—Henry and Paul, if she remembered correctly—looked around, frowning. "Her job is to find out who murdered this woman and bring them to justice. If your son is involved—"

That was when Henry and Paul hurried over, already arguing loudly. In seconds, Kate could no longer make out what any of them were saying. She looked over at Amanda, who was staring at her parents and future in-laws in horror.

The wind suddenly picked up, lifting Kate's loose hair off the nape of her neck. As more and more of the Trepalli clan emerged from the kitchen and came down the deck stairs to see what was going on, Kate stared at the arguing in-laws in dismay. John was chest to chest with Henry Trepalli and both of them were getting red in the face.

Dear God. Was this going to degenerate into a brawl?

"That's enough," she said quietly, almost to herself. Then she filled her lungs with air and bellowed in her best cop's voice, "THAT'S ENOUGH!"

Every face in the backyard turned to her. When she was sure she had the main culprits' attention—John and Henry—she stared at them fiercely.

"Look at you!" she said angrily. She looked at Camilla, Tina, and Rose. "All of you! Flying off the handle for no good reason. Marco will be back in a couple of hours—do you think he will be proud of your behavior?" She looked at John. "Do you think Amanda is proud of yours?"

Camilla opened her mouth but Kate raised a hand sharply to stop her. "That's enough," she said quietly. "I suggest you go back to your houses for now. I think everyone could use a break."

Camilla's face reddened and Tina's arms were still crossed, but their husbands nodded grudgingly. They gathered their wives and everyone—it seemed like fifty people but probably was no more than a dozen—slowly trickled out of the backyard and house.

Amanda turned a stricken face toward her.

"Aunt Kate—they're Marco's family…"

"Yes," agreed Kate equably. "But they're not allowed to behave like that."

John laughed shortly. "Thanks, Kate. For a minute there—"

"Don't," said Kate. She hadn't realized how angry she was until she heard his laugh. "You're just as bad as they are." His face colored and Rose patted his arm sympathetically. Kate was actually surprised that her sister had been the voice of reason in this whole affair.

Her phone vibrated and she pulled it out of her back pocket. There was a text from Dr. Kijawa:

PLEASE ATTEND THE MORGUE. INFORMATION ON AUTOPSY.

Thank God. She glanced up at her family.

"I have to go to the morgue. I'll check in with you all later."

And with that, she turned and left. As she tucked her phone away, she realized that her hands were trembling.

* * *

By the time she drove into the hospital parking lot, Kate had managed to unclench her jaw. She parked, turned the engine off, and sat in the Edge, taking deep breaths in and out until her shoulders relaxed.

It was only Tuesday. The wedding was on Saturday. Once wed, Amanda and Marco would take off on their honeymoon—location a secret—and both sets of relatives would return from whence they came.

The trick would be to keep things civil until then. Kate leaned forward slowly until her head rested on the steering wheel.

They should have eloped.

* * *

Dr. Kijawa opened the door to the morgue and let Kate in. The table in the middle of the room was empty and scrupulously clean. There was a whiff of disinfectant in the air, along with other smells that Kate didn't consider for long.

"Thank you for coming so quickly," said the doc, leading the way to the corner where she kept her desk. She gestured to the visitor chair and Kate sat down.

Dr. Kijawa also sat down and pulled a file folder toward her.

"As you suspected, Ms. Lawson died of asphyxia. My report will record her manner of death as a homicide." She pushed an eight by ten color photograph toward Kate.

It showed a close-up of Kelly Lawson's neck injury. It really was striking. A belt could have left those marks, but there would have to be some kind of decorations on the belt. Studs, maybe. Rhinestones?

"Her hyoid bone is still intact," continued Dr. Kijawa.

Kate looked up from the photo. "Lack of strength?"

"Not necessarily. It could be the tool used." Dr. Kijawa peered at the photo. "My guess would be a belt. If so, it would have distributed the pressure along its width. Not enough to break the hyoid, but enough to keep air from getting in." She frowned, her finger tracing the ligature mark. "It would have taken a long time to kill her. At least two or three minutes."

They both stared down at the photo. It took a lot of rage to sustain that kind of pressure for two or three minutes. To watch the victim struggle, then slow, then die. That kind of rage was personal.

"Was she sexually assaulted?" asked Kate slowly.

Dr. Kijawa shook her head. "No. In fact, there was no sign of recent sexual activity."

So what drove the rage that resulted in Lawson's murder?

"I will email you my preliminary report," said the doc, "and I will let you know when the toxicology results come in, and the analysis of the substance beneath her nails."

Kate stood up.

"Thank you, doctor." She wondered what Kelly Lawson could possibly have done to deserve such a brutal death. To end up naked in a canola field. It would be good to get DNA results back, but she wasn't holding her breath. Unless the killer had their DNA in the system, there would be nothing to compare with the DNA under Kelly Lawson's nails.

"I've sent the body up to Radiology," said Dr. Kijawa.

Kate's eyebrows rose. "Why?"

The doc placed her hands on her knees and looked down at them.

"I found evidence of old injuries," she said. "Scars that would be hidden under clothes. Healed breaks in her ribs. Missing teeth."

Kate looked down, too. "You suspect abuse."

"I do. I will let you know the results."

Kate nodded. If someone had been abusing Kelly Lawson, then her death could be a logical extension of that abuse.

"I found no recent bruising, however, except for that around her neck," continued the doc. "So perhaps I am wrong."

Kate took a deep breath, then regretted it. "I appreciate you dealing with this so promptly," she said. She headed for the door.

"Chief Williams."

Kate turned at the note in the doc's voice.

"There is one more thing." The doctor hadn't moved from her chair but the look on her face had turned grim.

"What is it?" asked Kate, steeling herself.

"Ms. Lawson was two months pregnant."

CHAPTER 10

Where are you?" demanded Kate. She could hear the clinking of glasses in the background.

"We're just having a beer and a snack," said Charlie, his mouth clearly full.

Kate glanced at the time on her phone, then put it back to her ear.

"The two of you have been hiding out for over four hours," she said sharply. "Mom and Fred are stuck at the house and Rose and John are trying to put Amanda back together again. You need to make sure Mom's okay."

One heartbeat. Two. Then Charlie said, "What the hell happened?"

So Kate filled him in and he sighed.

"This always happens at weddings," he muttered. "They should have eloped."

"I know, right?" Finally, someone who understood.

"All right," grumbled Charlie. "I'll drop Sean off at Amanda's to get the lay of the land and I'll go over to your place. I'll keep you posted."

"Thanks, Charlie," said Kate, suddenly remembering that she was supposed to be on leave and available to her mom. "I'm sorry to dump this on you."

"I know," said Charlie. "You didn't plan to have someone murdered in your jurisdiction."

They were just hanging up when she heard a car pull into the parking lot. She went to her window and saw McKell getting out of his Honda CRV. He looked stern under the bill of his cap, but then, he always looked stern.

She listened to the storm door slap shut and the thud of his boots on the linoleum and decided that if he stopped in the break room first, she would drag him out by his ear. But the footsteps came closer and she turned around to find him standing in her doorway.

"How did it go?"

He shrugged. "Trepalli kept it together but I was ready to jump through the mirror and strangle the detective."

Kate sighed and waved him to one of the guest chairs. She settled into her own chair and waited.

McKell placed his cap on the desk and leaned back. He had dark circles under his eyes and Kate wondered if they would ever go away. He didn't sleep well anymore. She didn't think it was physical pain left over from the sniper's bullet. She and McKell's brother spoke on a regular basis, keeping each other apprised of McKell's progress, and the brother had told her that McKell had admitted to nightmares.

"The guy was rough on Trepalli, clearly trying to rattle him. He asked all the standard questions about how he had met Lawson, what their relationship had been, had he known she was married, how long he'd been seeing her, where was he the night she died." He sighed and stretched his neck. "You know. He did what he was supposed to do."

Kate sighed, too. Yes, that was what the interviewer was supposed to do. "How did Marco answer?"

"He told the guy the same thing he told you. That he'd only met her the once and gave her his business card because she asked for it. He never saw her after that one time. He asked when did she die. Turns out he was at home with Amanda."

Kate nodded. Of course he was home with Amanda. It was

the day before the Trepalli and Williams clans were to descend on Mendenhall. But being home with Amanda wasn't a great alibi. A wife—or wife-to-be—could be suspected of providing a false alibi.

"There's something else," she told McKell glumly. "Lawson was two months pregnant."

"Oh, great," said McKell, shoulders slumping. "Trepalli's going to love that."

"Yeah." Kate sighed. "So, what about the interviews with Bragg's neighbors? Did you get a chance to go to Leaf Dental?"

McKell shook off his gloom and sat up straighter, pulling his notebook out.

"Yes, I spoke to all the neighbors who were around—three of them. The nearest neighbor reported that he sometimes heard Bragg yelling but he couldn't tell what about. He's an older gentleman and he wore a hearing aid. He said Kelly was pretty quiet, but friendly. She brought him chocolate chip cookies when she baked. Next was a man recovering from pneumonia at home. He's not normally home during the day since he and his wife both work, but he's met Bragg and thinks he's okay. His wife doesn't like him, though." He looked up from his notes. "She would be worth talking to, I think."

Kate nodded her agreement.

"Last one I spoke to was a teenage girl, home for the summer, and bored. They have one of those glider swings in the front yard and she spends a lot of time sitting there and scrolling through her tablet. She saw Kelly Lawson put suitcases in her car on Friday and leave. Bragg was at work. Later, when Bragg came home, she heard a lot of crashing and breaking sounds coming from his house. So, I'm not sure if Bragg actually kicked her out or if she left when he wasn't around."

Huh. Had Bragg lied? If so, was it to save face? Was there really a boyfriend?

The phone rang in the duty room and Charlotte answered, her voice floating back to Kate's office. The smell of burnt coffee filled the detachment, so familiar that she missed it when it was absent.

"What about her coworkers?" she asked.

"The dentist she works with most often was useless," said McKell with contempt. "He didn't even know she was married and she'd been working for him for almost a year. But I had better luck with the two dental hygienists, Lucy Bellingham and Jeanine Hurtubise. Nothing much from them. They said she was quiet and good at her job."

Kate expelled the breath she hadn't known she was holding.

"Dr. Kijawa suspects abuse," she said. "She's getting x-rays done and is going to see if there's a record of emergency room visits in Brandon."

McKell nodded. "We should check the ERs here and in Winnipeg, too. If he hurt her, he wouldn't want to raise alarms in his own backyard."

Had Calder Bragg abused his wife? Had the abuse escalated to murder? He could have left her body in the canola field on the Hurst farm to get her away from Brandon. If so, why did she have Marco's business card clutched in her hand? Had Bragg put it there to implicate Marco? It was too much of a coincidence to think that he happened to find a field that just happened to belong to friends of Marco.

"Chief?"

Both Kate and McKell swivelled to find Marco Trepalli standing in the doorway, wearing jeans and a white tee-shirt. Again, the thought flitted through Kate's mind: he and Amanda would make gorgeous babies.

"You survived," she said with a smile. She nodded him to the chair next to McKell.

"I have a whole new sympathy for suspects," he said, sitting down. Judging by the look on his face, he was serious. "You watched the interview?" he asked McKell.

McKell nodded. Marco had known he would be there, of course, for moral support as much as for having a witness.

"What do you think?"

McKell shrugged. "They're going to check your alibi, of course. And they'll check to see if anyone can disprove what you said about not knowing Lawson."

Marco's lips pursed, then parted on a gust of breath. "Let 'em. They can't prove that I knew her because I didn't." He looked at Kate. "Now can I please participate in the investigation?"

Kate's heart squeezed a little. She understood. Really, she did.

"No," she said.

He looked surprised. "Why not?"

She sighed. "Not yet, anyway. Dr. Kijawa says that Kelly Lawson was two months pregnant."

Sadness flitted over Marco's face and he shook his head.

"That poor girl," he murmured. "I wish—I wonder if she was reaching out for help when she approached me. Maybe I should have..." Then his face changed. "Wait a minute. You don't think—"

"No, of course not," said Kate firmly. "But it doesn't matter what I think. We have to cross all our t's, Marco."

A tide of blood turned his face and neck brick red.

"You want me to do a paternity test," he said bitterly.

McKell actually looked down and Kate almost cringed at the accusation in his voice. She knew better than to try and excuse herself, however. This was the job.

"I'll be getting a warrant for Calder Bragg's DNA, too," she said mildly. "Both the defence and the crown prosecutor will demand them. Better to be forthcoming."

Marco stood up abruptly. "Sure," he said and there was no disguising the fury in his voice. "That's what I'll tell Amanda. That you want my DNA for when the crown prosecutor asks for it. That'll be a great comfort to her. And I'm sure her father will feel great knowing that she's marrying a guy who may have murdered the woman carrying his baby. That's, you know, if there's a wedding at all."

"You don't need to tell her until it's over," Kate pointed out.

The look in his eye skewered her in place.

"If that's how you think," he said bitingly, "then it's no surprise you never married."

With that, he stormed out of the office. They heard Charlotte speak to him but he didn't answer. Then the storm door slammed shut. Moments later, the engine of his Mustang started up and he roared out of the parking lot.

After a while, McKell looked up.

"Well, that could have gone better."

CHAPTER 11

McKell had learned from the two dental hygienists that Kelly Lawson often went for lunch with a woman named Lisa Theopolis. They had no idea where she worked or anything else about her.

"I'll ask Martins to track her down in Brandon," said Kate.

McKell stood up. In the back of her mind, Kate noted the easy movement. He was almost back to himself. Except for the nightmares.

"I'm going back to Brandon at suppertime," he said. "I can stop in to see Theopolis at the same time, if Martins can locate her."

Kate nodded and watched him leave. She should be doing the interviews, tracking people down, obtaining DNA samples. Instead, she was going back home to see what awaited her.

She was just grabbing her cap and car keys when her cell phone rang. She dropped the keys back on the desk and fished the phone out of her pocket. Bert.

"Hi," she said.

"Hey," said Bert, his warm voice running through her like a balm. "Just checking to see how it's going."

She sighed.

"That bad, eh."

"Well, it could be better," she admitted. She closed her office door and went to stand by the window. The sky was a clear blue with no clouds. She told him about the confrontation between the Williams and Trepalli families that afternoon.

"Hoo boy," said Bert after she finished. "When's he getting interviewed? Things should settle down when it's done."

Kate sighed again.

"What?" asked Bert.

"He did the interview this afternoon and it went as expected. That's not the problem." Well, not the big problem, anyway.

"What is?" There was worry in his voice now. Bert liked Marco well enough, but he was very fond of Amanda. He treated her like a favorite niece, seeing as he had none of his own.

Kate considered her next words. Should she tell Bert? Was it a big secret? Marco was probably telling Amanda right now. Amanda would tell her parents. There was no telling who Calder Bragg would tell once they obtained his DNA. And all medical examiners' report became part of the public record of a case.

Still, it felt disrespectful to Kelly Lawson to discuss her personal life like it was juicy gossip.

She had a sudden memory of Lawson's long dark hair sweeping over her pale face.

"Never mind," she said finally. "I can't really talk about it. And I should get going. Who knows what they're all up to with no one to keep an eye on them."

Bert laughed, accepting her decision without demur. "Want me to come over?"

Yes. Yes, she did.

"How's your mom?" she asked instead.

It was his turn to sigh.

"Last night, she thought I was my dad. And she's not eating much."

Kate was quiet for a moment, trying to imagine that kind of hell. "I'm sorry, Bert."

"I know," he said. His voice got lower. "I know this is part of growing old. It just seems so cruel."

Well, it was cruel. To have memories stolen from you, piece by piece...

Bert saw his mom every day after work. He drove over to the Bessie Knowles Home and had dinner with her. Then they went over old photo albums, or played some of her favorite music. She loved the music.

Kate knew he didn't have much time left with his mom. She wasn't about to steal some of it away because she was feeling down.

"I'll be fine," she said. "Give your mom a hug for me." She had met Mrs. Langdon last year, before she went into care. She liked the old woman.

"All right," said Bert. "How about you call me tonight?"

"Will do," promised Kate.

"Love you, Katie," he said quietly.

"Love you, too, Bert." She hung up.

For one painful, gut-wrenching moment, Kate wanted Bert's arms around her more than she wanted to breathe. Then the feeling passed and she put the phone away.

Charlotte looked around, her eyebrows raised, when Kate walked into the duty room. Sunlight from the window by her desk gilded her brown hair. Today she wore a short-sleeved blue dress with a tight bodice and a knee-length full skirt and strappy sandals.

"Is Marco all right?" she asked.

Kate shrugged. "He will be."

Martins was on the phone at the duty desk and Friesen was at one of the common desks, typing on the keyboard. His dark blond hair was a little longer than usual. He glanced up, sensing her gaze, and smiled. His blue eyes crinkled up charmingly whenever he did.

She nodded at him and wondered if he was still dating Julianne Savoie, Amanda's friend and sometimes helper at the restaurant.

Martins finished on the phone and she went up to him, noting that the DC's door was shut.

"Did the DC ask you to locate a witness?"

"Lisa Theopolis?" He nodded. "Wasn't hard. She works for a law firm in Brandon. I've got her address, too."

"Good." McKell was like her. He didn't like to give a witness—or a suspect—advance notice that he was coming by. It might mean he'd show up and no one would be at home, but they both liked the element of surprise. People revealed a lot when they were surprised.

"I need you to obtain a warrant for a buccal swab from Calder Bragg," she continued. "Ideally, you could get it before the DC returns to Brandon. Talk to him about the details and justification."

"Yes, ma'am," he said.

"Also, can you check the Mendenhall ER and those in Winnipeg for any record of Kelly Lawson? Dr. Kijawa saw old evidence of abuse. She's checking with the hospital in Brandon. If you run out of time, please have Albertson follow up when he comes on duty. And let me know what you find out."

"Will do," said Martins.

She sensed Ben Friesen's and Charlotte's gaze on her back but ignored them. Once Martins found out the reason for the DNA sample, they would all figure out why Marco had been so upset.

"All right," she said to the room in general. "I'm going home." She looked at Martins. "Text me when you get the warrant." He nodded. "And call me if anything comes up."

"Yes, ma'am," he said. "Don't worry, everything's under control here."

Yes, she thought glumly. It was the home front she worried about.

CHAPTER 12

The black rental pickup truck was parked in front of the house, leaving the spot in front of the travel trailer for Kate. She got out of the Edge and followed the noise past the trailer and into the backyard.

There was a picnic table on her lawn.

"There you are!" called Rose.

Kate looked up at her deck to see her sister setting a covered platter on the round patio table. John came out of the kitchen carrying a platter in either hand. Kate blinked and noticed a barbecue in the corner of the deck, near the stairs that led to the lawn.

She didn't have a barbecue. Or a picnic table. Or platters, for that matter.

"Don't just stand there, sweetheart," said Mom as she came out of the kitchen carrying what looked like every single glass Kate owned on a tray. "Come help!"

Kate forced herself to move but once she got up to the deck, she stopped. Her kitchen looked like a tornado had ripped through it. There were bowls and dishes in the sink and on the counters. Something had dripped on the tile floor and been spread by hurrying feet. Bags of hamburger buns lay open on the counter. She blinked and noticed Fred leaning into the fridge. He emerged with a glass container—not hers—full of yellow liquid.

Then she noticed Amanda standing at the counter, shaping hamburger patties and pressing them flat on a plate. Amanda looked at her, her hands still working efficiently. Her eyes were bloodshot but there was a grin on her face.

"Don't worry, Auntie Kate, we'll clean everything up."

In the living room, Charlie and Sean were watching baseball, each one holding a bottle of beer. For a moment, she toyed with the idea of joining them.

"Could you bring this out to the deck?" asked Amanda, holding out the plate of patties.

Still a little stunned, Kate accepted the plate and turned to go out. Then she stopped and turned.

"There's a picnic table on my lawn."

Amanda nodded.

"Mom persuaded your neighbor, Mrs. Buckley, to lend it to us for the week."

Kate's mouth parted a little. Mrs. Buckley? The next-door neighbor could barely mutter "Good morning" when she saw Kate and now she was lending her picnic table? For a week?

"Go," urged Amanda, waving a greasy hand. A couple of drops of barbecue sauce—at least Kate hoped it was barbecue sauce—landed on the tile floor. "Dad's waiting."

Kate turned back to the door and almost bumped into John.

"Good," he said, taking the plate from her. "The barbecue is ready."

"I don't have a barbecue," said Kate automatically.

"You do now," said John. He gave her a reproachful look. "I can't believe you've lived here this long without a barbecue."

Kate followed him outside. Somehow, she had managed to muddle through fifty-five years without ever once feeling the need for a barbecue.

At least he wasn't mad at her.

"Lemonade?" asked Fred, handing her a glass.

Kate accepted it automatically and stood on her deck, looking around. Mom and Rose were at the deck table, arranging platters and covering them with tea towels to prevent insects from getting to the food. Fred was now at ground level, arranging glasses around the picnic table. Two of the chairs belonging to the round table on her deck had migrated to either end of the picnic table.

"Here, dear," said Mom, handing her the pitcher of lemonade. "Could you take this down to the picnic table?" She placed a tea towel on Kate's shoulder, to wipe down the pitcher or to cover it, Kate didn't know.

She glanced over her shoulder and spied Charlie in the living room. He was looking at her with a sympathetic grin.

She went down the stairs to avoid Mom and Rose's rushing about and set the pitcher down on the middle of the heavy wood table.

"Thank you," said Fred, lifting the tea towel from her shoulder and settling it over the pitcher.

"You're welcome," she said automatically.

He looked at her shrewdly and smiled.

"Apparently you took control of an escalating situation at Amanda's."

Kate felt the heat rise to her cheeks. Fred's smile widened.

"I wish I had been there," he added.

"Who told you?" asked Kate, setting her untouched glass of lemonade down on the table.

The sun was low and casting long shadows in her yard. A cool breeze caressed her bare arms, lifting the small hairs. She would need a sweatshirt soon.

"Rose told Hetty, who told me."

It still sounded strange to Kate to have a man call her mom by her given name. But Fred was a good man and he really did love Mom.

"I may have irreparably damaged relations between the two families," she admitted, sitting down on the end of the picnic table's bench seat.

Fred shrugged and sat down next to her.

"It's a wedding," he said. "They make people crazy."

Well, that was true.

"They could have eloped," he added.

Kate nodded and then gave him a half smile. "But Rose would never have forgiven her."

Fred patted her knee before getting up again. He leaned down to her.

"It's only for a few more days," he whispered. "We can handle anything for a few more days."

Kate grinned up at him, but before she could answer, her phone vibrated.

"Excuse me," she said, standing up to take the phone out of her jeans pocket. It was the detachment, Martins. Fred nodded at her and wandered back to the deck.

"OBTAINED WARRANT, DC ON HIS WAY TO BRANDON."

Good. She texted him back "OKAY" and slipped the phone back in her pocket. She looked over at the activity on the deck and, feeling slightly guilty, grabbed her lemonade and walked over to the back of the yard, where the land gave way to an escarpment overlooking the town of Mendenhall. It was always a pretty sight, but she preferred it at night, with the stars above and the lights of downtown below.

She took a drink of the lemonade and shivered at the sweet tartness of it. Another sip and she could feel her shoulders start to relax.

Judging by the number of seats at the picnic table, they weren't expecting anyone else for dinner. Did that mean that Marco would be having dinner with his family over at his house? Was that a mutual decision or were Marco and Amanda not talking to each other?

Kate sighed.

Did she need to apologize to anyone?

"All right, everyone!" called John from the deck. "Come and get it!" He closed the lid of the barbecue and carried a plate piled high with hamburgers to the table on the deck.

The smell reached her at the far end of her yard, enticing her forward. It felt like ages since she'd eaten last.

Charlie and Sean emerged from the living room, reaching the food first, and Kate almost rolled her eyes. Soon everyone was clustered around the table, reaching for hamburger buns, cheese, and condiments. There were two salads: a tossed one with red onion, baby tomatoes and feta cheese, and a potato salad with sliced eggs on top and a powdering of paprika. They both looked like Amanda's work.

Minutes later, they were all seated at the picnic table, handing the pitcher of lemonade down. Charlie and Sean offered to fetch beer for anyone who wanted it, but everyone was satisfied with the lemonade.

The breeze had turned a little cool, reminding Kate that she'd forgotten to put her sweatshirt on. But she was seated between John and Rose and was warm enough.

John leaned over, ostensibly to pour more lemonade in her glass.

"Psst," he whispered in her ear.

She glanced at him but he was paying attention to the pouring. "Yes?" she said.

He finished pouring and handed the pitcher to Rose.

"Sorry I was such an ass earlier," he said, finally looking her in the eye.

She raised an eyebrow. "Did Rose make you say that?"

"No, Rose didn't," said Rose on the other side. "In fact, Rose owes you an apology, too. We didn't mean to poop on your front porch. Or Amanda's."

In spite of herself, Kate smiled. When she, Rose, and Charlie were little, Dad always warned them not to poop on their front porch, by which he meant to be careful that an action taken in haste might have bad repercussions.

Mom smiled, too, obviously remembering the same thing.

"Wait," said Sean, hamburger halfway to his mouth. "What happened?'

Amanda laughed. "If you hadn't run off with Uncle Charlie, you would know."

Both Sean and Charlie blushed and the rest of them laughed.

* * *

By the time they finished eating, it was getting dark and the mosquitoes were out. Charlie and Sean offered to do the dishes as penance, but when Kate emerged with a sweatshirt from the spare room where she was staying while Fred and Mom took her room, everyone had pitched in to clear off both tables and clean the kitchen. Rose had even found the mop and was washing the stains off the floor tiles.

Kate stopped in the kitchen doorway and decided it was too dangerous to go in right now. She went to the dining room, caught Mom and Fred as they were walking into the fray, and settled them in the living room in front of the television.

"Too many bodies in there," she explained when Mom objected.

"She's right, Hetty," said Fred firmly, taking Mom by the hand. "Let the young'uns clean up."

Mom gave in gracefully, smiling at the new love in her life. Kate's heart squeezed a little as she thought of Dad, but he was long gone. It was a blessing that Mom had found someone else so late in life.

"Tea?" she asked, hovering next to them. "Coffee?"

"I'm fine, dear," said Mom, and Fred waved her off. He had found the remote control and was trying to figure it out.

Well, everything seemed to be under control inside the house. She went back out on the deck but Sean was just wiping down the round table. Two of the chairs were still by the picnic table, so Kate made her way to the lawn, noting that Mrs. Buckley had left her back porch light on. Kate didn't know if she had just forgotten it, or if it was to give Kate's yard that tiny bit more light.

Either way, it helped.

The picnic table was clear and had also been wiped down. As she grabbed one of the chairs, the first stars came out. It occurred to her for the first time that it would be nice to have a fire pit in the backyard. With a couple of chairs—maybe Adirondack chairs. It would be nice to sit around the fire at night, chatting with friends.

Not that she had a lot of friends, but Amanda came by often. And Bert was always here.

Well, wasn't that a sad observation? There were two people she could count on to visit her.

With a sigh, she turned to grab the other chair just as her

phone rang. She deposited the chair she was holding on the ground before pulling the phone out. McKell.

"You're back?" she said into the phone.

"Just got back," he confirmed.

She glanced at the time. Seven thirty. Long day for the DC. She fought off a wave of guilt. She was just going to have to accept that she couldn't be as hands-on with this case. No matter how much she wanted to be.

"What did you find out?" She grabbed the chair again and hauled it to the edge of the yard, where she could sit and watch the lights of downtown and wait for the rest of the stars to come out.

"No other neighbors reported hearing fighting from Lawson's home," he said. "Most people said that Bragg and Lawson kept to themselves. No parties. Hardly any visitors. Seems unusual for a young couple."

Kate shrugged, reminded of her earlier thoughts. "Maybe they don't have many friends here."

McKell was silent for a moment. Then, "Which begs the question: how long have they been here?"

Hadn't Bragg told her they had just moved to Brandon? She was going to have to pull her notes out to check. That's what came from having her attention divided.

"Did you get the swab?" she asked.

"No," he said. "According to the kid across the street, Bragg left home soon after you went to see him and hasn't been back since. The Brandon constable who came with me says Victim Services hasn't been able to reach him by phone."

It wasn't necessarily suspicious. He might have gone to be with family, or friends. Not many people wanted to be alone after getting news like that.

"I'll go to Brandon tomorrow," she said slowly. "See if I can catch him at home early." From the open door of the kitchen came the sound of laughter, Charlie's voice louder than the others. She wished they would close the door and keep the mosquitoes out.

"I can do that, Chief," objected McKell. "You stay with your family."

"I think my family could use the break," she said firmly. "And I'll be back early. What about Lisa Theopolis? Did you speak to her?"

"Yes," said McKell immediately. "And she says there was no boyfriend."

Huh.

"She and Lawson have been friends since Theopolis moved to Brandon six months ago. She says she never noticed injuries on Lawson, and Lawson never mentioned any problems at home."

"How close were they?" asked Kate.

"Pretty close, according to Theopolis. They went to the movies every week, had lunch a few times a week." He paused. "She was completely shocked to find out Lawson was dead."

"So… Lawson didn't go stay with her when Bragg threw her out?"

"Not according to Theopolis," said McKell.

"And nobody at work knew she and Bragg had separated?"

"No." She could almost see McKell shaking his head. "I have no idea where she was for the past few days."

Kate nodded and slapped at a mosquito on her neck. They would have to check hotels and motels. And bed-and-breakfasts. She wasn't gone long enough to have found and moved into an apartment.

It surprised her that Bragg had let her go. In her experience, an abuser never let go. And while it wasn't unusual for an abused woman to hide the abuse, it was unusual for an abused woman to have a close friend. Abusers controlled every aspect of a woman's life, including her friendships.

"So. Bragg says she had a boyfriend, but her good friend says she didn't. Neighbors heard shouting, but Theopolis says there's no trouble at home. Meanwhile, someone strangled Kelly Lawson and left her body in a field owned by Trepalli's friends, with his business card in her hand."

"I know," said McKell glumly. "I can't make heads nor tails out of it."

Kate nodded again. "Well, we're not going to figure it out tonight. I'll head into Brandon tomorrow to get the swab from Bragg. I'll take Boychuk with me again."

"All right," said McKell. She could hear the frustration in his voice. "Keep me posted."

"Will do," said Kate and she hung up.

She sat there in the dark, the phone in her hand, which rested on her lap, staring unseeingly at the town below. None of this made sense. What was Marco's connection to Kelly Lawson's death? Kate believed him when he said he had only met her once, months ago. But Lawson had kept his business card. And either died with it in her hand or someone had placed it in her hand after she was dead.

And placing her body in the canola field? On the Hurst farm? No matter how she looked at it, that seemed calculated to implicate Marco in the murder.

* * *

By eight thirty, Rose and John had left, taking Amanda with them. Or rather, Amanda drove them back to her house, since they had come in her car. As Kate stood in the open doorway watching them drive off, she wondered what they would find at the house. Finally she sighed and closed the door, turning back to the living room.

Charlie and Sean sat in the two easy chairs flanking the non-working fireplace. Sean was leaning forward, his elbows on his knees, looking at Mom and Fred, who were still sitting in the love seat.

"We're all morning people," said Sean earnestly. Kate smiled to watch his mobile face as he made his point. He was good-look-ing enough, she supposed, but more in a nondescript way. No, he would be like his dad, growing better looking as he got older. At twenty-six, he was tall like his dad, but with the slimness of a young man who hadn't entered the prime of his life yet. She had yet to hear of any serious relationship and might have thought he was gay if she hadn't seen him blush and stammer every time an attractive woman paid him any attention. It was endearing, really.

"We could go to Gimli," he continued, looking at his grand-mother. "You know, if you feel like it. I checked it out online and it's about an hour and a half to get there. It looks like a cool place and they have a beach!"

Everyone in the room smiled at his little-boy enthusiasm.

"We could ask Mom and Dad to come and maybe Amanda and Marco would like to come, too."

Kate looked down, suddenly overcome by the memory of the last time—the only time—she'd been to Gimli. The ghostly crying in the night, Amanda's strange reaction to the peninsula where they rented a cottage, then the attack... Amanda had almost died.

Kate doubted very much Amanda would be interested in returning to Gimli.

Charlie looked interested.

"What do you think, Mom?" he said. "A nice drive out, explore a bit, have some lunch..."

Mom and Fred exchanged a glance. Then Mom shrugged.

"It would be nice to see more of the area," she agreed. She glanced at Kate. "Don't even try to apologize," she warned. "You're trying to find out who killed that poor girl. If we're gone for the day, you can concentrate better."

Kate smiled but couldn't help feeling guilty. Some daughter she was.

"Then it's settled," said Sean with enthusiasm. He pulled his phone out. "I'll call Amanda and see who else wants to come. The truck can seat eight!"

Well, maybe it wasn't a bad idea. They didn't have the same history with Gimli. They would enjoy the Icelandic flavor of the small town and Lake Winnipeg was very impressive.

"So," she turned to her mother. "Did you bring your bathing suit?"

Mom blushed and Fred just grinned.

* * *

When the boys finally retired to the travel trailer and Mom and Fred to Kate's bedroom, Kate sat on the bed in the spare room and called Albertson.

"Hey, Chief," said Albertson. "Everything okay?"

She glanced at the time on her phone. Almost eleven o'clock.

Dammitall. Too late to call Bert.

"Yes, everything's fine. I want to take Boychuk back to Brandon with me in the morning. Will he be available?"

"Sure," said Albertson. She could imagine him sitting at the duty desk, his uniform crisp and freshly pressed, pushing his dark-rimmed glasses up his nose. Lately she'd noticed that he was letting his hair grow out a little, as if he was practising retirement. She swallowed a sigh. She was going to miss him.

"What time?" he continued.

Kate looked out the window. She had left the curtains and the window open and a cool breeze brushed over her, making her shiver in her tee-shirt.

"Let's say around six o'clock," she said. "I want to catch Bragg before he goes to work." If he was going to work. If he was even home.

"I'll let Boychuk know," promised Albertson. "Oh, by the way, we finally heard back from all the emergency rooms in a hundred-mile radius of Mendenhall. No one has any record of Kelly Lawson being brought in or treated, for anything."

Huh. What did that mean? Doctor Kijawa should be getting back to her soon with the results of the x-rays. Maybe she'd be able to tell how old the injuries were.

Maybe Bragg wasn't an abuser, after all.

CHAPTER 13

Once she had showered and dressed in her uniform, Kate wandered to the kitchen, where Mom was already puttering.

"Good morning, dear," she said with a smile. She was still in her nightgown with a light blue plaid robe over top, and a pair of fluffy blue slippers to match.

"Decided against leaving early?" asked Kate, accepting a cup of coffee. Not that they needed to leave early. Gimli wasn't that far. She reached in the cupboard for the sugar. Someone had moved it and she looked around for it.

Mom turned her attention back to the bread she was toasting.

"Well, it hardly seems necessary to show up there before the sun's even risen," said Mom calmly. "Everything will still be closed."

Kate smiled. "That's true. Might as well take your time." She found the sugar bowl on the counter and added a bit to her coffee.

Mom buttered the toast and placed them on a plate, which she pushed toward Kate.

"Do you think you'll find whoever killed that young woman?"

Kate glanced up from the toast. Mom was busying herself putting more bread in the toaster and didn't look at her.

For the first time, Kate realized that the case was really bothering her mother. This was the first time Mom had ever seen Kate on the job, or at least, involved in a case.

"It's early days yet," she said cautiously, "but I'm confident we'll find whoever did it."

Mom nodded but still didn't look up.

"Do you think it was someone she knew?" she asked softly.

Kate sighed. Yes, she did think someone Kelly Lawson knew had killed her.

"I don't know," she said. "We need to find out more about her."

The toast popped up and Mom buttered them. Kate pulled out the jam from the fridge and brought it to the counter. They both sat down at the stools and began to eat. After her last bite, Mom took a drink of her coffee and set the cup down.

"I hope you find him soon," she said quietly.

Him. Even Mom knew it was probably a man.

This time, Kate's sigh was quiet.

* * *

Kate pulled into the detachment parking lot, noting Stan Albertson's older pickup parked at the far end of the lot. Aside from his truck and the unreliable patrol car, and now her Edge, the lot was empty. Most of the constables parked at the back, in the compound.

The sky was lightening, revealing shreds of darker clouds. In the east, a pink glow filled the sky, heralding the sun's arrival. It was supposed to be warmer today but she shivered when the cool air hit her as she slid out of the SUV. Right now, it was cold.

The smell of fresh coffee greeted her as she entered the detachment, though the break room light was off. She walked over to the counter and placed her forearms on it. On the other side of the counter desk, Stan Albertson looked up from the duty log and grinned.

"Morning, Chief."

"Morning, Stan. How're things?"

"Quiet night," said Stan. "A couple of speeding tickets. A fender bender. A homeowner reported an intruder, but when we got there, it turned out to be the teenage son sneaking back in despite being grounded."

Kate nodded. Typical Tuesday night. She glanced around the duty room. Most of the lights were out, save for the one over Stan's desk and the desk lamp by the computer.

"Boychuk is on his way back," continued Stan. "They're just gassing up."

As if called up by the mention, a patrol car pulled into the parking lot, its headlights sweeping past the storm door, briefly flooding the entrance with light. Kate debated getting a coffee from the break room, then decided she wouldn't have time to drink it. She'd swing by Tim Hortons on the way out of town.

A moment later, the door opened and Boychuk stepped in, bringing the cool air in with him. Outside, the patrol car swung back out toward the road, silhouetting Boychuk briefly in its glare.

"Morning, Chief," said Boychuk. "Ready when you are."

Kate pushed away from the counter. "I've got the phone," she told Albertson. "Who's on today?"

"Jim O'Hara."

"I've got a job for him, and probably Charlotte when she comes in. We need to find out where Kelly Lawson was staying after she and her husband split up. She didn't stay at her friend's. So hotels, motels, bed-and-breakfasts in Brandon, to start off with. If we don't find where she stayed in Brandon, we'll have to expand the search."

Albertson nodded. "Want me to call Brandon and have someone meet you at the Bragg house?"

"No. We'll stop in when we get there. I don't want them showing up in front of his place before we get there." She didn't want to spook Bragg.

Boychuk stepped out again, holding the door open for her.

"Coffee?" he said hopefully as she led the way to her Edge.

"Yes, indeed," she said.

* * *

An hour and fifteen minutes later, fully caffeinated and with a constable from the Brandon Police Service following behind them, they parked in front of Calder Bragg's home. To her relief, Bragg's shiny red truck was in the driveway. While the curtains were drawn on the big front window, there was enough of a glow behind them to tell her that somewhere inside the house, a light was on.

They got out and waited on the sidewalk for the Brandon constable—Constable Satti—before walking up the narrow path to the front door. Kate nodded at Satti and he knocked. Not the "cop knock" that would wake the dead, but a solid, no-nonsense knock.

A moment later, the door opened to reveal Calder Bragg. He was barefoot and in loose pajama bottoms and a white tee-shirt. He held a towel in one hand. Half his face was shaved. His eyes were bloodshot.

"Hello," he said in surprise. "What's going on?"

"May we come in, Mr. Bragg?" asked Kate. No point doing this on the front stoop for all the neighbors to see.

He hesitated, then stepped back. The three of them trooped in. Kate and Boychuk automatically removed their caps and tucked them under their arms. Constable Satti hesitated a moment, then did the same.

Boychuk closed the door behind them. Bragg waited expectantly.

Well, no point in prolonging this.

"Mr. Bragg," said Kate softly, "did you know your wife was pregnant?"

The blood drained from Bragg's ruddy face, leaving two red splotches on his cheeks. He stared at her in disbelief.

"No, she's not," he said. "She wasn't."

Boychuk slipped quickly between Kate and Satti and grabbed Bragg's arm. Only then did Kate realize the man's legs were trembling.

"Let's sit down," murmured Boychuk, leading Bragg through the living room and into the dining room. Older table with mismatched but brightly painted chairs. Kate wondered if Lawson had painted them or Bragg. Boychuk sat Bragg down at the head of the table and he sat, too. Kate sat across from Boychuk, but Satti remained standing, within Bragg's view. Kate appreciated the sensitivity.

"She wasn't pregnant," repeated Bragg, staring at Kate. His

towel lay forgotten on the table. From the kitchen came the smell of fresh-made coffee. He had been shaving before having breakfast. Was he planning to go to work?

"I'm sorry, sir," she said gently, "but yes, she was. That's part of the reason we're here. We need to get a DNA sample from you to verify if you are the father."

His head jerked back as if he had been slapped.

"Who else would it be?" he demanded.

Light suddenly flooded the room. Satti had found the light switch. She nodded thanks at him. She hadn't realized how dark the room was. She studied Bragg's face but saw only outrage—and maybe a little hurt.

"Sir," she said carefully, "you mentioned that she had a boy-friend."

He hunched in on himself as if his stomach hurt and Kate suddenly felt as if she had punched the poor guy.

It's the job, she told herself. Do your job.

"Will you allow us to take a sample?" she asked softly. Out of the corner of her eye, she saw Satti turn to look at her but she ignored him. Yes, she had a warrant for the saliva sample, and if she needed to, she would enforce it. But she would rather get this guy's cooperation.

He looked half mad, half confused. Finally he shook his head and blinked hard. When he looked back at her, his eyes were very bright.

"What does it involve? Do I have to go to the hospital?"

Kate shook her head. "It's quite simple. Constable Boychuk has the kit." As she spoke, Boychuk dug into his jacket pocket and removed the plastic tube. He unscrewed the top and removed the wand. "See? It's nothing more than a glorified cotton swab. He swirls it around inside your mouth and then you're done."

Bragg's hands rubbed first his face, then his short hair. The play of muscles in his powerful arms promised they would have their hands full if he decided to object. But then his shoulders sagged and he shrugged.

"I guess I want to know, too," he muttered. This time, there was no disguising the tears in his eyes.

Were these the reactions of a man who had killed his wife? Maybe. But it was clear to see there were no scratches on the man's arms or hands. Kate would have to widen the scope of the investigation.

Boychuk leaned over and swept the cotton-tipped wand around the inside of Bragg's cheek. He withdrew it and screwed the wand back into the tube. He pulled out a pen from his shirt pocket and began to fill in the information on the tube itself.

"Thank you," said Kate. "Before we leave, I do have a couple of questions."

Bragg's sigh was ragged and tired. He nodded at her to proceed.

"How long were you married to Kelly?" she asked.

His eyes closed in pain.

"We celebrated our first wedding anniversary last month."

"Did you get married in Brandon?"

He opened his eyes and looked at her in surprise.

"No, we moved here when I got the job at Balderson Industries. We were married in Vancouver."

Kate nodded, noting from the corner of her eye that Boychuk was busy taking notes.

"So, that's where you met? Vancouver?"

Bragg nodded. "Yes. Why? Is that important?"

She smiled. "We never know what's going to be important. That's why we ask so many questions. Were either you or Kelly married before?"

He shook his head.

"Is Kelly's family back in Vancouver? Her friends?"

He was still shaking his head.

"No family. As for friends, she didn't really have any. You might check with her old employer. I might be able to find the name around here somewhere."

"That would be helpful," agreed Kate. "So, you didn't know each other very long before you married?"

He smiled.

"Not really. We fell in love right away and got married just before we moved here."

Kate got the sense that this man knew very little about the woman he'd married. Maybe that was the way Kelly Lawson had wanted it. If that was her real name. The fingerprint search had come to nothing. Whoever Kelly Lawson was, she wasn't in anybody's system.

"Is that where your family is?" she asked. "Vancouver?"

He nodded. "Well, Richmond, but close enough."

She stood up. "Do you think you can find the name of her employer in Vancouver? Then we'll get out of your hair."

He nodded again and stood up, too. "Give me a minute," he said. "I think she kept a file."

He disappeared into the back of the house and Kate took the opportunity to look around. Beyond the dining room she could see the kitchen. It was small, with a linoleum tile floor and laminate counters. The cupboards had a fresh coat of yellow paint, which did a lot to cheer the room up. The yellow matched the yellow on one of the dining room chairs.

Boychuk stood up, tucking his notepad away, and Satti was already halfway to the door by the time Bragg returned, holding a file folder.

"She's very organized," he said with a smile. Then the smile faltered. "Was very organized." He held the folder out to Kate.

She took it and opened it. Inside were pay stubs from a Davis Street Dental. She flipped through them. Two years' worth. Where had she worked before that? Davis Street Dental would probably have a resume for her. Or Leaf Dental in Brandon.

She plucked one of the stubs from the folder and handed the folder back to him. "If you don't mind, I'll hang on to this one."

"Sure," he said. His mouth clamped shut on whatever he had been about to say. Probably something like, "She won't mind," or "She doesn't need it anymore."

She could feel Boychuk and the constable almost vibrating in their eagerness to leave. She understood. It was hard to be in the presence of grief. But there was something else she needed to understand.

"Sir, when we first interviewed you, you told us that your wife had a boyfriend. Did she tell you that?"

Another pause.

"No, I didn't hear it from her." This time there was curiosity in his voice.

That was interesting. Lawson's friend at the law office wasn't aware of any boyfriend. Bragg had also told them that he had kicked Lawson out, but that wasn't quite true, was it? The neighbor kid had told McKell that she had seen Lawson load up her suitcases when Bragg was away at work.

"Then how did you find out?" she asked.

"Her boyfriend came to the house and told me."

The tingle started at the base of Kate's spine and traveled all the way up to her scalp. Boychuk's whole body tensed.

"When was this?"

"The day before I kicked her out," he said after a moment. "Kelly had left early for work but I was getting ready to leave for Winnipeg, to install a machine in a client's factory. He pulled in behind my truck and came right up to me, the arrogant little pr—" He stopped himself and finished with, "jerk."

"What did he tell you?" she asked, trying hard to keep the eagerness out of her voice.

"That Kelly was finished with me and that if I didn't leave her alone, he would kill me."

"Whoa," said Boychuk reflexively.

"Yeah," said Bragg. "I thought that was pretty rich, coming from him."

"Why's that?" asked Kate.

"He barely came up to my chin," said Bragg in an aggrieved tone. "I must have outweighed him by sixty pounds!"

Huh. That was interesting. It took a lot of chutzpah to face a bigger man and claim his wife.

"Did he give his name?" she asked.

"No. I told him to get the hell off my property and he did."

"Can you describe him for me?"

He sighed in frustration. "Fine. He was maybe five feet four, a hundred and thirty, a hundred and forty. Brown eyes. A half-assed beard. Short hair. Brown."

"Thank you," said Kate, as Boychuk scribbled madly. "What did Kelly say when you told her?"

"Not much," said Bragg in a low voice. She was pretty sure he was fighting back tears. "She slept on the couch that night and was out of the house by the time I got up. She must have come back after I left because when I got home from work, she had packed her things and gone."

Kate could feel his heartbreak. Heck, she wasn't doing so well herself.

"Thank you for telling me, Mr. Bragg," she said softly.

"I have no idea why you needed to know that," he replied.

Well, for one thing, it gave her another viable suspect.

"Every bit of information helps. One last thing before I leave. What was he driving?"

"A Chevy Silverado," he said promptly. "King cab. White, with a gray stripe running along the bottom. 2002 or 2003."

* * *

They drove back in silence. The sun was at exactly the wrong angle and finally Kate had to pull out her sunglasses. In spite of the glare, she loved this time of day, when the sun cast long shadows over the fields. Through the car's vents came the smell of sweet hay, which had become her favorite scent. Next to coffee.

Bragg's reaction this time seemed much more... natural? He seemed genuinely grief-stricken that his wife might have been pregnant. Maybe yesterday the shock had robbed him of his senses. And really, was there a right way to react to the news that someone you loved had been murdered?

She kept going over what she had learned from him. This man who had accosted Bragg at his own home. Why hadn't Bragg told her that when she first notified him of Kelly's death?

Because he'd just found out that his wife was dead. Too shocked, maybe.

Maybe.

"All right," she said, thinking out loud. "Kelly Lawson had no friends in Vancouver that Bragg knew of. She had only one friend in Brandon, Lisa Theopolis. None of the injuries the doc documented were recent, except for the bruising around Lawson's neck. Theopolis said there was no abuse at home and no boyfriend. But Bragg met the boyfriend." She stopped, momentarily stumped.

"So where is this guy now?" wondered Boychuk. "Did Lawson really leave with him? Maybe Bragg killed her in a rage because she was planning to leave him."

Kate nodded.

"But there were no scratches on him. Maybe she left with the boyfriend and he killed her. He could be the one who abused her in the past."

There was more and more traffic coming from the east. She glanced at her dashboard clock. Almost eight o'clock. A lot of folks in Mendenhall and surrounding areas worked in Brandon.

"He didn't seem to know a lot about her past," continued Boychuk, staring out the windshield. The sun didn't seem to bother him at all. His brown hair looked like he'd been running his fingers through it, but it just grew that way. "I mean, I don't care how much of a whirlwind romance it was, you'd think he'd know something about her friends or where she came from or went to school. I mean, you can only have so much sex. After a while, you have to talk to each other."

Even as the heat rose up her cheeks, Kate laughed. He glanced at her and smiled sheepishly.

"Sorry, Chief."

"You're right," said Kate, sobering. "It's almost as if she deliberately kept him in the dark about her past. We need to find out more about her."

Boychuk nodded. "Didn't your preliminary report say that the doctor took scrapings from under her fingernails?"

Kate always prepared a draft preliminary report that was accessible to all her constables—and Charlotte. That way, everybody could be up to date on the case.

"Yes," she said. "But God knows when we'll get the results back. Or the toxicology report, for that matter. At least we'll get the

DNA results back more quickly. Or part of them, anyway."

And that was only because they were asking the lab to compare the DNA of Calder Bragg and Marco Trepalli against that of the fetus. To determine paternity. That result could open up another avenue of investigation if it turned out Marco was the father.

Please, God, she sent up a silent prayer. Don't let it be Marco.

And if the paternity test said neither Bragg nor Marco was the father? Then she'd have to wonder about this boyfriend.

Boychuk had been thinking about something else entirely.

"Bragg was wearing a tee-shirt. I didn't notice any scratches on him. Did you?" he asked.

Kate shook her head. She knew exactly where he was going with this.

"If Kelly Lawson struggled with her assailant, she would have scratched his face, maybe his arms," continued Boychuk.

"Yes. In particular, she would have scratched up his hands, trying to get him to loosen whatever he was choking her with." She had seen it before, in other cases.

"If it was a he," murmured Boychuk.

Yes, if it was a he. In her mind's eye, she saw again the photograph Doctor Kijawa had shown her, of the bruising around Lawson's neck. Deeply indented parallel lines, with deep marks at regular intervals, as if from studs or rhinestones. A belt. But was it a man's belt, or a woman's? Her belt or her assailant's?

"Call O'Hara, please," she said. "Tell him about the Silverado and get him to put a BOLO out for it. I want to speak to the driver."

CHAPTER 14

Kate dropped Boychuk off at home and drove to the detachment, still mulling over what needed to be done. McKell was already in, though he normally only showed up around nine. They tag-teamed: she came early and left early; he came later and left later.

To her surprise, Trepalli's 1965 silver Mustang was parked in visitor parking.

Her stomach tightened in dread. What was he doing here?

She walked into the detachment, carrying the plastic tube with Bragg's DNA and anticipating the worst. She automatically glanced inside the break room. Trepalli sat on the battered, red leather loveseat, leaning back and looking dejected, while McKell leaned a hip against the counter, arms crossed. They both looked up at her.

"What's the matter?" she asked, stepping into the break room and closing the door behind her. "What happened?"

Trepalli went from looking dejected to looking miserable.

"I think the wedding is off."

Kate barely controlled a gasp. Her stomach turned to ice and her mouth dried up.

"Why?" she demanded, then wondered if it was her business to ask. Did she care whether or not it was her business? No.

"Why?" she asked again when he didn't reply. She took a good look at him, noting the circles under his eyes, his dishevelled hair, his wrinkled shirt.

McKell glanced at Trepalli, then sighed.

"He told Amanda that he had to provide a DNA sample, and why."

Trepalli looked up at her. His eyes were bloodshot.

"I tried to explain it to her, tell her that it was standard procedure, but she got so mad." He blinked up at Kate. "I've never seen her mad like that."

Kate took a deep, trembling breath. No need to panic. This was just part of the pre-wedding jitters.

Right?

"I told him this sort of thing always happens before a wedding," said McKell. His voice was calm. "I should know."

Well, that was true.

Kate set the tube down on the small table under the window and sat down sideways on the hard-back chair so she could face her young constable. She rested one forearm on the table and looked at him.

"I know the Lawson thing happened at the worst possible time for you," she said. "Your family is here. Her family is here. You're trying to get ready for the biggest day in your lives." Both McKell and Trepalli were looking at her, clearly wondering where she was going with this. She wanted to point out that their problems didn't amount to a hill of beans compared to the murder of Kelly Lawson and finding out who killed her. But that was probably not productive. "You're both worried about how the families will interact. If future in-laws will like you. Approve of you. This is probably the most stressed you will ever be in your lives."

She was trying for reasonable. Calm. What she really wanted to do was shake the boy out of his funk.

"Maybe you and Amanda need to take some time away from everyone," she suggested. "Go to Winnipeg for the night. Find a nice bed-and-breakfast. Decompress."

Trepalli was already shaking his head.

"There's still too much to do," he began.

Kate raised an eyebrow at him. "Between the two families, there are probably fifty people able to help. They can spare you for one night."

He managed a small smile at her exaggeration.

"There is an awful lot of them, isn't there?"

Kate nodded, not trusting herself to speak right then. If she did, she was sure the word "elopement" would fall out of her mouth.

The boy stood up and straightened his shoulders.

"Anyway. I came to give the DNA sample, not to cry on your shoulders."

Kate and McKell both looked at him, their heads cocked at identical angles.

"You look like hell," McKell pointed out.

"Did you sleep in a barn?" asked Kate.

Trepalli shrugged. "I slept in the car."

"In the Mustang?" asked Kate with a wince. "For Pete's sake. That can't have been comfortable."

"No, ma'am, it wasn't," agreed Trepalli. He took a deep breath and looked at McKell. "Do you want to administer it, DC?" he asked.

McKell straightened finally and nodded. "I'll be right back." He left, closing the door behind him.

Trepalli looked down at Kate. "Thanks for the pep talk," he said softly.

Kate stood up into a sunbeam. "Just remember, Marco. She's as scared as you are, but she loves you with all her heart. You two will work it out." She wanted to go to the house herself and shake some sense into Amanda, but that really wasn't her place.

McKell came back in a moment with the small rectangular box containing one of the DNA kits. He hadn't bothered wiping the dust off it.

Kate watched as McKell repeated the same procedure Boychuk had done with Bragg, then resealed the tube with its swab.

"I'll take it," she said, putting her hand out.

"I can send one of the constables to Winnipeg with the samples," said McKell. "Might be quicker than waiting on a courier."

Everyone wanted the results as soon as possible.

Kate kept her hand out. "I'll go. My whole family is gone to Gimli for the day and this will give me a chance to see Bert."

McKell slapped the tube in her hand. "Don't forget to fill in the information on the label," he said.

Kate nodded and slipped both tubes in her pants pocket. She glanced at Trepalli as she headed for the coffee pot.

"You can't hide out here forever," she pointed out, pulling a clean cup from the cupboard.

The storm door slammed shut and they all looked at the closed break room door, but no one came in. Trepalli sighed.

"All right. I'm going back." He looked like a soldier about to face the enemy.

McKell slapped him on the shoulder and strode out of the break room, leaving the door open. Kate finished putting a bit of sugar in her coffee and stirred it. She picked up the mug and looked at Trepalli.

"This is the woman you plan to spend the rest of your life with," she said conversationally. "If she's not up to being a cop's wife, better you find out now."

Then she walked out.

* * *

She found McKell at his desk. Together they watched through his window as Trepalli climbed into his Mustang and drove off. By mutual, if silent, agreement, they didn't discuss him.

"Any issues with Bragg?" asked McKell as she sat down in his padded visitor chair. Outside his office, she could hear Charlotte on the phone. O'Hara was busy filing occurrence reports and cross-checking them with the online duty log.

Kate sipped her coffee. "No. He gave us the sample willingly. He was totally shocked to find out she was pregnant. Heck, even she might not have known." She sighed. "I don't know, Rob. He looked pretty good as a suspect, but now I'm beginning to have my doubts."

McKell sat back in his swivel chair and laced his fingers over his flat midriff. "Still, we can't cross him off the list."

No, they couldn't. Kate summarized what Bragg had told them.

"At least we have a mystery boyfriend to add to the list, aside from Marco. We need to find out more about Kelly Lawson. Maybe talk to Theopolis again to see if Lawson had any other friends. We need to go back in her history. Bragg doesn't seem to know a whole lot about her past. And find out about her boyfriends, if we can."

"Sounds like she was hiding something," said McKell when she finished.

"I agree. Can you dig into her history? Here." She fished inside her jacket and pulled out the evidence bag with the pay stub Bragg had given her. "She worked at Davis Street Dental in Vancouver before she and Bragg left for Brandon. See what you can find out about her. Maybe get a resume from them. Or from Leaf Dental in Brandon. Find out who her friends were, where she lived. You know."

"Yes, I know." McKell smiled and Kate shrugged in apology. He knew what he was doing. "Maybe we can check into Bragg a little more, too. From when he was in Richmond."

"Good idea. Also, we need to know where Kelly Lawson spent her last days."

McKell nodded and added that to the list he was compiling on the yellow pad on his desk. "O'Hara and Charlotte are already on it."

That could take a while. There were a lot of hotels, motels, bed-and-breakfasts, and rooms to rent in Brandon. Not to mention Mendenhall and Winnipeg.

Kate stood up.

"We need to follow up with Jane Hurst's farm workers." She pulled out her notepad from her back pocket and flipped through it. "Frank and Giuseppe. You'll need to touch base with Hurst for their particulars."

Before she could continue, he picked it up. "You want to know if they knew the woman, where they were the night she was placed in the field, if they know Marco."

Kate nodded jerkily. She hated this aspect of the case—that Lawson's body had been left on the farm of friends of Marco's.

"Someone knew Marco was friends with the Hursts," she said slowly. "I'll stop in at the Hurst farm on my way back from Winnipeg. We need to know why Marco is tangled up in this."

McKell nodded. The look on his face was grim.

"I would hate to think that woman was murdered to implicate him."

Kate didn't answer. Marco's connection to Kelly Lawson was tenuous, at best. According to him, they'd only met once, briefly, last year. Yet, she had hung on to his business card. Why? Because she was attracted to him?

Or because she feared she might need a police officer one day?

CHAPTER 15

Dr. Kijawa made room for Kate in between two patient appointments. She led Kate back to her examination room and waved her to a chair before settling in at her desk. Today the doctor wore a pretty flowered skirt that swirled around her dark legs as she walked. The toenails peeking through the open sandals were painted a candy apple red.

She dug around on her desk and finally found the folder she was looking for. She pulled a sheet of paper out.

"Your victim was either a daredevil or she was an abused woman," she began without preamble. "She'd had both clavicles broken, at different times. Radius and ulna on both arms have been fractured at various times. Fractured cheekbone. Fibula cracked on one leg, broken in the other. All injuries show signs of extensive remodeling."

Kate's lips had pressed into a thin line. Now she said, "You mean, signs of healing?"

Dr. Kijawa nodded. "Yes, these injuries happened sometime in the past, over a long period of time."

Kate thought for a moment. "Can you tell when the last injury happened?"

The doctor scanned the sheet, following along with her finger. Finally she looked up.

"According to the radiologist, the most recent injury is perhaps three years old."

Huh. That left Calder Bragg out as the abuser, then. Not only had she never known of an abuser who stopped abusing his regular punching bag, Bragg and Lawson hadn't even met by the time the abuse stopped.

If Bragg was telling the truth.

"All right," said Kate on a sigh. "Anything else?"

"The substance beneath her nails was leather," said Dr. Kijawa. Her face showed no expression but Kate knew her well enough by now to know that impassivity hid anger.

Leather. Kelly Lawson had scratched something made of leather. Gloves?

"I have sent it and a DNA sample of her fetus to the lab in Winnipeg," continued the doctor.

"Oh." Kate pulled the two tubes from her pocket. "I'd hoped to bring everything in person to the lab. Maybe express our wish for expedited results."

Dr. Kijawa's eyebrow rose sardonically. "Hope springs eternal, I see." She turned to the laptop on her desk and scrolled through her email. "Ah. Here." She read a few lines, then scribbled some numbers on a yellow sticky note. "This is the file number from the lab. Tell them you wish to add those two samples to the ones I sent over."

Kate stood up and accepted the sticky note.

"Thanks, Doc. I appreciate your quick work on this."

Dr. Kijawa nodded stiffly. "This poor child deserves our best work, Chief Williams."

"Yes, she does," agreed Kate somberly. It looked to her like Kelly Lawson had been dealt a terrible hand in life. The least she could do was find whoever had ended it.

* * *

She spent the drive to Winnipeg turning the case over in her mind, only surfacing occasionally to note that the day had turned out gorgeous. Her family had picked a great day to go to Gimli.

Kate had never actually been to the lab in person, so it took some searching to find it. The building looked like something out of the Soviet era, a block of brown brick and practically no windows. It was in the north of Winnipeg, close to the airport. She drove by it twice before she realized it was the right place. It didn't help that they had placed the name of the lab in modest-sized letters near the top floor of the building. She had been looking for a sign on the lawn, or at least above the door.

Once inside, an efficient young woman with a name tag that read "L. Bachman" at the receptionist desk took her samples, handed her a receipt, and promised to add the samples to Doctor Kijawa's original submission.

Kate barely had time to request expedited processing—a request greeted by a pitying smile—before she found herself back on the sidewalk.

Sheesh.

She should really go back to Mendenhall and help McKell with the long list she had left him, or maybe stop at the Hurst farm to interview the workers, if McKell had been able to set it up, but she could take an hour and have lunch. With any luck, Bert would be free.

She sat in her car in front of the lab and flicked through her list of contacts until she found Bert. The sun shone through the passenger window, warming the interior of the car to the point she had to turn the key over and open a window.

Bert answered on the third ring.

"Hey, beautiful. I missed talking with you last night."

"I'm sorry," she said. "It was really late by the time everyone went to bed. How about I make it up to you with lunch?"

"Good timing," said Bert cheerfully. "I just finished one meeting and the next isn't until two. Lola's in fifteen?"

Kate nodded. "See you there."

Lola's was a small diner on Ellis Avenue, tucked between two businesses on a street that seemed to have grown up hodgepodge, with homes interspersed among the businesses, with dilapidated buildings practically leaning on brand new condo buildings. Kate liked it.

It took her almost fifteen minutes to get to the diner, thanks to lunchtime traffic. Seemed like everyone was determined to get all their errands done over lunch. She pulled into a parking spot a block from the diner and walked up. Bert was already there. He stood up when she walked in and she smiled. She could see in his eyes the longing to take her in his arms—and she longed to hug him, too—but they were both in uniform.

Instead, he waited for her to sit down and then slid into the booth across from her. Lola's was a throwback to the fifties, with bright red stools fronting the long counter and a series of booths across from them. A linoleum tile floor and Formica-topped tables completed the look. A display case next to the cash register tempted the onlooker with everything from baklava to brownies. Kate always tried to avoid looking in that direction.

The place was half full, with two booths still free along with most of the stools. By the time they finished lunch, there wouldn't be an empty spot in the diner.

She tossed her cap on the seat next to her and studied Bert. He looked crisp and neat in his white, short-sleeved, open-necked shirt with the Winnipeg Police Service patch on the shoulders. He'd gotten lots of sun over the summer and looked tanned against the white of his shirt. His red hair was burnished almost to gold thanks to the sun, and his copper-penny eyes looked clear and untroubled, which was a relief to her. He had made peace with slowly losing his mother to Alzheimer's.

"Do I pass muster?" he asked, though he had been studying her, too. Was it only two days ago they had seen each other? It felt like much longer.

"You'll do," she said flippantly, then grinned at him.

The waitress arrived with two menus and set them down in front of them, followed by a glass of water each.

"Specials are on the board behind the cash register," she said. "I'll be back to take your order."

They could have saved her the time, since they always ordered the same things.

"So, how are you?" asked Bert, studying her face.

She smiled. "I'm fine. I miss you."

He sighed softly. "I miss you, too, Katie."

They stared at each other for a few seconds, the weight of the unsaid between them. The bell above the door rang as an older man came in and sat at the counter.

Finally Bert smiled. "What did you do with your family?" he asked.

Kate took a deep breath. "They all went to Gimli for the day."

The smile left Bert's face. He had been with her last summer when they barely saved Amanda from Daniel Bergstrom. She knew he was in no hurry to return there.

"So," he said finally. "Did Marco and Amanda go, too?"

She arched an eyebrow at him. At that moment, the waitress returned.

"Have you decided?" she asked politely. She was probably in her early forties and wore a form-fitting uniform that would have been current in 1956. Still, she had the figure for it. She kept her brown hair in a ponytail, completing the look.

Kate ordered her regular salad but requested feta cheese and Bert ordered his regular Reuben. She knew they would end up splitting both meals, so she requested an extra plate.

When the woman left, Kate turned back to Bert.

"Of course, they didn't go. I'm not sure what Marco's family is up to today."

He sat back and looked at her, frowning.

"What happened?"

Damn it. The man knew her too well.

"Bert, it's all wrapped up in the case. I can't really discuss it."

He stared silently, then finally blew his frustration out on a gust of air.

"I hate that we can't tell each other everything."

Kate nodded.

"I know. Me, too. I can tell you this: Marco and Amanda are having a hard time with this."

His lips pursed as he considered what she had said.

"So. Amanda is mad that Marco is involved—maybe involved—

with this dead woman."

Well, he already knew that. It was hardly news. She nodded. "Marco figures the wedding may be off."

He nodded slowly and clasped his hands on the tabletop. "As you know, I've never been married, but I hear these jitters are common."

Kate rolled her eyes. "It's hard to take it seriously when I'm dealing with a murder."

He smiled gently at her. "Maybe. But this is the most important thing in their lives right now, murder not withstanding. Cut 'em a little slack."

Geez. Amanda, maybe. But Trepalli was a police officer, for Pete's sake.

Then lunch arrived and Kate decided to deal with Amanda and Trepalli later.

CHAPTER 16

Bert walked her back to her Edge and opened the door for her. Before she could climb in, he leaned in and kissed her thoroughly. Her heart skipped a beat, and by the time they both came up for air, she felt a little dazed.

"We're in uniform," she murmured against his cheek.

"Sue me," he said cheerfully. He gave her a fierce hug, then loped toward his green Honda. She watched him get in and buckle up, then waved a goodbye.

Finally she slid in behind the steering wheel. She loved her job, and she really liked Mendenhall, but this living in two different cities was starting to wear on her. They saw each other maybe once during the week and on weekends. It always felt like they were visiting.

Before leaving the parking lot, she called the detachment.

"Mendenhall—Hi, Chief," said O'Hara.

"Hi, Jim. Any luck finding where Kelly Lawson was staying?"

"Not yet," said O'Hara, "but we're only about halfway through the list."

This case was getting on her nerves.

"All right," she said. "Let me know what you find out. What about the Hurst farm workers? Did we get information on them?"

"The DC was working on that," said O'Hara. "Hang on, I'll

transfer you."

"Wait!" she said. "What about the BOLO on the Silverado?"

"Nothing yet," said O'Hara, "but we have to give it time. Transferring."

A moment later, McKell came on the line.

"Hi, Chief. Their names are Frank Alford and Giuseppe Russo. Neither one has a record. Alford is from Churchill and Russo is a landed immigrant. Been here five years. Both have been working for the Hursts for over four years. They're at the farm now."

Kate finished writing in her notebook and closed it.

"All right, thanks," she said.

"Are you still in Winnipeg?"

"Yes, just leaving. Why?"

"I could get Holmes to meet you there."

Kate considered. Did she need anyone with her? Not really. She'd just be talking to the two farmhands—just to cross her t's and dot her i's—and follow up with Hurst about her relationship to Trepalli. No reason to pull anyone off patrol for that.

"No, I'll be fine," she said. She glanced at the clock on the dashboard. Almost two thirty. Damn. She had wanted to be back early enough to make dinner for everyone. "Looks like I'll be back in the office by about five."

"All right," said McKell. "Hopefully we'll have something more on Lawson by then."

They hung up and Kate set off, heading west. The lunchtime traffic had eased, leaving mostly transport trucks and other commercial traffic on the roads. As she hit the Trans-Canada, she saw more and more farmers in their fields, taking in the crops. It was perfect weather for it. Hopefully the weather would last for the wedding.

Forty-five minutes later, she pulled into the long Hurst driveway, trailing a plume of dust behind her. The fields of sunflowers were shorn but the canola still stood tall, even though she had released the scene back to the Hursts.

Two pickup trucks, one white, the other a rusty brown, were parked in front of the Hurst farmhouse next to an older red sedan.

She looked up at a movement in the farmhouse window and

saw two small faces peering out at her from a main floor window. That was the sitting room, if she remembered correctly.

She sighed. Kids.

As she walked up to the porch, the door opened, revealing Jane Hurst. She wore jeans and a faded denim shirt with the sleeves rolled up. Her curly blonde hair was in two braids today.

"Mrs. Hurst," greeted Kate.

"Call me Jane," said Hurst automatically. "Mrs. Hurst is my mother-in-law."

Kate grinned and nodded.

"My officer called you?"

"Yes," said Hurst, stepping back to let Kate in. The house felt gloomy after the glaring sunlight, but after a moment, Kate's eyes adjusted. Something smelled good. Stew? Chicken? Her stomach thought about rumbling, but she was still full of lunch.

"You want to talk to Frank and Giuseppe, right?" said Hurst, leading the way into the kitchen. As Kate passed the opening into the sitting room, two little figures appeared in the doorway as if by magic.

"Tallie and Jamie," called Hurst, "time to go play outside."

"Yay!" cried the older kid, a girl. She grabbed her little brother's hand and rushed past Kate and Hurst into the kitchen. A moment later, Kate heard a door slam.

All right, then.

"Actually," said Kate, following Hurst into the bright kitchen, "I have a few questions for you, if you don't mind."

Hurst turned toward her, but her glance went to the window. Reassured her children were in sight, she looked at Kate.

"What did you want to know?"

Before she could stop herself, Kate asked, "How are the dogs?"

Tears filled Hurst's blue eyes and she turned away.

"They didn't make it."

Dear God. "I'm so sorry," said Kate. Anger quickly replaced dismay. What kind of monster killed two innocent dogs?

The same kind of monster who killed a woman and left her naked in a field.

"Thank you," said Hurst. She quickly wiped her face and turned back to Kate. "I hope you find the bastard who did this." She smiled tightly. "All of it."

Kate nodded. As with the last time, she sat at the island while Hurst turned on the electric kettle and placed a wire mesh ball filled with loose tea in a teapot.

"We're working on it. So, I just found out that you know one of my constables."

Hurst blinked at Kate for a second, then her face cleared.

"Oh, you mean Marco." At Kate's nod, she continued. "Yes, we met him a few years ago when he dated the younger sister of a friend of mine." She leaned in conspiratorially. "They were completely wrong for each other, but sometimes you have to let people find that out for themselves."

Kate nodded in agreement.

"Are you close?" she asked conversationally.

Hurst stared at her for a moment, clearly surprised at the question. Then she seemed to realize that this wasn't a social call.

"I don't know that I would say close," she said slowly. "We like him and Amanda a lot. They come over for dinner once in a while and we go over there once in a while, though it's a lot more involved when we go." She nodded at the window toward the kids. "There's the age difference, of course," she continued. "Almost eighteen years. I think of them a little bit like my older kids." She smiled. "So, all right, maybe close."

Kate nodded. So, a naturally occurring friendship. Could it be that whoever had left the body in their field had meant to implicate the Hursts, and Trepalli's business card in Lawson's hand was just a coincidence?

Yeah, not likely.

"How long have you been friends?" she asked.

"About, oh, I'd say five years."

The water finished boiling and she poured it over the tea ball.

"Do you know anyone who resents your relationship with Marco and Amanda?"

Hurst returned the kettle to its stand then turned to look at Kate.

"What's going on, Chief Williams?" She crossed her arms over her chest.

Kate chose her words carefully. "We have evidence connecting Marco with the young woman you found. It seems unlikely that her body was left here by pure coincidence."

Jane Hurst walked back to the island and stood staring at Kate, separated by a slab of marble.

"He knew her?"

Kate nodded.

"And he knows us." Hurst's eyes took on the faraway look of someone thinking hard. After a moment, she focused on Kate and placed both hands on the island top, leaning forward. "Is someone trying to implicate Marco in her murder?" Her face had gone white and now her hands gripped the edge of the island top.

Kate shrugged. "I don't know. I need to understand what the link is between the dead woman, Marco, and you."

Hurst looked down at her hands and thought some more. Finally she shook her head.

"I really don't see a connection," she admitted.

Neither can I, thought Kate. She watched Hurst pour the tea into cups and considered. The only logical thread she could see through this morass involved Calder Bragg. Maybe Lawson had used the threat of contacting Marco to get her husband to not abuse her. Maybe Bragg had decided to find out what he could about Marco and followed him to the farm one day. Maybe when Lawson decided to leave, he snapped and decided to get rid of her and frame Marco at the same time.

Maybe, maybe, maybe.

"When's the last time Marco came by?" she asked impulsively.

Hurst stopped wiping down the counter with a dishcloth and looked up at the ceiling, as if she'd find the answer there.

"A month ago, maybe?" she said. "Oh, hang on." She walked over to a door on the other side of the refrigerator and opened it. It turned out to be a pantry and on the inside of the door was a calendar. She flipped the page back to the previous month and read the entries in the crowded squares. "Exactly a month ago," she said, closing the door and heading back to Kate. "On July 28. A Saturday."

Kate nodded and jotted the information down in her notebook. She had no idea what use it was, but at least she had it.

"All right," she said. "Maybe I could speak to Giuseppe first."

Hurst nodded and grabbed her tea before heading to the back deck through the sliding glass doors in the kitchen. Kate watched as she grabbed a metal rod from a nail in a post that supported the pergola over the deck and ran it vigorously around the inside of a metal triangle, making a godawful clanging sound.

It worked, however. A few minutes later, two men emerged from around the corner of the house and, after greeting the kids who were playing in a sandbox, came up the stairs to the deck. Hurst spoke to them briefly, then nodded to the sliding glass door.

One of the men separated from the small group and headed inside. He was in his late twenties, maybe early thirties, with a clean-shaven baby face, brown eyes, and thick brown hair under a red, sweaty ball cap. He wore jeans and work boots and an old, faded tee-shirt with a tractor on it. His face and arms were deeply tanned.

He came inside and wiped his boots on the area rug in front of the doors. Doffing his cap, he looked at Kate.

"Hello," he said. "My name is Giuseppe Russo. You wish to talk to me about the poor woman?"

His Italian accent was so thick that Kate had trouble parsing the words through the lilting cadence. She replayed the words in her head and a split second later than it should have taken her, she caught on.

"Yes," she said. "Please have a seat." She waved him to one of the stools at the island and wasn't surprised when he took the one farthest from her.

"How long have you worked for the Hursts?" she asked, to break the ice.

"Since I come to this country," he said, his words tumbling over each other. "I came on a student visa and now I am permanent immigrant!"

Kate swallowed a sigh. Between his accent and his rapid-fire speech pattern, this might take a while.

In the end, it didn't. Giuseppe—"call me Joe"—didn't have anything to add to Hurst's story. No, he didn't know Kelly Lawson. He'd been at work on Saturday because it was harvest time, but Sunday was a day off. On Monday, "Signora Hurst" had called him and told him not to come in. He'd been shocked to learn of the poor "signorina" and had been relieved when the Hursts decided to harvest the canola field last.

She learned nothing new from him, in spite of which she had a hard time getting him to stop talking. The fact that a dead person had been found on the farm had clearly affected him. Finally she told him he could go and could he please send in Frank.

"Si, of course," he said, standing up. He headed for the door, putting his cap on, but then paused before opening it. He turned back to her. "I hope you find who did this terrible thing," he said in a low voice. "That poor lady... and the dogs..." He shook his head. "Such a person does not deserve to walk among us."

And with that he slid the door open and went out to the deck.

Kate stared at his retreating back thoughtfully. She agreed with him. Whoever had done these terrible things, they had to be locked up.

Frank Alford was the antithesis to his colleague. Where "Joe" still had baby fat, Alford was a tall, rangy man with long, lean muscles. He was at least twenty years older than Russo and was balding, with graying hair. His eyes were a startling green against the tan of his face. He wore dungarees over a plaid cotton shirt with the sleeves rolled up. Like Russo, however, he wore a stained ball cap, which he removed when he walked in from the deck. He wiped his work boots carefully on the mat but stayed where he was.

"Mr. Alford?" said Kate.

He nodded.

"Please sit down," said Kate, nodding to the stools. There were four stools at the island. Kate sat at one end. Where Russo had sat at the farthest end, Alford picked a stool that was closer. He kept one stool between himself and Kate, which was respectful, she thought.

She started with the same questions she had asked Russo and learned that he had started working for the Hursts over nine years ago. He worked at the Hurst farm and at another nearby farm. He'd moved to the area from Ontario maybe fifteen years ago.

After a few minutes, Kate realized she was sweating. This man made her work for every word he gave her. Not that he was unwilling to help, she thought, but he was a naturally taciturn individual. She was willing to bet he had never married.

No, he didn't know Kelly Lawson. He didn't see the body. He hadn't worked on Saturday or Sunday; he was working on the other farm on those days.

She finally decided to cut him loose. The interview was more painful than it was worth.

"Thank you for your time, Mr. Alford," she said. "I'll let you get back to work."

He stood up with a nod and grabbed his cap from the neighboring stool. But when he got to the doors, he turned back to her.

"I was here on Sunday night," he said.

Kate's eyebrows rose. "I thought you didn't work here on Saturday or Sunday."

"Didn't. Come for dinner every Sunday night."

Kate could see it. Hurst was just the kind of woman to take him under her wing for a home-cooked meal once a week.

"Did you see or hear anything unusual?" she asked.

He remained silent for so long that she straightened her back with interest.

"When I was leaving," he said, looking her in the eye, "at around nine o'clock, I saw a white pickup with a gray stripe at the bottom. Looked like an older Chevy. No box. King cab. It was too dark to see who was driving or read the license plate, but it wasn't a Manitoba plate."

Holy cow. Kate scrambled to write it all down, fighting the shakes that the surge of adrenalin brought on.

"What kind of plate...?" she asked.

He shrugged. "I would just be guessing."

"And if you were to guess?" she pressed, trying to keep her

impatience in check.

He hesitated. "I would guess B.C. Not Alberta. Not Saskatch-ewan."

Well, that was interesting. B.C. plates had blue writing on a white background. Alberta and Saskatchewan were red and green, respectively. Manitoba plates were all over the place, but the most common ones were black letters on a scenic background.

"Where did you see the truck?" she asked.

"I was just coming out of the driveway onto the Three Fifty," he said. "Drove away from me, heading for the Trans-Canada."

Kate waited but he didn't add anything.

"Anything else?" she prompted.

He shook his head once. "No. Didn't even remember until you started asking. The Chornovil farm shares the access road with the Hursts. Might be someone they know."

"Might be," agreed Kate.

But she didn't think so.

CHAPTER 17

It was past five by the time she made it back to the detachment. To her surprise, Charlotte was still there. She sat on the edge of her desk, her capris revealing her shapely, sun-tanned legs and her sandals showing off her tangerine-colored nail polish.

What was it with nail polish lately?

"Hello," said Kate as she walked into the duty room. O'Hara nodded at her but didn't say anything as he was on the phone. Hearing her voice, McKell came out of his office.

"The gang's all here," murmured Kate. But they weren't really. Usually at this time, two patrol officers would be in the break room, eating dinner. Then they would switch off with the other two. But it was summer and the late afternoon sun was warm and inviting. They might be sitting in one of the local parks to eat their lunches.

The duty room smelled of the citrusy floor cleaner the janitor used and the fresh air from the open door to the compound.

"Did you learn anything?" asked McKell quietly, so as not to disturb O'Hara.

His graying, receding hair was kept to under an inch high—never shorter, never longer. She had no idea how he managed that.

"Maybe," she said. On the twenty-minute drive from the Hurst farm, her excitement at Alford's news had dissipated. None of it made sense. How could Alford have seen Lawson's boyfriend driving away from the access road? The timing was all wrong. It was much too early in the evening. Jane Hurst had said her dogs had barked in the middle of the night, which meant Lawson's body had been dumped in the middle of the night, not at nine o'clock.

They would check with the Chornovils, of course, but the truck was probably not connected. Alford could easily have been mistaken about the plate. And in the dark, the gray stripe could have been any other dark color.

She briefed McKell and Charlotte on what she had learned—and not learned—from the farmhands. O'Hara hung up and swivelled on his stool to listen, his gray eyes serious. He didn't smile much in general, but he never missed a thing.

"Did you talk to the Chornovils?" he asked.

Kate shook her head. "No. I'm already late." She glanced at the clock above the duty desk opening. Five thirty. She was so late. "As soon as they come on duty, I'd like Albertson to send Boychuk and Tourmeline back to the Hurst farm to interview the husband. His name is Elliott Hurst."

"He wasn't there?" asked McKell, crossing his arms over his chest.

"He works in Winnipeg," said Kate. "Jane Hurst handles the day-to-day operations of the farm and looks after the kids."

O'Hara nodded and wrote the information down on a yellow pad. Then he turned and looked at her expectantly. Not much for words, was O'Hara.

"Then I'd like them to go talk to the Chornovils. I assume they're a family operation, too. They share an access road with the Hursts." She told him what Alford had told her about the pickup truck. "I doubt it will amount to much," she finished.

McKell nodded. "Too early to be dumping the body," he said.

Kate sighed. She wanted a coffee, but there was no time. She needed to get back home before her family disowned her.

"What about you?" she asked, taking them all in with her glance. "Any luck?"

O'Hara nodded at Charlotte and she straightened on her impromptu seat.

"We found where Kelly Lawson was staying," she said. Sunlight filtered in through the window by her desk, bathing her in gold. She reached behind her and picked up a small notepad. "Lakeside Suites, on 26th Street. She checked in on Friday." She looked up at Kate. "They didn't know she was dead. I had them pack up her belongings. The Brandon cops are holding them for us."

All right, then. That was something, at least.

"I can send someone to pick them up," said O'Hara.

Kate considered. Was there a rush? Finally she decided she wanted Lawson's belongings here in Mendenhall.

"Yes," she finally said. "Send someone to pick them up. And question the staff at the hotel to see if they noticed anything strange, or whatever, about Lawson." She glanced at the clock again. She could get Albertson to send Tourmeline and Boychuk, but that would take them off patrol for hours. Better to send someone from day shift. Whoever went would end up doing overtime. She sighed. "Who needs the overtime?"

O'Hara shrugged.

"I'll find out."

"All right," said Kate. "Good work," she told him. "You, too," she told Charlotte. "Now go home."

Charlotte grinned and slid off the edge of the desk. "Just waiting on you," she said cheerfully. She grabbed her bag from the bottom drawer of her desk and sashayed out. Even O'Hara grinned.

"How about you?" she asked McKell just as the phone rang. O'Hara turned away to answer.

"Let's sit down," said McKell, nodding toward his office.

Kate glanced at the clock again and followed him in. She closed the door so as not to be distracted by O'Hara's low rumble.

"What are you late for?" asked McKell.

Kate sighed. "Life in general, I think. I'm surprised Rose hasn't called yet to demand to know where I am."

McKell grinned. "I contacted Davis Street Dental," he said. "Lawson worked there for two years before moving to Brandon." He pushed a few sheets of paper across the desk toward her. "They emailed me her resume."

Kate glanced at the top sheet. There were dates in the left-hand column and a list of employers on the right. She studied the addresses for the employers and then looked at McKell.

"She never stayed anywhere longer than eighteen months. Davis Street was the longest job she ever had."

McKell nodded. "And she traveled east to west, then east again, starting in Toronto and ending in Vancouver before finally moving to Brandon."

Huh. Did she have itchy feet? Problems with the law?

"We haven't had time to call each of her previous employers," continued McKell. "We only got the resume maybe an hour before you got here. It seems they had placed her file in storage. We had to wait for the person to retrieve it, scan it, and email it to us."

It might have been easier to ask Leaf Dental for Lawson's resume.

So, tomorrow, then. Kate realized her shoulders weren't quite as tense as they had been.

"That's good," she murmured. "We finally have something to work with."

McKell nodded. "I can get going on it first thing tomorrow."

"I can help, too," she started, then stopped. She had no idea what was happening tomorrow.

McKell grinned at her. "I'll keep you posted if I find out anything."

Kate nodded glumly. She hated having her attention divided like this. She stood up.

"What did you find out about Marco's relationship to the Hursts?" asked McKell.

She sat back down. "Nothing, really." She told him what Hurst had told her about their relationship and McKell frowned.

"Well, that seems pretty innocent," he said. "So did the murderer want to implicate Trepalli or the Hursts?"

Kate shrugged. That was the question, wasn't it?

* * *

The rental pickup wasn't at the house. Kate pulled into her driveway and turned the engine off, all the while trying to see if anyone was inside the house. Charlie and Sean wouldn't have dumped Mom and Fred and gone drinking, would they?

She shook her head as she got out of the Edge. No, of course not. Charlie had a well-honed sense of survival.

The smell of barbecuing meat reached her and she took a deep breath. Ah, summer. Unfortunately, the enticing smell wasn't coming from her place. A few houses down, four or five little kids screeched in the front yard as they ran through the sprinkler in their bathing suits. Kate smiled. She remembered doing that when she was a kid.

The minute she walked into the house, the silence screamed at her. Had they gone to Amanda and Marco's? Without telling her?

A little miffed, she tossed her keys into the ceramic bowl on the half wall separating her front entrance from the living room and took her work boots off. Before going to change into her civvies, she opened the kitchen window and then walked out onto the deck, leaving the French doors open to let in fresh air. Long shadows made her lawn look like velvet. Again, she took a deep breath of the summer air.

"Nice evening."

She jumped and whirled, only to find her neighbor, Mrs. Buckley, staring at her from across the fence, a startled look on her face.

"Geez," said Kate, placing a hand dramatically over her chest. "I think I lost a year off my life."

Mrs. Buckley smiled. She was a tall, thin woman with faded red hair that she always kept in a bun at the back of her head. With her high cheekbones and brilliant blue eyes, she reminded Kate of the actress Katharine Hepburn. Kate judged the woman might be in her mid-seventies.

"Didn't mean to startle you," said Mrs. Buckley.

Kate smiled and walked to the edge of the deck. If she climbed down to ground level, she would have to stand on tiptoe to see the woman.

"Thank you for lending us your picnic table," she told her.

Mrs. Buckley nodded graciously and placed her hands on top of the fence. She had a gardening claw in her right hand.

"You're welcome," she said. "I don't get much use out of it since my daughter and her husband moved to Kingston."

"That's a long way," commiserated Kate. "Job?"

"She's with the Forces," said Mrs. Buckley.

Ah. "I expect you don't want to be following them around the country," said Kate with a smile.

"The last thing a young couple needs is for the mother-in-law to be tagging along," said Mrs. Buckley tartly. "I was lucky that her first posting was in Shilo. At least I got to see them regularly."

Kate nodded. Canadian Forces Base Shilo was maybe half an hour from Mendenhall. Perfect distance. Her phone rang and she jumped again.

"They might feel differently once the grandchildren start coming," she pointed out. "Excuse me." She pulled the phone out of her pocket and glanced at the screen. Rose.

"Hi," she said, turning away from Mrs. Buckley with a small wave. "Where are you guys?"

"We're just getting into town," she said cheerfully. "They're going to drop me and John off at Amanda's before heading home." She paused for a moment, then added quickly, "Why don't you join us? Just in case we need reinforcements?"

Kate's eyes closed briefly. Reinforcements. In case the Trepalli clan was there, she meant. Did that mean that Amanda had been alone with the Trepallis all day? Surely Marco wouldn't have done that to her, no matter how mad they were at each other.

Well, hell. Now she had to go and see for herself.

"I'll be there in fifteen," she said and hung up.

As she went inside to change, she wondered what they could possibly have been doing in Gimli for so long.

* * *

To her surprise, none of the Trepallis were there, not even Marco. Kate parked behind the black pickup and made her way to the back of the house. Plastic tables were set on either side of a makeshift aisle in the tent, and white plastic chairs had been placed around the tables. Two long tables sat on either side of the main opening. If she remembered correctly, that was where all the food would go.

At the far end of the tent was a wooden dais about nine inches tall. That was where Marco and Amanda and the marriage commissioner would stand.

By her count, there had to be space for at least fifty people inside the tent, and dozens more at the tables on the deck.

They had two days left to decorate the tent, place tablecloths on the tables, set flower arrangements on each table, get all the food ready.

She took a deep breath. It was going to be a zoo.

"Hello, dear."

Kate turned to see Mom and Fred looking down at her from the deck. They each held a tall glass of something light and fizzy. She was willing to bet it was ginger ale and not anything alcoholic.

"Hi!" she said. "How was Gimli?"

"It was lovely," said Mom. She looked a little tired, but her eyes were bright and she looked happy to be standing.

"We met friends of yours," said Fred. He placed an arm around Mom and squeezed her a little closer.

"Alice and Jakob Petterson," said Mom.

Kate looked from one to the other. Her heart was beating faster.

Alice and Jakob Petterson. She hadn't seen them since last year. When they almost lost Amanda.

Mom smiled and Kate walked around to the steps. Inside the kitchen, Charlie and Sean were placing dishes in the dishwasher. Did that mean they had had dinner? Charlie looked up and caught her eye. He grinned and she waved.

She walked over to Mom and kissed her cheek.

"So what did you do?"

Fred urged Mom toward one of the round tables on the deck and Mom sat. He waited until Kate sat down, too, before taking his own seat.

"We explored the town when we first got there," said Mom. Her nose and cheeks were pink from the sun, and so were her bare arms. "We found a wonderful bakery that made excellent coffee."

Kate smiled. She remembered the Gimli bakery.

"Then we decided to go to Petterson's," said Fred, picking up the tale. His own face showed no trace of sunburn. He was a hat man, clearly. "And that's where we met Alice and Jakob."

Kate nodded. That was where she had met the older couple, too. The store was a throwback: it carried everything from bathing suits to rakes, with designer scarves and kitchen equipment thrown in for good measure. She had liked them immediately. They had been instrumental in helping her close the Bergstrom case.

The sun was dipping toward the horizon and a breeze rose up, bringing with it the smell of cut grass and wild roses. Kate closed her eyes and turned her face toward the sun.

"They invited us to lunch at their place," continued Mom. "Did you know they had a home on the lake? Quite beautiful."

No, she hadn't known that. She opened her eyes and squinted at her mother.

"They certainly took to you," she said.

Mom shrugged modestly. "We're about the same age," she explained.

"Alice told us what happened last summer," continued Fred.

"No wonder Amanda didn't want to go," murmured Mom.

"There you are!" said Rose, emerging from the kitchen with a glass of beer in her hand. "We had the loveliest day!"

She plunked herself down on the empty chair next to Kate. Her face turned serious. "I hadn't realized that was where Amanda almost drowned."

Kate nodded. It wasn't really that Amanda almost drowned. It was that Daniel Bergstrom almost drowned her. She remembered very clearly how upset Rose had been when she found out. First Amanda was shot and then she was almost drowned. Rose had almost driven to Mendenhall from St. Lambert to fetch her daughter.

Instead, Amanda had moved back to St. Lambert. And then Trepalli had gone there to woo her back.

"Why didn't you tell us?" continued Rose. "We could have gone somewhere else."

Kate took a deep breath and smiled at her sister. "It's not Gimli's fault. It's a great little town and it has a beach. People from all around go there all summer long. It's just that last summer's events are still pretty fresh in our minds. Where's Amanda?"

"Inside," said Rose somberly. "Talking with her dad." She looked at Mom and shrugged. "She's really having second thoughts."

Oh, for Pete's sake!

"Is this still about Marco being a witness in the case?" she demanded.

Fred looked at her in surprise and even Mom's eyes got wider at her tone, but really, this had gone far enough.

"Where's Marco?" she asked, looking around as if he would materialize.

"He spent the day with his family," said Rose. She hesitated, then looked troubled. "He didn't spend the night here."

"That's because he spent the night in his car!" Kate felt like she was about to explode. After everything those two had gone through, were they really going to blow it on this?

At that moment, John emerged from the kitchen, hands in his jean pockets, wearing a light gray sweatshirt with the sleeves pushed up his forearms. His white hair gleamed in the lowering sun. He looked thoughtfully at Rose and shook his head slightly.

"It's not looking good," he said.

Kate stood up abruptly, her chair scraping back. She was angry, so angry that she could barely control herself.

"I'm going to talk to her."

Rose stood up, too, looking alarmed, but Kate turned toward the door.

"Wait," said Mom.

Kate stopped. She hadn't heard that tone of voice since she was a teenager. It was the steel hiding in the velvet that always made them pay attention to that tone when they were growing up.

Hetty Williams stood up and brushed out the wrinkles in her linen shirt.

"I'll talk to her." Without looking at any of them, she limped toward the kitchen door and disappeared inside.

Kate and Rose looked at each other. They waited one beat, then two. When they judged that Hetty was out of sight, they rushed for the kitchen door. Once inside, Kate turned to Rose.

"Where?"

"The spare room," whispered Rose.

Sean and Charlie stopped loading the dishwasher and turned to look at them.

"What's going on?" asked Charlie.

"Shhhh!" said Kate and Rose at the same time.

They scuttled through the kitchen doorway and into the modified living room, turned left toward the hallway that led to the bedrooms. As they approached the closed door to the spare room, they slowed down and tiptoed closer.

Behind them, Charlie and Sean followed uncertainly, casting questioning glances at each other but at least keeping quiet.

They heard Amanda's voice first.

"—can I trust him?" Her voice quavered with tears. "First he's called in to an interview and now they want his DNA? Did he sleep with this woman? Did he father a child with her?"

"That's what you're worried about?" asked Mom calmly. "Shouldn't you be worried that he killed her?"

"Oh, of course he didn't kill her," said Amanda indignantly, her voice rising. "He's not that kind of man!"

"But he is the kind of man who would cheat on you and have unprotected sex with a woman he's just met. I'd say you were better off without him," said Mom.

Kate and Rose glanced at each other, then they looked over their shoulders at Charlie. He raised an eyebrow at them.

Yes, this was exactly the same kind of reverse psychology their mother had used on them when they were young.

"Grandma!" said Amanda, horrified. "How can you say that? You don't know him the way I do."

"I'm sorry," said Mom calmly. "I thought you were wondering if you knew him at all? You're clearly having second thoughts about this wedding. Maybe deep down, you realize he's capable of cheating on you. Capable of murder."

Kate found herself holding her breath. Holy cow. Was that really what Amanda thought? Felt? If so, she really shouldn't go through with the wedding. No matter what Kate thought.

She believed her young constable was completely innocent, but she wasn't the one marrying him. If Amanda had any doubts, any at all, she should call the whole thing off.

After a long silence, Amanda's voice came through the door clearly.

"I know you're only trying to help, Grandma," she said, her voice cold, "but this is more complicated than you seem to realize."

"No, it's not," said Mom. "How do you think he feels, knowing the woman he's planning to marry is wondering if he's capable of cheating on her? Of maybe killing? You either trust him or you don't. You either stand by him or you let him go. Stop dithering and make a choice."

Kate's adrenalin suddenly surged as she realized that Mom was about to step out of the bedroom and find them all standing there, eavesdropping. She turned around and swept the other three before her, rushing them out of the living room/dining room just as the door handle to the bedroom rattled and Mom came out.

Kate shoved Charlie and Sean toward the dishwasher and pulled Rose with her out the kitchen door and onto the deck. They barely made it back to the table, joining Fred, who looked at them with a bemused expression, and John, who just shook his head at them, before Mom emerged onto the deck and limped toward them.

Fred stood up and waited for her to join them. He seated her and then glanced at Kate over Mom's head. Kate just shook her head minutely. He shrugged and sat down next to Mom.

"How did it go?" he asked, pushing her glass toward her.

Mom took a deep breath. "I have no idea. I hope I helped her see things more clearly."

They all remained silent for a moment. The last of the sunlight peeked past the neighbor's house, casting shadows onto the deck while placing the top of the table in sunlight.

Sean and Charlie joined them, bringing chairs from the dining room with them. They each carried a beer.

Kate finally sighed. "Well, I'm hungry. If you've all eaten..."

"We haven't eaten," said Mom cheerfully. "We've ordered pizza."

Kate's mouth instantly started watering. Pizza sounded wonderful.

"What's with all the dirty dishes, then?" she asked Charlie.

"Seems Amanda and her friend Julianne were cooking most of the day," he replied. "The fridge downstairs is full of food. You know. For the wedding." He looked at Rose questioningly but she just shrugged.

"That Julianne is hot," said Sean suddenly. They all turned to look at him and he blushed. "Well, she is!"

They all laughed at him and Kate said, "Sorry, kiddo, but she's been seeing one of my constables for a while now."

He looked crestfallen. "Story of my life," he muttered.

"Sure," said Kate with a straight face. "Because you have so much trouble attracting women."

Mom and Rose burst out laughing and Kate grinned at him.

The doorbell rang and John jumped up.

"I'll get it," he said and headed inside. They heard voices and then the door closed and he returned to the deck.

"Pizza's here," he said.

They all got up as one. Clearly everyone had developed a good appetite. Kate let them all cluster around the kitchen counter and went to knock on Amanda's door. When she got no response, she stuck her head inside. Amanda was sitting on the edge of the double bed, staring at the wall.

She and Marco had given up their room to her parents and taken over the room that they usually used for storage. A utilitarian shelf unit stood against one wall, stacked with cardboard boxes and plastic tubs.

"Amanda?"

Amanda turned to look at her. Her expression was solemn but she had stopped crying.

"Yes, Aunt Kate?"

"Pizza's here."

Amanda nodded.

"Thank you. I'll be there in a minute."

Kate left her there but kept the door open so Amanda could

smell the pizza and hear the hubbub in the kitchen. If anything could draw the girl out, it was having people invading her kitchen.

Minutes later, Amanda emerged onto the deck, carrying a plate with a slice of pizza and a glass of water. Sean had already fetched an extra chair and they all moved over to make room for her at the table.

Conversation flowed around the girl for a while before she joined in. By the time Sean and Charlie reached for the last two slices, she slapped their hands away and closed the box, informing them that Marco would be hungry when he came home.

Rose and John exchanged a glance.

It was promising.

CHAPTER 18

Marco still hadn't returned by the time Kate left with Mom, Fred, Sean, and Charlie. But Rose and John were there so Amanda wouldn't be alone. And Kate knew Trepalli wouldn't stay away forever. He was hopelessly, deeply in love with Amanda. If she wanted him, he'd be there. If she didn't want him, she was a fool.

The night had gone cool but everyone was reluctant to stay inside, so they dug out sweaters and shoes and retired to the deck. Kate brought out the good scotch and placed the bottle, glasses, and ice in a bowl with tongs on a silver tray Mom had given her years ago. She carefully opened the kitchen door and extended an elbow to turn off the kitchen light and the deck light, plunging the deck into darkness.

"Hey," said Charlie as she closed the door and made her way to the table. Someone had removed the umbrella and leaned it against the corner of the wall.

"Just watch," said Kate, setting the tray down.

So they did. After a moment, Sean said, "Wow."

Wow, indeed. This was one of the reasons Kate loved her little house. It was perched on an escarpment that overlooked downtown Mendenhall and when her neighbors had their lights off—like tonight—the sweep of sky and stars seemed to fill the world.

Charlie stood up and walked to the edge of the deck, looking up. "Not bad, Sis," he murmured.

Kate nodded smugly and began to add ice to the glasses.

"No ice for me," said Fred.

She poured and handed everyone a glass before holding hers up. "Here's to having a wedding on Saturday."

"Hear, hear," said Fred.

They all sipped and there were appreciative murmurs all around. Even from Mom.

"So, what do you all feel like doing tomorrow?" asked Kate.

The wash of stars provided enough light to show Mom glance at Fred.

"I'd rather not go for another long drive," she said finally.

"We haven't seen much of Mendenhall," Fred pointed out.

"Apparently there's a nice walk along the Assiniboine River," said Sean.

Kate looked at him.

"What?" he said defensively. "I googled it."

At that moment, her phone buzzed in her pocket and she jumped.

"Excuse me," she said, standing up. She pulled the phone out of her pocket and looked down at the screen.

GOOD TIME TO CALL?

It was from the detachment.

She turned back to the group. "I'll take this inside." She headed inside and made her way to the living room, keeping all the lights off. When she was sitting in her favorite chair, she called the detachment.

"Hi, Chief," said Albertson. "Is this a good time?"

"Yes," said Kate. She realized she still had her glass in her hand and took a sip. Peaty, smoky, smooth. Wonderful. "What do you have?"

"Boychuk and Tourmeline are back from the Hurst farm. They interviewed Elliott Hurst. He was at work in Winnipeg when his wife found the body. We can confirm with his employer tomorrow, if you like."

"Yes, do that," said Kate. She doubted Elliott Hurst had anything to do with Kelly Lawson's body being left on his farm, but she had to be thorough. "Where does he work?"

"He's an engineer at a place called Wind Energy Labs."

All right. That was Hurst taken care of. "Did they go to the Chornovil farm?"

"Yes. It belongs to an older couple, Bridget and Elmer Chornovil. It's a family-owned operation. The kids are taking over after this last harvest, and Bridget and Elmer are going to move into Mendenhall proper."

Well, that was more information than she needed.

"What did they say about the truck?" she asked patiently.

"They don't know it," he said. "In fact, they don't even know anyone from B.C." He paused and she could hear paper rustling. "The access road isn't accessible directly from their farm. You have to drive down the Three Fifty and turn onto the access road. So the truck wasn't coming from their place."

Huh. Kate leaned back and stared into her darkened living room. What was a truck with B.C. plates doing on a farm access road at nine o'clock on a Sunday night?

Maybe casing the area? Trying to find the best place to leave a body? Wouldn't the murderer have cased the location before then?

Maybe not. Maybe not if the murder was unplanned. Or not planned well.

"I've asked the crew to keep an eye out for the truck," said Albertson. "Maybe we should ask Brandon to do the same."

"Yes," she said slowly. "Give them a call. Tell them the driver is a person of interest in the murder of Kelly Lawson. Ask them to note the license plate number but not to stop it." She wasn't sure why—but they didn't have anything serious to hold the driver on. And she didn't want him leaving Manitoba. "And maybe ask Winnipeg to keep an eye out, too."

If the driver was the killer, why was he still here?

"Will do," said Albertson. "And Tattersall is back from Brandon with Lawson's belongings. There's nothing much there, Chief. Just clothes and personal hygiene stuff. But there is a power cord for a cell phone."

Holy hell in a handcart. A cell phone. Why hadn't it even occurred to her that Kelly Lawson had a cell phone? Everyone had a cell phone these days. She wasn't normally this stupid.

How much time had she wasted?

"We have to find which carrier she was with," she muttered, aware that her face was burning in embarrassment.

"Yes," agreed Albertson. "We'll start as soon as offices open in the morning."

"If we don't find the right one in Manitoba," said Kate, "expand the search to B.C." Lots of people didn't bother changing carriers when they moved.

When she hung up, she stayed in the living room, thoughts swirling uselessly through her mind. She wasn't normally this disorganized. This frazzled. This was the entire reason she had always chosen to work far from her family.

They were a distraction. All those interpersonal dramas, those demands on her time... she couldn't be a good cop if she was constantly worried about her family.

She wondered what else she might have missed. They had found Lawson's body two days ago and were still no closer to finding her killer. She had no suspects to speak of. Oh, there was Calder Bragg, the husband, but nothing about him screamed "murderer." There was Trepalli, but she was only including him as a formality. Then there was the driver of the mysterious white pickup with the gray stripe at the bottom.

The driver was probably back in B.C. by now.

She sighed wearily.

"Sounds like you've got a lot on your mind," said Charlie from the kitchen doorway.

She looked up, noting how his dark bulk filled most of the doorway. Had he always been that wide? Or had he bulked up from all the scuba diving he did in his job as a marine biologist?

He detached himself from the doorway and entered the living room, moving carefully as he wasn't used to the layout. Finally he sat down in the easy chair by hers.

"What's going on?" he asked. "Are we making your life difficult?"

She looked at him, but couldn't decipher his expression in the darkness.

"Charlie," she said patiently, "you always make my life difficult."

He laughed. "Yes, but normally not when you're trying to solve a murder."

She shrugged and sighed again.

"I'm just frustrated. I feel like I can't get a good grasp on this case."

"Maybe because we're distracting you," said Charlie. "Why don't you go in tomorrow and try to figure this out? Those of us who want to will go for a hike down by the river. I'm thinking we should ask Marco's family if anyone wants to join us."

Kate's eyebrows rose.

"Is that a good idea?"

"Oh, sure," said Charlie, his shape leaning back. "We're going to be sort of related to these people come Saturday. We had better get used to each other."

"That's very nice of you, Charlie." And it was.

"Well, I'm a very nice guy," he said.

"And modest, too," she added.

He laughed. "We can plan for a late lunch somewhere, and you can join us. Then you can go back to work and we'll go to Amanda's to see what else needs doing."

A weight she hadn't even realized she was carrying suddenly slipped from her shoulders and tears pricked her eyes.

"Thanks, Charlie. That'll be very helpful."

He stood up. "That's what big brothers are for. Now, it's getting on to my bedtime and I'm pretty sure Mom is ready for bed, too."

He was right. When they got back to the deck, Sean and Mom were loading up the tray with the used glasses and Fred held the bottle of scotch in one hand while he pushed the chairs in with the other.

Half an hour later, Sean and Charlie had retired to the trailer and Kate sat in her spare room with the lights out, staring out her window at the stars filling the space between Mrs. Buckley's roof next door and the window frame while she waited for Mom and Fred to finish getting ready for bed.

She glanced at the time on her phone. Almost ten thirty. It was a little late, but Bert wouldn't mind.

"Hi, sweetheart," he answered after two rings. "How are you?"

The moment she heard his voice at the other end, her whole body relaxed. She lay back against the pillow and saw nothing but stars outside her window.

"Fine," she said. "It's good to hear your voice."

CHAPTER 19

The day dawned cool and a little cloudy, and Kate put on her light uniform bomber jacket before leaving the house.

At breakfast, Mom had worried that it might rain for the wedding in two days, but Kate checked the forecast and reassured her that there was no rain expected for at least a week. Farmers would appreciate that.

Now as she drove down the quiet streets of Mendenhall, most of them still waiting for the first kiss of sunlight, she wondered if there was even going to be a wedding. She stopped by the Tim Hortons and grabbed four black coffees and a bunch of sugar packets and creamers before heading for the detachment.

Most businesses were still dark this early in the morning, but she did see one man jogging on Main Street. He ignored the lights, as there was no traffic to speak of. The smell of the coffee filled her car and she breathed deeply of the lovely aroma.

She pulled into the detachment parking lot and parked her Edge in her assigned spot.

She had planned her arrival just before shift change. She wanted to be there when Albertson briefed O'Hara, just in case there were new developments.

As she walked into the detachment, closing the storm door behind her, voices floated to her from the duty room. Then Albertson leaned over the duty desk to look into the hallway.

"Hi, Chief," he said cheerfully. "You're just in time. O'Hara's here."

Kate noted his bloodshot eyes, the bags under his eyes, and the gray stubble on his cheeks and chin. Stan Albertson was beginning to look old. These long overnight shifts were for younger people. She wouldn't want to go back to them.

She entered the duty room and placed the tray of coffees at the end of the counter. O'Hara's gray eyes lit up and he looked to her for permission. She grinned and handed him a cup.

"Thank you," he murmured.

She pushed the bag with the creamers and sugar packs toward him and turned back to Stan.

"Help yourself," she said.

He hesitated, then took one. "Normally I'd say no, but I have to stay up today if I'm going to sleep tonight." This had been his last night shift for this rotation. He was about to be off for four days. Like most of them, he didn't want to waste any of his precious days off sleeping during the day.

She grabbed a cup and stirred in some sugar before going over to sit at Charlotte's desk. She pulled out her notepad and grabbed one of Charlotte's pens, then looked up. Stan Albertson and Jim O'Hara were both looking at her with identical quizzical expressions.

"Go on with your briefing," she waved them on. "This way you won't have to repeat for me."

Albertson nodded and turned back to O'Hara, who, even though he was standing on the floor and Albertson was seated on the stool on the platform, still towered over the older man.

Albertson proceeded to brief O'Hara on what had happened overnight, which wasn't much, as Wednesday nights—like most weeknights—were usually quiet. A dispute between two neighbors that resulted in fisticuffs. A drunk and disorderly at Earl's Hangout—if there was going to be a D&D, Earl's was where it would happen. Street racing on one of the rural roads.

Then Albertson pulled a pad of paper toward him.

"As for the case, we're now looking for a white pickup with a gray stripe at the bottom, with B.C. plates. We've got a BOLO out for it in Brandon and Winnipeg, too, with a do-not-approach. We interviewed the husband, Elliott Hurst, last night. He says he was at work but you need to confirm that this morning. The name and phone number of his employer are in the duty log."

O'Hara nodded and waited.

"The DC will continue interviewing Lawson's previous employers to see what we can learn. We got her possessions from Brandon last night. There was a phone charger cord, but no cell phone. We need to learn which service provider she used. Maybe Charlotte can do that?"

O'Hara nodded again.

Albertson looked at Kate. "Did I forget anything?"

Kate shook her head. "No, but I think we need to check Calder Bragg's past, as well as Lawson's. Maybe check ViCLAS," she said. Though she doubted if the Violent Criminal Linkage Analysis System would have anything on him.

"We might have better luck with CPIC," Albertson suggested.

He was right. The Canadian Police Information Centre contained information on a wide variety of subjects, from people on parole to dental records. She nodded.

"Yes. Check with CPIC and maybe contact Richmond RCMP, just in case." That was where Bragg was from, and local police often knew a lot more than made its way into databases. "And contact Bragg's employer." She leafed through her notebook until she found the name. "Balderson Industries. See if we can get his resume."

From outside came the sound of cars pulling in. Shift change.

"Do we think Bragg is good for it?" asked O'Hara.

Kate shrugged and stood up.

"Honestly? No. But no stone unturned and all that." She grabbed her coffee and, still clutching her notebook, headed for her office. She wanted to call Bragg before he left for work.

The sun hadn't worked its way to her side of the building yet and her office was a little cool. She debated turning the light on but finally decided against it. She could see well enough. She closed the door behind her.

Sliding in to her ergonomically designed chair, the one she had bought herself to protect her sometimes touchy back, she switched her computer on and sipped on her coffee while it booted up. After a minute, she set the coffee down and pulled her notepad toward her.

Male voices rose in the duty room as two shifts converged for the handover. If she were a bad guy, this was when she would commit her crimes, when there were no patrol officers on the street. She and McKell had actually toyed with the idea of staggering the shift change, so that there was always one set of constables on patrol, but the logistics just hurt her head. Even McKell had been daunted.

She found the right page and picked up the hand set. She punched in Bragg's number and waited, listening to one ring, two… After the fourth ring she was just about to hang up when the call was picked up.

"Yes?" said a man.

"Is this Calder Bragg?" asked Kate.

"Speaking," said Bragg.

"Sir, this Chief Williams in Mendenhall. Do you have a minute?"

There was a pause, then he said, "Sure. What do you need?" Resignation threaded through his voice. She could well imagine that he was sick of hearing from her.

"Did your wife have a cell phone?"

"Yes. She took it with her."

"Do you have the phone number?"

"Just a sec," he said. After a moment, he recited the phone number and she jotted it down.

"Thank you."

CHAPTER 20

By the time McKell showed up—at eight o'clock, a full hour earlier than he normally did—the BOLO for the truck had been updated, O'Hara was on the computer checking ViCLAS and CPIC, Charlotte, who had also come in early, was on the phone trying to find which service provider Lawson had used, and Kate was in her office, on the phone with Balderson Industries' one-person human resources department.

The damned woman refused to share Bragg's resume.

"Ma'am," explained Kate. "This is a murder investigation. If I have to, I'll get a warrant."

"Why don't you do that, Chief Williams," said the woman, unperturbed. "At Balderson Industries, we take the privacy of our employees seriously."

Whereas she and the entire Mendenhall police force were apparently willing to run roughshod over their constitutional rights.

"Thank you for your time," said Kate and disconnected.

A part of her wanted to drive over to Balderson Industries and slap the woman upside the head. Instead, she called Bragg at work.

"Chief Williams," he said, after barely two rings. "This is becoming a habit."

She smiled. "And you are being very patient, Mr. Bragg. I appreciate it."

"What do you need?" he asked, clearly unimpressed with her appreciation.

She hated having to ask him. It would be so much better to obtain the resume from his employer, with him none the wiser. That way he couldn't call previous employers and warn them. Or threaten them.

On the other hand, that damned woman would probably tell him anyway.

"I'm sorry to bother you with this, sir," she said, "but I need a copy of your resume. I was hoping to avoid disturbing you with this routine stuff, but your HR person refuses to give it to us without a warrant."

"That's Darlene," said Bragg. She thought she could hear a smile in his voice. "She doesn't give up information easily." He sighed. "Why do you need my resume? Do you want to check my references?"

Kate decided to go for the truth.

"Something like that. As part of the investigation, we have to speak to people who knew you before you came here. It's part of the background check."

There was a long silence at the other end. In the background, she could hear the clanging of metal against metal and the thrum of something big and mechanical.

Finally Bragg sighed. "I don't have my resume on me," he said. "It's on my laptop at home. I'll go to the office and tell Darlene to email it to you. Will that work?"

"Yes, it will. Thank you, Mr. Bragg." She gave him her email address and disconnected. Then she leaned back and sat with her elbows on the chair's armrest and her fingers laced across her belly.

She was pretty sure Bragg wasn't the killer. But it was still mighty strange that he'd been going in to work every day since she had notified him of his wife's death. Grief took people in different ways, but still…

The sun had finally moved to the front of the building and now sunlight flooded her little office, warming it considerably. She stood up to take off her jacket and hung it on the coat rack in the corner by the window. Cars were driving by on the main drag, sunlight glinting off roofs and roof racks as they passed by.

A sharp knock turned her around.

"Come in," she said.

McKell opened the door and walked in. As usual, he was impeccably groomed, though she noticed a small shaving nick on his chin. His blue eyes were alight with interest.

He sat down in one of her visitor chairs and a whiff of his cologne reached her. Something pleasant and citrusy.

"We have to find that pickup," he said, his eyes following her as she resumed her chair.

"For all we know," said Kate, "he's back in B.C. by now."

McKell waggled his head. "If it's our guy, he's gone to a lot of trouble to implicate the husband," he stuck out his index finger. "And Trepalli, what with dumping her body on the farm belonging to friends of his and planting Trepalli's business card in her hand." He extended his next finger. "I'll bet you anything he's sticking around to see what happens."

Kate doubted it. It would be incredibly risky to stick around. But the man—if this was their man—had disposed of Kelly Lawson's body in a very calculated way. Where had he killed her? The Brandon officers hadn't found anything in her suite when they picked up her things. Nobody at the hotel had seen anything that raised suspicions.

Kate was beginning to form an opinion of Kelly Lawson, but she needed more information.

"Let's keep going," she said slowly. "I'll take part of Lawson's resume and we'll try to get through it this morning."

McKell nodded and stood up. "I'll make a copy and we can split it."

Kate followed him out into the duty room. It was still cool since the sun wouldn't reach Charlotte's window and the storm door to the compound until later in the afternoon. O'Hara was on the phone, nodding at something the other person was saying.

As McKell disappeared into his office, the smell of fresh coffee enticed her into the break room. Charlotte looked up from stirring sugar into her coffee.

"Hi, Chief," she said. She wore the familiar plastic hair band to keep her bangs out of her face. Kate suspected she was growing out her hair again. Today she wore a pair of green capris, leather sandals, and a tailored, short-sleeved plaid shirt that looked a little cool for this time of the morning.

"Any luck?" asked Kate.

"No, ma'am," said Charlotte, shaking her head and setting her loose curls to shivering. "I've got a list of about half a dozen service providers between here and Vancouver, but so far only one service provider was open, and that was the Winnipeg one."

"Oh." Kate looked guiltily at the younger woman. "Would it help if I had a phone number for you?"

Charlotte raised an eyebrow. "I would think so, yes."

Kate grinned sheepishly. "Sorry. I'll get it for you in a minute."

Charlotte rolled her eyes good naturedly. "Don't we need a warrant to request that information?"

Kate shrugged. "First, we need to determine the service provider. Then we get the warrant. It would be so much easier if we had her phone."

Charlotte nodded but looked down at the floor.

"What's the matter?" Kate asked the young woman, suddenly worried. In the two years Kate had been chief of police in Mendenhall, they had dealt with murders, attempted murders, cold cases involving murder; she had been shot, Amanda had been shot, Bert had been cattle prodded... she would never have thought life in a small Prairie town could be so dangerous. Was it affecting Charlotte?

"Nothing," said Charlotte, glancing up only to look back down. "It's just... I mean... I feel so useless when we're dealing with cases like this. All I do is phone around. Make sure we have supplies. Keep the coffee going. I should be doing more."

Kate blinked at her admin assistant. Where was this coming from?

"You know we couldn't run the detachment without you, right?" she asked.

Charlotte gave Kate a quick smile.

"Thanks, Chief, but a trained monkey could do that job."

Kate's head tilted to one side.

"Um, no, they couldn't. If you weren't doing that phoning around, one of the constables would have to do it. This stuff," she waved around the room, "the phoning around, the interviewing people, the searching of databases... that drudgery is all police work. It's the work we have to do to get the answers we need. Police work is very boring ninety percent of the time."

Charlotte picked up her coffee cup and smiled at Kate.

"You're absolutely right," she said cheerfully. "So I'd better be getting back to it."

Kate watched her walk out of the room, wondering what that was about. She went to the counter and took a mug down from the cupboard. A moment later, she was back in her office, looking at the photocopies McKell had left on her desk.

Lawson's resume was three pages long, but the first page and a half, the most recent employers, was crossed off. Apparently McKell would be doing those. Kate scanned her pages and counted four different employers, ranging from Vancouver to Calgary. How many places had the woman worked? She was only twenty-four.

She would go from east to west, starting with the oldest job. She looked at the date, did a quick calculation, and figured Lawson had been twenty-one when she worked at the Henderson Dental Clinic in Calgary. She'd been there two months, then moved to Edmonton. Four months, then on to Terrace and Williams Lake, all in B.C., all for a few months before she moved on. There were no references listed, only the standard "references available upon request."

Kate blinked, superimposing a map of Alberta and B.C. over the various towns Lawson had worked in. All that hopscotching around... Had she been running?

She wiggled her computer mouse to wake up her computer and peered down at the clock. Almost eight forty-five. That would be seven forty-five in Alberta and an hour earlier in B.C. Too early for B.C. She could try the Alberta ones. Someone might be in.

She called the two Alberta dentists. Both were open but neither had anything pertinent to add about Kelly Lawson. "Nice" and "good hygienist" weren't going to get Kate anywhere. She suspected that they never had a chance to get to know her.

She'd have to wait another hour or two to call the B.C. dentists. McKell wouldn't be having much luck, either, since all his references were in B.C.

In the meantime, she might as well check her emails. Had her family left for the walk around the trail yet? Probably not. It was still early and the hike would only take about an hour and a half. She pulled out a sticky note from her drawer and wrote "MAKE RESERVATION" on it and then stuck it to the edge of her monitor. She was supposed to call Betty's Restaurant and reserve a table for ten for lunch. It wouldn't be nearly enough room if the Trepallis decided to join the Williams family on the walk, but Kate suspected the Trepallis wouldn't come.

They would still be mad at her for treating Trepalli as a witness.

Which reminded her... She pulled out her notepad and flipped through the pages until she found Kelly Lawson's cell phone number, which Bragg had given her. She jotted it down on another sticky and walked it over to Charlotte, who looked up from her screen with a smile.

Back at her desk, Kate opened her email program and stared in dismay at the dozens of new emails awaiting her attention. For Pete's sake.

As she was staring, a new email popped up from a DVerlaine@ Balderson.com. She blinked at it for a few seconds before realizing the "D" must stand for "Darlene." She opened it, but there was no message, only an attachment entitled "Bragg Resume."

Surly woman.

But good for Calder Bragg. He had come through. She opened the attachment and sent it to the printer. Then she filed the resume under the LAWSON CASE subfile folder before getting up to fetch the printout.

She entered the duty room just as O'Hara stepped down off the platform. He looked surprised to see her.

"What is it?" asked Kate. She grabbed the sheets from the printer and turned to face him. Charlotte turned to her and before O'Hara could speak, said, "That phone number has a B.C. prefix, but there are ten carriers in B.C. It'll take a while to narrow it down."

Kate nodded. "Okay." That was just the start. Once they figured out which carrier Lawson had used, they would have to obtain a warrant. That they would be able to obtain one wasn't in doubt, but it would take time, and it would take even more time for the carrier to comply.

"Ma'am," said O'Hara, capturing her attention again. "Bragg isn't referenced anywhere in ViCLAS or CPIC, and the Richmond RCMP have no record of him, either formally or informally. The guy's a boy scout."

"I always knew they had to be out there," she murmured. "I just never thought I'd meet one."

O'Hara grinned and returned to his stool on the platform just as McKell emerged from his office.

"Nobody's open yet on the west coast," he said, waving Lawson's resume in one hand. There was an edge of frustration to his voice that Kate rarely heard. This damned case was getting to them all.

"Nothing to do about it but wait," she said calmly. She glanced at the clock above O'Hara's head. Just past nine. "I'm going to call Doc Kijawa to see if she's got anything else for us."

"Fine," said McKell grumpily, going back to his office.

Charlotte looked up from the phone she had tucked between shoulder and ear and gave Kate a grin, which she returned.

Five new emails had come in by the time she returned to her desk. For Pete's sake. Then she caught an unfamiliar address: lbachman. Who was L. Bachman? Then she glanced at the subject line: EXPEDITED LAB RESULTS.

Her heart jumped and she dropped the mouse.

Holy...

She grabbed the mouse and clicked on the line.

"Dear Chief Williams, this is just a note to let you know we processed the samples you brought in yesterday. The results are attached. (We don't normally process samples this quickly, but Deputy Chief Langdon of the WPS emphasized the urgency of this case.)

Laura Bachman"

Kate reread the message and then clicked on the attachment, then clicked again to open the PDF. Up popped a page with three columns. The left-hand one read "Locus PI," the second and third ones read "Allele Sizes." Above the second column was "BABY LAWSON" and above the third one was "MARCO TREPALLI."

Kate ignored all the numbers in the columns—they meant nothing to her—and skipped to the bottom of the page, which read:

"The alleged father is excluded as the biological father of the tested child."

Relief washed through her, leaving her trembling. She had known—of course she had known—that Marco wasn't the father of Kelly Lawson's baby, but there was nothing like having proof.

She scrolled down to the second page, which detailed the same test but with Calder Bragg, and scanned the conclusion:

"The alleged father is not excluded as the biological father of the tested child. Based on testing results obtained from analyses of the DNA loci listed, the probability of paternity is 99.9998%."

As relieved as she had been to read Marco's test results, now grief stabbed through her. Calder Bragg would have been a father.

Whoever had killed Kelly Lawson was also responsible for the death of her baby.

She took a moment to collect herself and then called Doctor Kijawa at the clinic. The receptionist informed Kate that the doc was in with a patient. Kate left a message to have the doc call her when she was free and hung up.

She sat still for a few long minutes. She felt as if she had been put through the wringer. In the duty room, low voices murmured. Then a dog yipped, startling her. She debated going into the duty room to see what was going on but instead went to her window and peered out. An unfamiliar car was parked in visitor parking. Clearly, the owner of the dog.

Returning to her chair, she went about dealing with her email. As she responded and deleted, each according to its destiny, she wondered just how bad it would have been if she had stayed away for the week as she was supposed to do.

After a while, she glanced at the clock and picked up the handset to call Betty's. A few minutes later, she had reserved the small patio at the back of the restaurant. Mom would like it—it had trellises covered in ivy and other flowering plants. It could get cool at this time of year, but judging by the sunshine out there, that wouldn't be a problem.

Another half hour of clearing out her email and Kate decided it was late enough to start calling previous employers.

She started with Calder Bragg's resume, just because that was now the only outstanding element in her investigation of him.

He had attended the Southern Alberta Institute of Technology and had only had two jobs since graduating, unlike Lawson, who had flitted from position to position. Kate called both employers and both had nothing but good things to say about Bragg. Good worker, honest, played well with others. The most recent employer said how sad he was to see Bragg go, but understood that his new wife had wanted a change.

Kate hung up and sat staring out the window at the pale blue sky.

So, moving had been Lawson's idea. Bragg hadn't mentioned that. He'd said they moved because of a job offer. Did Balderson Industries poach him away or did Bragg apply to the Brandon company?

Did it matter?

Her cell phone rang, startling her. She jotted down a note on the yellow pad on her desk so she wouldn't forget to ask Bragg, then pulled out the phone. It was Bert.

"Hi," she said.

"Hi, yourself," said Bert. "Just checking in to see how you're doing."

They chatted for a few minutes, then Kate said, "So I hear I have you to thank for expediting my lab results?" She wasn't sure how she felt about it.

Bert hesitated at the other end.

"Well, the lab owner owes me a few favors," he said.

Kate sighed softly. "So I jumped the queue." That didn't feel right at all, even if she was relieved to get the results so quickly. It wasn't right that she should move to the front of the line just because she knew Bert.

"Yes, you did," said Bert calmly. "You have a murderer still out there, and that DNA information could make all the difference in finding him quickly." His voice dropped lower. "And this was just about the only way I could help you."

Kate smiled. She decided she could live with it. She might have done the same for him if their roles had been reversed.

"Thank you," she said finally. "That must have been some favor."

"What did you learn?" he asked, not answering her implied question.

"I only got part of the results back. I'm waiting to talk to Doctor Kijawa about the biological results."

"What about the paternity tests?"

How did he even know? Had she told him? Or had someone else? Part of her stirred in anger, but maybe she had told him?

She sighed softly. She was uncomfortable sharing the results of the paternity tests with him, despite his help. Still. It wouldn't hurt anything.

"Calder Bragg was the father."

Bert was silent for a while. "Poor guy," he said finally.

Kate had always thought Bert would have liked to have been a father. He had never settled down with any woman long enough to have to decide. And now he was with Kate, and she had made her own peace with motherhood a long time ago. It wasn't for her. And now she was past the age for childbearing. If Bert stayed with her, he would never be a father.

"I have to go," said Bert. "A meeting."

"All right," she said softly. "Let's talk tonight."

"Tonight. Love you."

"Love you, too."

CHAPTER 21

Kate spent the next hour talking to Kelly Lawson's earlier employers, or waiting for them to call her back. One dental office had closed down. Those she could speak to all said the same thing about Lawson: she was a hard worker, efficient, capable, and smart.

But Kate noticed that while the earliest employers spoke of her sweetness and youthful enthusiasm, later ones spoke of her being quiet and reserved. What had changed?

She was just about to get up and see how McKell was faring with his own interviews when Charlotte knocked on the doorjamb.

"She was with B.C. Mobile," said the girl without preamble. "They confirmed it but won't release any information without a warrant."

Kate nodded. She had expected it.

"All right," she said. "I'll—"

At that moment, McKell appeared behind Charlotte, the expression on his face telling her he had something.

Charlotte looked over her shoulder and jumped in surprise just as Kate said, "What is it?"

"Her next-to-last employer, the one in Williams Lake?"

"Yes?"

Charlotte stepped aside so the DC could go inside. Then she

leaned against the doorjamb. Clearly she wanted to hear this, too.

McKell sat down in one of Kate's visitor chairs. A slanting sunbeam rested on his shoulder.

"I spoke to Lawson's boss there. There was an incident about three years ago. Lawson's boyfriend showed up at the dental practice, shouting at Lawson and threatening her. They called the police and he was taken away, but the boss never saw Lawson again. Next thing you know, she pops up in Vancouver, at yet another dental clinic."

Kate took a deep breath to still her trembling. They were getting close.

"We need to talk to her friends from Williams Lake," she said.

McKell nodded.

"There was one girl at the clinic that she was close to, according to the dentist, but she isn't working there anymore. Her name is Eleanor Bakshi. The dentist thinks she moved to Edmonton."

"We have to find her."

"Working on it," he said, standing up. Kate stopped him before he could leave.

"Charlotte found Lawson's service provider."

He smiled tightly. "We're getting closer."

Kate nodded.

"You work on finding Bakshi. I'll work on the warrant."

"I can type up the form," said Charlotte, straightening. Kate suddenly remembered their discussion in the break room. Charlotte was as much a part of her team as any of the constables. If she was unhappy in her role, Kate had to find a way to fix it.

"Thank you," she said. "As soon as it's ready, I'll take it to the justice of the peace."

* * *

By the time she got to Betty's Restaurant, she was late. She had worked on the form with Charlotte and then spent almost the next hour waiting for the justice, who was in a meeting. At that point, the justice was late for her own lunch appointment, so Kate swore in the information and left the form with the justice, who saw no problem issuing the warrant, save for time.

"Come back at one thirty," she said. "I'll have it for you."

On the way to the restaurant, Kate suddenly realized that she needed to call Calder Bragg to give him the results of the paternity test. It, too, would have to wait. She was not going to tell him he had lost both his wife and his baby while rushing to get to the restaurant.

Betty's was an older, one-story building—probably from the '50s—with wood siding, large picture windows, and a recessed door. With its blue tile floor and mustard and terracotta walls, it always reminded her of a Mexican restaurant, but Betty's didn't serve Mexican food. Instead, it concentrated on fancy soups, elaborate salads, and some of the best sandwiches she had ever had, all on homemade bread.

And they didn't serve any pop.

All the tables were full. Everyone glanced up at her entrance but she was used to that. The waitress caught her eye and Kate pointed to the door in the corner, the entrance to the patio. The waitress nodded and Kate threaded her way to the door, nodding to the people she knew and raising a hand in acknowledgement to the mayor, who seemed to be having a lunch meeting with two other men.

The sun caught her in the eyes as soon as she opened the door and she blinked away the reflexive tears.

"There you are," said Rose, taking her by the arm and leading her forward. Kate resisted a little until she could finally see clearly. Then she blinked. Holy... The entire patio was taken up with Williamses and Trepallis.

"Geez," she blurted out. "Are you all here?" She would never have a chance to eat before she had to pick up the warrant.

The table—tables end-to-end—erupted in laughter and she found herself sitting at the head of the table at the only empty chair left. Mom and Fred were about halfway down the table, sitting next to Marco's cousins. Charlie sat at the opposite end and Sean sat next to a pretty little thing that Kate didn't remember meeting. Rose resumed her seat next to Camilla on one side and Tina on the other. John sat across from her with Marco's father, Henry, on one side and Tina's husband, Paul, on the other.

Marco and Amanda sat on opposite sides of the table, conspicuously too far apart to talk. Marco nodded to her but Kate was too far to read his expression. He wasn't smiling. Amanda was busy talking to Charlie.

A vine-covered trellis protected the patio from the sun overhead and a gentle breeze swirled though, cooling them down and bringing with it the scent of wild roses.

She had Camilla on her left and Henry on her right. Now Camilla leaned over and patted her bare arm.

"Amanda took the liberty of ordering ahead," she said with a smile. "Or we would have overwhelmed the poor staff."

Kate nodded and remembered to smile.

"Good idea," she murmured. "So, what have you been up to?"

Camilla wore a short-sleeved, green-and-yellow cotton shirt and cropped white pants. She had sunglasses pushed up on top of her thick dark hair. Now she shrugged.

"We've been driving around," she said. "Some of us have been to Riding Mountain Park—such a lovely place!—others went to Winnipeg, shopping. Henry and I went for a walk with your family on a trail by the riverbank."

"Sounds lovely," said Kate. And it did. Well, maybe not the shopping part. "I take it we're just about ready for the big day?" She studied Camilla's face carefully, looking for signs of trouble, but Camilla just shrugged.

"As ready as we can be today," she said. "Tomorrow will be busy. We will finish decorating, add the tablecloths, that kind of thing. The flowers and the cake arrive on Saturday morning and so does the rest of the food." She leaned toward Kate. "I think the girl is preparing to feed a small country."

Kate grinned, but before she could say anything, the food arrived. There were bowls of soup for everyone and platters of sandwiches cut in quarters. Next came pitchers of exotic juices.

The noise level jumped as pitchers and platters were passed around. Kate saw grins on faces and for the first time since she got there, she relaxed. Everyone was talking to everyone. There was no tension. John and Henry were deep in conversation and Charlie and Paul were laughing. Then she glanced at Marco and Amanda, who were clearly avoiding each other.

Dammitall. This was getting tiresome.

By one fifteen, she had eaten a big bowl of soup that had lemon grass and chicken and coconut, she thought, and half a roasted vegetable sandwich. She was so full she couldn't wait to get back to her car so she could discreetly loosen her belt.

She wanted to know how the river walk had gone but there was no chance to talk to Mom or Rose privately. Mom looked happy, chatting with the cousins, so clearly it hadn't been bad. She also wanted to know what plans they had for the afternoon, but again, there was no opportunity to talk. At last she stood up and pushed the chair away. It scraped loudly on the paving stones, quieting all conversation. All faces turned to her.

"I have to go," she said, addressing herself to Mom and Rose. "I'll catch up with you at dinnertime. Okay?"

She could have kicked herself for the last word. What would she do if they objected? Say "fine" and sit down again?

"No problem, dear," said Mom, even though Rose frowned slightly. "We know you're working on an important case."

Kate's mouth twisted slightly but she only nodded and waved a goodbye before heading back into the restaurant. Behind her, the noise level rose again as people resumed their conversations.

She stopped at the cash register and paid for everyone's meals. The amount made her gulp, but it was a gesture of goodwill, and really, it was the least she could do for constantly abandoning her family. She left a healthy tip and was rewarded with a beaming smile from the young man at the cash register.

A moment later, she stood on the sidewalk outside Betty's, breathing deeply and wishing she could walk back to the detachment. She would need her car, however.

The door to the restaurant opened behind her and she turned to see Amanda coming out.

"Hello," said Kate, surprised to see her. "You okay?"

Amanda's blue eyes were dark with anger.

"Where do you get off telling Marco I'm not fit to be a police-man's wife?"

What? Kate stared at her, too shocked to even blink.

"What are you talking about?" she asked. A man walked by, looking at Amanda, but he flinched away when she glared at him.

"You told Marco to think twice about marrying me."

Kate shook her head slightly.

"Did he tell you I said that?" she asked, unsure what was going on. A car drove by, music so loud she could feel it in her chest.

"I'm paraphrasing," replied Amanda bitterly.

She was really angry. And then Kate remembered being in the break room with Marco when he provided a DNA sample.

"What I told him," she said truthfully, "was that he needed to be sure you could handle being a cop's wife, and that if you couldn't, it was better he should find out now. And if you have doubts, you should rethink this marriage thing, too."

Splotches of red appeared on Amanda's cheeks, but her lips were almost white.

"How dare you stick your nose in our relationship?" she said, her voice so low Kate had to strain to hear it.

Now Kate was getting mad. She had stood up for these two throughout their whole courtship. She had risked her life to save Amanda, not once, but twice. She had defended Marco to Rose and John.

"You made it my business, and everyone else's, when you started having second thoughts about marrying him," Kate pointed out. "You invited everyone here and then, at the first sign of trouble, you started wondering if you should marry him. Now you're both miserable. Well, pee or get off the pot!"

Amanda crossed her arms over her chest and a cold look came over her face.

"That's pretty rich from a woman who won't marry the man she supposedly loves, but won't let him move on."

Kate felt as if someone had punched her in the gut. The blood drained from her face and she watched open-mouthed as Amanda turned on her heel and went back inside.

CHAPTER 22

She picked up the paper warrant from the justice and asked her to send it to her electronically, too. It would help expedite getting it to B.C. Mobile.

When she got back to the detachment, Charlotte was sitting at the duty desk, replacing O'Hara while he took a lunch break.

She saw Abrams in the break room, but no O'Hara.

"He had errands," said Charlotte, just as the phone rang. Kate nodded and glanced into McKell's office on her way to her own. The good DC had stepped out. She closed her office door and leaned against it.

Holy cow.

Had she screwed up? Had she butted in where she had no business?

Amanda had been so mad...

She suddenly remembered what Marco had told her when she first informed him he would have to do a paternity test. He had said it was no surprise she wasn't married.

Her eyes closed as she felt the heat rising in her cheeks. Dear Lord. Clearly he and Amanda had discussed her marital status and both thought she wasn't fit to marry.

Was that why she had avoided marriage? She had always thought it was because being a police officer was all consuming, but maybe deep down, she had known it wasn't for her. And she had seen how many marriages broke up as a result of the job. She hadn't wanted that heartbreak for herself.

Was that unreasonable?

Did she resent Marco and Amanda for wanting to take a chance?

But for Pete's sake! Here they were, two days before the wedding, and they weren't speaking to each other!

She desperately wanted to talk to Bert, but that wouldn't be appropriate at all. He had asked her to marry him last year and she had said no. Nothing in her life had changed, no matter how much she loved him. He had been furious with her at the risks she had taken, but that was the job. She didn't want to be torn between the demands of the job and the needs of a husband.

She opened her eyes and looked around at her office. Her small, cramped office. The sun had gone around the building, leaving the front in shade. It was cool in the room, even though the sky through the window was blue with the last of summer.

Was this what she would remember at the end of her days? A life spent in offices like this?

Her cell phone rang and she let it ring twice before finally fishing it out of her pocket. She really didn't feel like talking to anyone, but she still had a job to do.

To her relief, it was the doctor's clinic.

"Chief Williams," she said.

"Good afternoon, Chief," said a woman's voice. "Dr. Kijawa has a cancelation at two o'clock. Do you want it?"

"Yes," said Kate promptly. She glanced at the time on the screen. She had ten minutes. "I'll call her at two."

While waiting, she checked her email. Sure enough, the justice had sent her an electronic version of the warrant. Kate forwarded it to Charlotte, then walked out of her office.

Charlotte looked up from what she was writing as Kate placed the warrant on the duty desk in front of the girl.

"I emailed you the electronic version," she said.

At that moment, O'Hara walked in, carrying a cotton bag filled with groceries. Kate blinked at the sight of that big man carrying a tote bag. He removed his cap and frowned.

"Anything wrong?" he asked.

Kate shook her head. "No. We have the warrant for B.C. Mobile. Let's see if we can light a fire under them to give us her records."

O'Hara nodded and stepped into the break room, probably to put the perishables away in the fridge. He wasn't married or seeing anyone that Kate knew of, so he was responsible for all his own cooking. She wondered how his dad was doing. He was in a long-term care home in Winnipeg and O'Hara visited him on his days off.

The thought brought her back to Bert and his mother, and she shied away from it, instead going back to her office.

Dr. Kijawa answered on the first ring.

"Good afternoon, Chief," she said.

"Hello, Doc," said Kate. "Any updates?"

"You received the results of the paternity test?"

"Yes," said Kate. "The husband was the father." And she still hadn't told Marco about the results of the paternity test. She would have to call him. Wouldn't that be fun.

"So sad," said Dr. Kijawa. Then she took a deep breath, as if to clear out the sadness. "I, too, have received results." She paused slightly. "I am surprised at how quickly they came." She waited a beat, two, then moved on when Kate didn't say anything.

"Toxicology reports nothing untoward in her blood," she said. "She was not drugged, nor did she have any alcohol in her system. As for the substance under her nails, we already knew it was leather. The lab confirmed it was tanned cow hide."

Kate nodded, even if the doctor couldn't see it.

"Is that it?" she asked.

"Yes," said Dr. Kijawa. "I am sorry it is not more."

Kate sighed.

"Can't be helped. Thank you, doctor."

She was about to hang up when the doctor cleared her throat.

"Yes?" said Kate.

"Did the girl have any family?"

Kate shook her head. "Not that we've been able to locate." The doctor took a deep breath and let it out on a sigh. "That poor child."

* * *

Kate sat back in her chair, drumming her fingers on the desk and staring at the wall in front of her. Thoughts swirled around in her mind like tumbleweeds in an empty lot.

Who had Lawson's boyfriend been? Nobody McKell spoke to at the Williams Lake dental clinic had known his name, and before they could ask Lawson, she had disappeared.

They might learn more if they could find Lawson's friend, Eleanor Bakshi. If they could get the man's name, they could run a search through ViCLAS and CPIC. The Williams Lake RCMP would have a record of him, if nothing else. After all, they had taken him away.

But she needed a name.

And where was the truck? Maybe McKell's intuition was wrong and the man had gone back to B.C., having wreaked his havoc. Possible, maybe even likely, but a small part of her stubbornly resisted believing that.

He had gone to the trouble of planting Marco's card in Kelly Lawson's hand, and risked driving around with a dead body so he could dump her in a canola field belonging to Marco's friends. He would want to see what came of it.

Marco had undergone a pretty thorough security check before becoming a police officer. If there had been something hinky in his past, it would have been flagged. Still, it might be worth talking to him.

In any case, if the boyfriend had it in for Marco, he would stick around to watch the fireworks. So why couldn't they find his bloody truck?

If he was smart, he would have gotten rid of it.

Huh. He might have abandoned it somewhere. It wasn't that easy to get rid of a vehicle within a town. He hadn't abandoned it in Mendenhall—her constables would have found it by now. Brandon? Or Winnipeg? Or somewhere between those two cities?

Both those jurisdictions were already looking for the truck. If it was there, someone would find it.

Finally she picked up her phone and stared at it. There was no avoiding it any more. She had to call Marco.

The line rang five times before rolling over to voice mail. She listened to Marco's voice telling her to leave him a message and he'd get back to her. She hung up. Was he avoiding her?

Probably.

Was she still invited to the wedding? Was there still going to be a wedding?

Oh, dear Lord, this was exhausting.

They should have eloped. Then this whole mess could have been avoided.

She pulled up the texting app and selected Marco's number. Then she wrote: "HUSBAND IS THE FATHER OF THE BABY," and hit send.

She glanced at the clock on the computer. Almost two thirty. A wave of fatigue rolled over her, reminding her that she hadn't been sleeping that well all week. Too many things to worry about.

She didn't want to call Bragg now. He would be at work and she didn't want to deliver the news that he had lost his baby along with his wife where he would have no privacy. Better wait until after dinner.

* * *

When she went to fetch a coffee, O'Hara was in the break room, rummaging in the refrigerator. All Kate saw was his bum sticking out. He didn't see her until he finally emerged from the depths of the refrigerator, holding a can of ginger ale triumphantly in his hand. His face went red when he saw her.

"I knew I'd left one in there," he muttered.

Kate grinned at his discomfiture.

"What if the boyfriend abandoned his truck in Brandon or Winnipeg?" she said, trying out her theory. "He might have rented a car, or even bought another one."

"Or traded in his truck for another vehicle," said O'Hara thoughtfully. He looked at Kate. "A car's not cheap. He might have wanted the trade-in value. We need to call dealerships in Brandon and Winnipeg. And used car lots." He looked a little daunted, and Kate didn't blame him. How many dealerships would there be between those two cities? A hundred? Two hundred?

More than they could handle alone.

She sighed in frustration. Now that the thought had occurred to them, they couldn't unthink it. At least Mendenhall didn't have any car lots.

"We can handle the Brandon lots," she said. "I think. We'll need help with the Winnipeg ones."

"Maybe Bert can lend us a couple of constables?" said O'Hara.

Kate nodded. "I'll call him."

O'Hara nodded and passed her to go back to the duty room while Kate helped herself to a cup of coffee. She stirred some sugar into it and stood staring down at it for a moment.

Maybe she wasn't sleeping well because she was drinking too much coffee.

At that moment, the storm door opened and McKell strode in. He glanced inside the break room and changed course when he saw her.

"Any luck locating Bakshi?" she asked.

"Yes," he said, pulling a mug down from the cupboard. Kate moved over to give him space. "But she was busy for a few hours." He glanced at his watch. "She should be available any minute now. I'm going to try calling again."

"Where is she?" asked Kate.

"She's in Red Deer," said McKell. "And she's not a dental hygienist anymore. She's teaching at an elementary school. Class should be out soon."

That had to be more fun than looking inside people's mouths all day.

They walked out of the break room, McKell letting her go first. In the duty room, O'Hara was on the phone. Kate glanced at Charlotte, who was just hanging up her own phone. She turned a frowning face up to Kate.

"I've emailed B.C. Mobile the warrant," she said. "But it could take some time."

Kate set her cup on the corner of Charlotte's desk. Today Charlotte wore a pair of white capris and a fuchsia-colored top with a boatneck and three-quarter-length sleeves. Her slip-on shoes were made of canvas printed with a wild array of flowers.

"Rob?" called Kate. When he popped his head out of his office, she nodded him over so as not to disturb O'Hara on the phone.

"O'Hara and I think our suspect may have gotten rid of his truck," she said. "He may be driving something else by now. Either he abandoned the truck, or he sold it, or he traded it in for another vehicle."

Charlotte caught on before McKell did.

"There are hundreds…" she began, her face paling.

McKell's expression changed as he realized what she was saying.

"I know," Kate said, putting a hand up. "I figure we can handle Brandon. Charlotte, maybe you can go online and print out a list of all the dealerships and used car lots in Brandon. Then we can split it. Rob, you can help when you finish with Bakshi, and O'Hara can call in one of the constables to help."

"What about Winnipeg?" asked Charlotte, already turning to her computer.

"I'll call Bert to see if they can help."

"This is going to take time," warned McKell.

Kate shrugged. "I know. But I've run out of ideas. If anyone has a better one, I'm all ears."

She looked from Charlotte to McKell, who both shook their heads.

"All right, then. And Charlotte, if we haven't heard back from B.C. Mobile by tomorrow morning, I'll call the president of the company."

She went back to her office and called Bert, but he was in a meeting. He called her back an hour later.

"Hey, Katie," he said when she answered. "How are you?"

As always, the sound of his voice eased the tension out of her shoulders.

"Fine," she said. "But I have a favor to ask."

She could almost see his eyebrows rising. She never asked him for help. It was a point of pride. But there was pride and then there was foolish pride.

"A professional favor, I take it?"

"Yes." And she explained what it was she hoped for. When she was done, Bert whistled softly.

"That's a lot of calling around."

"I know," she said. "We're handling Brandon but—"

"Not a problem," he interrupted cheerfully. "Would you believe we've got two summer students working for us? We can barely keep them busy enough, so this should keep them occupied."

"Thank you," she said with relief. "Thank you, thank you, thank you."

"Oh, don't worry," he said, his voice dropping. "I'll think of some way for you to repay me."

Even from an hour away, the man could still make her blush.

"Now," he continued, his voice back to normal. "How's it going with the family? Did you tell Marco about the paternity results?"

Kate sighed and even to her ears it sounded woebegone.

"I tried calling him," she said glumly. "I think he's avoiding me. So I texted him the results." She leaned back in her chair and considered putting her feet up on the desk. With her luck, someone would walk in.

"Really?" Bert sounded surprised. "That seems out of character."

"You want out of character?" she asked. "Amanda yelled at me at lunchtime and told me to mind my own business. I think I may be uninvited to the wedding." She didn't tell him what Amanda had said about their relationship.

To her shock, Bert started laughing.

"What's so funny?" she demanded.

He managed to control himself.

"Weddings. They bring out the crazy in people."

Well, that was true. "They should have eloped," she muttered.

"In this case, you may be right."

She sighed again. "I have to go, Bert. Phone calls to make and all that."

"Okay," he said. "I'll keep you posted."

They hung up and Kate glanced at the time. Almost four o'clock. She didn't know how late dealerships and used car lots stayed open. Better get going.

* * *

She was on the phone with a woman at the Subaru dealership when she heard McKell's familiar tread on the linoleum floor. A moment later, he appeared in her doorway, practically filling it with his excitement. She waved him to a seat.

"I've just checked with our sales folks," said Sabine Wellars, "and I can confirm that we haven't bought any pickup trucks at all in the last month. We've sold some cars, however."

"Can you check your records?" asked Kate. "You get the buyers' names and addresses, correct?"

"Yes," said the manager, "but I don't think we can release that information."

"It's public information," said Kate patiently. "Motor Vehicles will get the information, too."

"Yes, I guess that's true," said Wellars, but her voice was full of doubt. "I'll have to check with my manager."

Kate hung on to her patience with both hands. At this rate, it would be next week before they got through all the dealerships in Brandon.

"Once you do, just email me the list, please," she said and finally hung up. She took a deep breath and looked up at McKell, who was looking at her with sympathy.

"Tell me you've got something," she said.

"I've got something," he said.

"Hang on," said Kate, and raising her voice, called out, "Charlotte, Jim!"

She heard the scrape of the stool on the platform, and moments later, Charlotte and O'Hara stood in her doorway. O'Hara stepped back to let Charlotte in and they both stood, looking expectantly at Kate. She nodded to McKell.

"Go ahead, Rob."

McKell kept his gaze fixed on Kate.

"Spoke to Eleanor Bakshi," he started. He glanced at O'Hara and Charlotte. "She was a friend of Kelly Lawson's when she worked in Williams Lake." He turned his attention back to Kate. "She and Lawson hung out at work and at lunch only, because Lawson's boyfriend wanted her home right after work."

Kate's lips pursed. That was the sign of an abuser, trying to control her access to other people.

"She said Lawson didn't talk much about him, but sometimes she would come to work injured. Never her face, though. She would always have a good reason for the injury. She fell or she walked into something or... whatever. We've all heard it before."

O'Hara and Charlotte both nodded grimly.

"Anyway, Bakshi remembers the incident with the boyfriend showing up at the dental practice very clearly. She says she and Lawson were both working with a patient when the boyfriend stormed in demanding to see Lawson. He terrorized the receptionist until Lawson showed up, still in her mask and gloves. He yelled at her and called her terrible names—Bakshi refused to repeat them—and then he tried to haul her out of the building. But one of the patients in the waiting room called the police and another guy—a big guy, apparently—forced him to release Lawson and stopped him from leaving when he realized the cops were coming."

He took a deep breath and Kate found herself leaning in.

"The cops came and took him away, kicking and screaming. The dentist told Lawson to go home, that they would handle her patients. So she left. And as we know, she never came back. Bakshi went over to her apartment after work but Lawson wasn't there. Bakshi never saw or heard from her again."

He pulled his notebook out of his shirt pocket.

"And before you ask, yes, she remembers the guy's name. He's Christopher Adamos."

CHAPTER 23

According to the Canadian Firearms Program, Christopher Adamos had never registered a firearm nor did he have a license for one. That didn't mean he didn't own one, of course.

Kate stared at her screen, willing it to divulge more information on the man who had—probably—killed Kelly Lawson. They had contacted the motor vehicles department in British Columbia and confirmed that a Christopher Adamos did indeed own a 2002 Chevy Silverado, white with a gray stripe. And they provided the license plate number, which would make finding a possible trade-in or sale that much easier, as well as a Vancouver address.

But it was still taking so much time.

McKell had talked to the Williams Lake RCMP only to learn that Adamos had been charged with disturbing the peace and fined. Charlotte had spoken to the Vancouver police department but they had no information on Adamos.

She glanced at the time on her computer screen. Five forty-five. She had to go. There wasn't much to do here until tomorrow anyway. Most of the car dealerships in Brandon were closed, or about to close.

She'd already sent Charlotte home and Abrams back on patrol. Who would have guessed that a town with fewer than fifty thousand people could have so many dealerships? They would have to pick it up in the morning. Bert had promised to call her later with an update from Winnipeg.

She had to get back home to her family. She winced, wondering if Amanda had told Rose about their argument.

Then she remembered that she still had to call Calder Bragg. She almost groaned out loud.

She got up from her desk and went over to her door. She could hear the faint murmur of McKell's voice coming from his office. O'Hara sat with his back to her, busy writing in the duty log. From her open window she could hear the faint thrum of cars on the street. She took a deep breath of air that smelled slightly of burned coffee, and closed the door.

Finally she walked over to her window and pulled her phone out of her pants pocket. She called up the directory and tapped Calder Bragg's name. The phone rang once, twice, three times before being answered.

"Chief Williams," said Bragg patiently. "How can I help you?"

Kate braced herself. "Are you home, Mr. Bragg?"

"Yes," he said cautiously. "Why?"

She looked down at the windowsill, knowing she was about to turn this man's world inside out. Again. "I've received the results of the DNA tests," she said softly. "Kelly was carrying your baby."

There was a long silence at the other end. Then she heard a soft thud, and for a moment, she worried that he had fainted; but then he spoke again.

"Why wouldn't she have told me?" he whispered.

"It's likely she didn't know herself," said Kate. "It... she was very early in her pregnancy. Women don't always know in the beginning, especially with a first pregnancy."

Oh, for Pete's sake. As if she knew what she was talking about. But her words seemed to give him solace.

"Yes," he said softly. "That could be." Then a sob tore through him. "Dear God, why is this happening?"

Tears pricked Kate's eyes and she cleared her throat.

"Sir, is there someone I could call for you?"

"No," he said, barely regaining control. "There's no one."

And with that, he hung up.

* * *

When she got home, one of the white sedans was parked in front of the house and the pickup was parked in the driveway in front of the trailer. The hike and lunch must have gone really well if the Trepallis were visiting the Williamses.

She parked behind the sedan and cut across the lawn to the front door. They might all be sitting on the back deck, but Kate wanted to change out of uniform first. But when she walked in, she saw Mom standing in the kitchen doorway, her hands clasped in front of her waist, and Fred standing behind her, one hand on her shoulder. They both turned to look at her, identical grim expressions on their faces. Mom had tears in her eyes.

"What?" said Kate, the door still open behind her. "What is it?"

A movement caught her eye and she turned to see Charlie sitting in her chair and Sean in the other one. Both looked miserable. Camilla and Henry sat on the love seat in front of the big window, their expressions hidden in the glare from the window.

It smelled like spaghetti sauce and candlewax in the house, which surprised Kate as she didn't think she owned any candles.

She stepped in and closed the door behind her. Keys still clutched in her hands, she looked from face to face.

"Will someone please tell me what's going on?"

After a moment, Camilla Trepalli stood up and smoothed down her cream-colored linen top.

"The wedding is off," she said softly. "They've canceled it."

A trembling started in the pit of Kate's stomach and made its way to her hands. She stuck them in her pants pockets, still clutching the keys.

"I'll go talk to Amanda," she said, her voice breaking.

Charlie shook his head and stood up.

"Don't bother," he said. "Marco's the one who broke it off."

* * *

Camilla and Henry left soon after. Both families decided to meet at Kate's house in the morning for breakfast and to discuss the situation. Once they had gone, Kate turned to her mother.

"I don't think I have enough dishes."

Mom shrugged. "We'll make do."

Kate turned and went to the guest room to change, but ended up sitting on the edge of the bed, looking up at the slice of sky she could see through the window.

The flowers were supposed to arrive tomorrow—both the ones for the tables under the tent and Amanda's bouquet. Julianne would have been there all day to help with the last of the food. Julianne was also supposed to bring Amanda's wedding dress from her house—where Julianne had been keeping it hidden from Marco—to Kate's house, where Amanda would have prepared for the wedding.

Now, none of that was going to happen.

Trepalli had left the house to Amanda and her parents and was staying with Stan Albertson and his wife for a few days. Kate would have thought he'd go to Ben Friesen, but then she remembered that Friesen was dating Julianne. Marco wouldn't want to be there.

He could have moved into the house where his parents were staying, of course, but he wouldn't want to talk about the canceled wedding. Stan and his wife, Beth, were older, more experienced. They wouldn't press him.

Kate leaned over and rested her forehead against her knees. She sighed heavily, her breath hot on her knees. The cancelation of the wedding brought her thoughts swirling back to Bert.

Did Marco and Amanda feel about each other the way she felt about Bert? She'd never loved anyone the way she loved him. She was never as content as when he was with her. She knew he still wanted to marry her, but what if she screwed it up? Everything was good now—why risk it?

And what about his heart? Thanks to an undiscovered heart murmur, he'd almost died when he got cattle-prodded. What if they got married and he died?

She didn't think she could survive that.

She sighed again, and this time tears pricked her eyes.

A soft rap at the door straightened her. She wiped the tears from her eyes and said, "Yes?"

The door opened to reveal Bert in beige cotton pants and a short-sleeved green tee-shirt.

"Hey," he said softly. "Your mom sent me to check on you. She said you'd been here for a while."

Kate stood up. Another tear trickled out. She couldn't seem to stop them.

"I was just getting changed," she said thickly.

Bert nodded and came into the bedroom, closing the door behind him.

"What are you doing here?" asked Kate. "When did you get here?"

He shrugged. "Just a minute ago. I took tomorrow off. I figured I could help out with your family while you're busy with this case. Your mom told me what happened."

He looked sad and that got the tears going even faster. In three steps he was holding her.

"It's all my fault," she hiccupped. "I should have minded my own business and let them work it out."

Bert rubbed her back and held her close.

"What exactly did you do?"

Kate reached in her pocket for a tissue but found only keys there. She looked around and found a box on the dresser. She wiped her nose and her eyes before answering.

"I told Marco that if Amanda couldn't handle being a cop's wife, it was better to know now. And I told Amanda that if she had any doubts, she should rethink this wedding." She grabbed more tissues as the waterworks were firmly on now.

He put an arm around her shoulders and led her to the foot of the bed, pushing her to sit. "Do you honestly think you're the only one to tell them that? I gave Amanda the unvarnished truth about cop marriages and how long they last. I'm sure Marco's friends all warned him to be sure she could handle the stresses before marrying her." He sat down next to her and nudged her shoulder with his. "We know they love each other, but sometimes that's not enough."

At that, Kate lost all control of her tears and Bert took her in his arms, rocking her gently until the storm had passed.

* * *

"We're waiting until tomorrow to start calling," said Rose. She had come over after dinner and now they all sat on the deck, listening to the crickets chirping and watching night fall.

Kate sighed and took a sip of scotch. The bottle was getting perilously low. Mom and Fred sat side by side, holding hands. Everyone was subdued.

"Where's John?" asked Bert. His chair was close to Kate's and his knee found hers.

"He took Amanda for a drive," said Rose. "They used to do that when she was a teenager and something had upset her." She looked away and sighed softly.

"Calling who?" asked Sean. He, more than the rest of them, had been very quiet all evening. Kate couldn't tell if he was sad or angry.

Charlie, on the other hand, was clearly angry.

"Everyone they invited," said Rose. "The tent company. Her friend Julianne. There's so much food…" She sighed again. "Anyway, Camilla and I are splitting the list of invitees. John is calling the tent company. Amanda will have to call her friend Julianne."

"What about Marco?" asked Charlie, practically biting the words off. "If this was his idea, shouldn't he get his ass in gear and help?"

Rose looked at her brother. Expressions were hard to read in the incidental light from the dining room, but Kate and Rose were both familiar with the sound of anger in his voice.

"His mother will share their list with him," said Mom out of the darkness. "There's no point getting angry, dear."

"Really?" said Charlie. "I disagree. He waited until everyone had flown across the country to be here before pulling the plug. I'd say that's a good reason to be mad."

"Well," said Kate, standing up. "It was the only way to actually get you here, so I'm grateful for that. More scotch, anyone?"

Rose laughed and after a moment, so did Charlie. He could never stay angry.

"Not for me," said Mom. "I'm going to bed."

It was a bit early, even for Mom, but they said their goodnights to her and Fred, and then stayed on the deck a while longer. The odd mosquito found Kate's bare ankles but there was a nip in the air and the mosquitoes were few.

"Why wait until tomorrow?" asked Kate, circling back to what Rose had said.

"Camilla and I are hoping that they'll come to their senses by morning."

Kate nodded but didn't say anything. She would never have thought that Marco Trepalli would be the one to cancel the wedding. He loved that girl. And Amanda loved him, too. They were so suited for each other.

Stay out of it, she warned herself.

"I should get going," said Rose, standing up. "It's going on nine and I want to be home when they get back."

Kate walked her sister inside, where Rose picked up her purse, and then to the front door. She could hear water running in the bathroom. She had left her car keys in the spare room and hurried to get them. John had dropped Rose off, so now Kate would have to drive her back.

She found Rose on the stoop, watching the stars. They were dimmer in the front of the house than in the back, thanks to the streetlights, but still beautiful.

"I can see why you love it here," said Rose quietly. "This is much more your style than Vancouver or Toronto ever were. I like the people here."

"So do I," said Kate. "Rose, I... I'm so sorry if I had any part in this."

Rose turned toward her.

"Because of what you said to them?" At Kate's start, she continued, "Yes, Amanda told me about it." She laughed softly. "Kate, John and I talked to Amanda when she first told us they were getting married. Was she sure she knew what she was getting into? Mom and Dad had a version of that same talk with me before I married John. He was a geologist, for pity's sake. He would never be home. He wouldn't make any money. We warn the ones we love because we love them. And sometimes, only someone you love will tell you the hard truth."

She looked up at the sky again.

"Everything Mom and Dad said about John was true but I didn't care. I wanted to marry him and he wanted to marry me. What it boils down to is if talking can dissuade you from marrying the person you love, then you shouldn't marry them."

Kate took a deep breath of the night air, redolent with the ghosts of earlier barbecues, and nodded.

She took Rose home. John and Amanda weren't back yet, so she walked her to the house and accepted a goodnight hug from her sister.

"Lock the door," she said automatically as she turned away.

"Yes, Mom," laughed Rose. But she locked the door.

Kate walked to the driveway, but instead of getting into the Edge, she turned left and followed the driveway to the back of the house. The tent filled the space, looming like an abandoned circus tent. Under it, the plastic tables and chairs gleamed skeletally.

She turned back, her heart aching, and went home.

Charlie and Sean had already retired to the camper, though she could see lights on. She went inside the house and locked the front door. She'd been leaving the deck door unlocked for the boys, if they should need to come inside in the middle of the night. She wasn't worried about intruders. The boys would hear anyone trying to get in.

Besides, she had a gun.

Bert was waiting up for her at the kitchen counter. He held a glass of water. She walked over and wrapped her arms around him.

"Thanks for coming tonight," she whispered in his ear. "I'm so glad you're here."

He placed a big hand on the back of her head and stroked her hair.

"Always, my love." He pulled away from her and set the glass down on the counter. "Let's go to bed."

* * *

She slept better that night than she had in weeks, comforted by Bert's arm over her, and was deeply asleep when her phone rang, startling her out of a dream of John at the bottom of a deep gulch, waving a rock hammer at her.

She scrabbled for the phone on the bedside table and finally accepted the call. It was the detachment.

"Yes," she said, still groggy.

"Chief, it's St-Ives." His French accent always seemed more pronounced at night. Maybe it was because he didn't talk as much at night.

"Yes, St-Ives," she replied. "What's going on?" She pushed her blankets off and swung her legs out. The bedside clock read four forty-five. There would be no going back to sleep now. Behind her, the bed sagged as Bert shifted to one elbow.

"We just got a call from Brandon, ma'am," said St-Ives. "I thought you would want to know right away. Monsieur Bragg's house burned down tonight."

CHAPTER 24

She wore the same uniform she'd worn the day before, as all her clean ones were in her bedroom, now occupied by Mom and Fred.

"I can go with you," said Bert, tucking his tee-shirt inside his jeans. Kate finished putting her hair up in a bun at the back of her head and considered. Finally she shook her head.

"Would you mind staying here and letting Mom know that I had to go?" she asked. Mom had been upset last night. For the first time, Kate wondered if her mother felt guilty, too.

"Sure," said Bert easily. "I'll look after them," he promised.

Kate turned away from the mirror and gave him a quick hug.

"Thank you," she whispered.

"You're not going alone, are you?" he asked in her ear. No amount of whispering could hide the concern in his voice.

"Not if I can help it," she said.

She left Bert in the kitchen, making coffee as quietly as he could. She walked across the lawn to her car, glad she had left it parked on the street. She might still wake the boys up when she started it, but at least it wouldn't sound like it was next to their beds.

She started the car and put the heat on. Mornings were definitely getting cooler. She pulled out her phone and tapped Trepalli's number. It rang four times before he answered. She knew he would. He would know that she would never call at this hour unless it was urgent.

"Chief?" he said, his voice groggy. "What's the matter? Is it Amanda?"

"No," said Kate crisply. "Do you still want in on the case?"

"Yes," he said immediately, sounding much more awake.

"Do you have a uniform with you?"

"Yes, ma'am."

"Then get dressed. I'll be at Albertson's house in ten minutes." She hung up.

Ten minutes later, she pulled up to Albertson's house, which was still dark. The whole world was still dark though the sky was lightening in the east. It smelled damp.

Before she could text the boy, a shadow detached itself from the house and came loping up to the car. She unlocked the door and Trepalli slipped in. The dome light came on, revealing his freshly-shaven cheeks, pressed uniform, and polished boots.

How did he always manage to look like he'd walked out of a police recruitment brochure?

"Chief," he said by way of acknowledgment.

"Trepalli," she replied. She pulled away from the house and drove slowly down the residential street, not wanting to wake any more people than she already had.

"What's going on?" asked Trepalli, belatedly putting his seat belt on. He placed his cap on the dashboard.

"First, coffee," muttered Kate as she headed toward the Tim Hortons.

Five minutes later, she'd had her first sip and felt she might just survive the day. She pulled the car out onto the empty street and headed for the highway.

"I got a call from St-Ives," she finally told him. "Calder Bragg's house burned down last night."

"That's Kelly Lawson's husband," he said, then, not waiting for her confirmation, "Was he hurt?"

"No," she told him. "He was able to get out safely."

"Was it arson?"

That had been Kate's first thought, too. It was too much of a coincidence that the house just happened to burn down in the middle of a murder investigation.

"That's what we're going to find out," she said.

"Do you think Adamos set the fire?"

She glanced sideways at him. He was awfully well informed for someone who was supposed to stay out of the investigation.

"I don't know," she said. "But it wouldn't surprise me."

He nodded and concentrated on his coffee, as if aware he'd said too much. Just under the smell of coffee, she caught a faint whiff of cedar. The boy had even had time to slap on aftershave. She hadn't even brushed her teeth.

They passed very few cars on the Trans-Canada Highway, but there were lots of transport trucks and even a few buses. Kate watched the fields on either side grow more and more defined as the morning progressed. She was reminded of Jane Hurst's canola field and the stink of it.

After fifteen minutes of silence, she sighed.

"Did you not tell her about the paternity test results?" she asked.

He kept looking straight ahead.

"No."

"Why not?" she asked, flabbergasted. "That would have set Amanda's mind at ease, surely."

He turned to look at her and she glanced at him, but couldn't make out his expression in the gloom.

"Because it's not trust if she needs proof."

After that, she couldn't think of anything to say and they remained silent for the rest of the trip.

By the time they reached Brandon, the sun was cresting the horizon, throwing long shadows in front of them. Kate drove to Third Street, where two fire trucks were still blocking the street, their lights flashing. An EMS truck stood idle by the curb, its back doors open. One firefighter was spraying water on the houses on either side of what was left of Calder Bragg's home.

Kate and Marco parked six houses down and walked to the scene, taking in the destruction. One wall remained standing, and one brick chimney. Everything else had tumbled down. Smoke still rose from the ruins, filling the air with a choking cloud. Kate automatically put her hand over her mouth and nose.

On either side of the clump of emergency vehicles, people in various stages of night wear were staring at what was left of Calder Bragg's home.

At least no other homes had caught fire.

Kate ducked around the EMS truck, Trepalli right behind her, and collared the nearest firefighter, a young woman whose face was black with soot.

"Who's in charge?" asked Kate.

Without a word, the woman pointed toward a man giving instructions to two other men, who took off at a run. He turned toward Kate just as she reached him, taking in her uniform in one swift glance.

"Can I help you?" he asked gruffly. His glance kept going to the smoldering ruin, as if checking that it hadn't caught again while he wasn't looking.

"Mendenhall Chief of Police Kate Williams," she said, not offering to shake hands. She'd learned never to shake a firefighter's hand at the scene of a fire. "This is Constable Trepalli."

"Chief Sigurdsson," he replied. "What are you doing here?"

Kate suppressed a smile. She liked a person who didn't beat around the bush.

She nodded toward Calder Bragg's house.

"The man who lives here is part of an investigation we have underway in Mendenhall. Do you know what happened yet?"

Sigurdsson took off his helmet and scratched his head. His gray hair was plastered to his skull.

The man's exhausted, she suddenly realized. She wondered how long they had been fighting the blaze. And it must have been quite the blaze, judging by the remains.

"Too soon to tell," he said, replacing his helmet. A breeze blew the smoke toward them and Kate squinted against the sting. "The fire investigator can't get in yet." He hesitated, looking down at Kate from his six-foot height. "But if I were to hazard a guess, I'd say yes to arson. Witnesses reported a strong smell of gasoline before the fire swallowed everything."

Trepalli shifted next to her, reminding her of his presence.

"Do you know where the homeowner went?" she asked.

Sigurdsson shrugged. "The EMTs checked him out and decided he didn't need to go to the hospital. He said he woke up from the smell of smoke and was able to get out quickly. He even managed to save his car."

Kate glanced at what was left of the driveway. Sure enough, Bragg's Lariat was gone.

"That was lucky," said Trepalli noncommittally.

Sigurdsson looked at him for the first time. "Yes. That doesn't happen very often."

"Do you know where he went?" asked Kate, as the EMT truck started up and began to pull away.

"No," said Sigurdsson. "But he was talking with the EMTs if you want to know more."

Trepalli took off at a run, easily catching the slow-moving vehicle. He slapped the driver's window to attract his attention and the truck stopped.

"I can get a report to you as soon as we finalize the investigation," said Sigurdsson. "Do you have a card?"

Did she have a card? Kate blinked and wondered if she had left them at home. Then she remembered she was wearing her jacket. She fished through the inside pocket and pulled a card out.

"Thank you, Chief," she said, handing it to him.

"You're welcome." Pocketing the card, he turned back to the burnt wreck. She was dismissed.

Trepalli came back as the EMT truck began rolling again.

"They said he was going to stay with friends," he told her.

Kate's eyebrows rose. Bragg had given her the distinct impression that he didn't have any friends.

* * *

"I'm surprised the BPS wasn't on site," said Trepalli as they got back into Kate's Edge.

"So am I," said Kate. She looked at the fire site down the street, still smoking but now hazy with morning light. "They knew it was his house—they called the detachment to let us know." Even as she spoke, she pulled her phone out and punched the listing for the detachment, putting it on speaker phone.

"Chief," said St-Ives. "What did you find out?"

Kate's eyebrow rose in irritation. She didn't answer to him. He answered to her. She took a deep breath and blew it out silently.

Don't overreact, she warned herself.

"Nothing much," she said. "Do you have the name of the person who called you from Brandon?"

"Yes," he said promptly. She heard him clacking away on the keyboard for a few moments, then he came back. "A Sergeant Harris. Probably the duty sergeant."

"Call him back, please. I need to know where Calder Bragg is."

"Yes, ma'am," he said promptly. "Were they not on scene?"

"They were not," said Kate. "Let me know what you find out."

"Will do, Chief." He hung up.

Kate immediately tapped the listing for Calder Bragg. She wasn't surprised when he didn't answer. She left a message on his voice mail, asking him to call her, then sent him a text with the same message.

Her coffee was long gone, and now she was hungry. Up the street, near the corner of Park Avenue, someone pulled out of their driveway and turned onto Park. She glanced at the clock on the dashboard. Almost seven.

Marco's stomach growled and she glanced at him.

"Sorry," he said, his color high. "I didn't have supper last night."

Kate's grin faded. Yeah, last night was probably bad for him. She examined him a little closer, but except for slightly bloodshot eyes, he didn't look particularly tired.

Ah, youth.

"All right," she said, almost to herself. "Let's get some breakfast. Maybe he'll call me back in the meantime."

"Maybe he went to work?"

Kate paused in the act of turning the key in the ignition. She stared out the windshield, not really seeing anything.

Could it be? Why not? He'd gone to work after finding out his wife had been murdered. She still thought that was strange, but she'd been doing this long enough to realize grief took people in different ways.

"Let's go eat," she said finally. "We can call Balderson Industries from the restaurant."

* * *

St-Ives called as she was parking in front of Leo's Diner. A dozen pickup trucks and cars were already parked there, despite the early hour. That was usually a good sign.

"What did you find out?" she asked when she accepted the call and put it on speaker.

"Bragg is staying at the Holiday Inn on 18th Street," he said.

Huh. So much for staying with friends. Out of the corner of her eye, she caught Trepalli looking at her. He had noticed it, too.

"All right," she said. "Thank you." She cut the connection and slid out of the car before slipping the phone back in her pants pocket.

They walked to the door in silence, both lost in thought, and entered to the almost debilitatingly delicious smells wafting over from the kitchen. They snagged the last empty table in the corner. Kate removed her cap and placed it on the windowsill while Trepalli hooked his over the chair back.

They waited for the young waiter—he couldn't be more than fifteen, for Pete's sake—to bring them coffee.

As Kate stirred a bit of sugar into hers, a wave of fatigue rolled over and she felt her shoulders slump. With an effort, she straightened and looked over the menu card. She didn't know why, really. All she wanted was toast.

"If we assume it was arson," said Trepalli slowly, "are we also assuming that Adamos did it?" He kept his voice low so as not to be overheard.

Before she could say anything, the young waiter came back

and stood smiling down at them, clearly waiting for their order.

Kate asked for a glass of orange juice to go along with her toast. Trepalli ordered the special—two eggs scrambled, hash browns, sausages, and pancakes. Kate stared at him and he shrugged.

"I'm hungry," he said as the waiter left.

"Yes, you are," she agreed. "It's a natural assumption that Adamos did it, but we have no evidence yet. We have to wait for the fire investigator to finish."

Marco looked at her and it was her turn to shrug. Of course she thought Adamos had done it. First he killed Lawson, then he tried to frame Trepalli, then he burned down Bragg's house. It all made a twisted kind of sense.

"We have to find the bastard," said Trepalli.

"First we eat," said Kate. She never did her best thinking on an empty stomach. She glanced at the big clock over the lunch counter. Almost seven thirty.

"Why don't you call Balderson Industries?" she suggested. "Ask to speak with Bragg." Bragg might be ignoring her calls. If so, he might have asked the receptionist at Balderson to screen his calls. She pulled up her list of recently called numbers and found the one for Balderson Industries. She read it out to Trepalli and waited as he punched it into his own phone.

After a moment, he sat up straighter and said, "Hello. May I speak with Calder Bragg, please?"

He listened for a moment, then said, "I see. Thank you." Then he hung up.

He looked at Kate.

"Calder Bragg doesn't work there anymore. He quit."

CHAPTER 25

They finished breakfast in silence and went to the Holiday Inn. Bragg wasn't there. He'd never even checked in.

Had he taken the news of the baby's death harder than she had thought? First he lost his wife, then he found out he'd lost his baby, then his house burned down.

"Do you think he's all right?" asked Marco as they left Brandon behind.

Kate shrugged. "I don't know." The more she thought about it, the more worried she became. It had been one blow after another, with no time to recover in between. Maybe he just wanted to get away from the scene of all his heartbreak, but what if he planned to hurt himself?

"Call St-Ives," she said finally. "Have him put a BOLO out for Bragg's truck. Emphasize that it's for a welfare check only."

"It'll be O'Hara on the desk by now," said Trepalli. "Where do you think Bragg is going?"

Kate pulled the visor down against the glare of the sun. "He's from the Vancouver area. Maybe that's where he's heading."

Trepalli got on the phone and filled O'Hara in on what was happening.

They drove in silence for a few more miles while Kate took

stock of all the balls tumbling through the air. Something felt off. She felt off balance, as if she had forgotten to do something. She kept her gaze on the road ahead while considering everything they had done to date on the case.

Finally, one element floated to the surface of her mind. It wasn't a big thing, but it was a loose end that she might as well snip.

"Call O'Hara back," she said, then added, "Please." She re-arranged her thoughts until they made more sense. "Ask him to call Vancouver PD and check on Christopher Adamos' last known address. If he's living with someone, could they interview that person."

Maybe he had a roommate. Or maybe he was living with his mom. Or a sibling. It was worth a try.

"Good idea," said Trepalli, pulling his phone out again. "Maybe his neighbors know what he's been up to."

Kate nodded but Trepalli was already talking to O'Hara.

By the time they arrived in Mendenhall, Kate couldn't wait to get out of her jacket. The sun had been beating through her wind-shield all the way home. And the coffee and orange juice had finally caught up to her.

As they walked into the detachment, they heard Charlotte's voice ringing through the entrance hall.

"It doesn't matter if you've never heard of Mendenhall." Her voice was so cold Kate felt instantly cooler. "You have the warrant. I expect those records within two hours or your company will be in contempt of court."

The handset banged down so hard Kate was afraid the receiver had broken.

She and Trepalli glanced at each other. Finally Trepalli, braver than she, advanced slowly toward the duty room opening. Kate fol-lowed behind.

O'Hara was sitting on the stool at the duty counter, cautiously watching Charlotte, who stood at her desk, fists on her hips, star-ing down at her phone as if daring it to ring.

"Everything okay?" asked Kate.

O'Hara glanced at her sideways, his gray eyes wider than normal. Kate didn't blame him. She didn't think she had ever heard Charlotte raise her voice.

Charlotte turned toward them, her eyes snapping with residual anger. Her color was high and her usually full lips were pressed into a thin line.

The girl took a deep breath and expelled it on a gust of irritation. She wore black capris and a long, sleeveless paisley shirt that buttoned up the front.

"God save us from petty bureaucrats," she muttered. Then she straightened her shoulders and smiled. "We should have those phone records soon," she said. She sat down and pulled her keyboard toward her. "And if we don't, I'm going to fly to Vancouver and personally kick that nitwit in the shins."

O'Hara turned toward them, grinning. Marco grinned, too, but was wise enough to keep quiet.

"Nothing to report?" asked Kate, heading into the duty room.

"Not yet," said O'Hara. "Still too soon. As for the dealerships, they should all be open by now. Tattersall is coming in to help, and the DC will be here any minute. Between him, Tattersall, Charlotte, and me, we'll finish this up in a few hours, tops."

Kate nodded. "I'll keep going on my list and help cut down the time."

"I'm here," said Trepalli. "I may as well be useful."

Kate gave O'Hara the nod and he explained to Trepalli what they were doing. Kate eyed her young constable, wondering if she should send him home. Or to Albertson's, at least. She doubted he wanted to go back to the house he shared with Amanda right now.

Kate sighed and headed for the washroom.

When she got back to her office, she closed the door and opened the window to let some fresh air in. Then she settled at her desk and called Bert. He answered on the first ring.

"Hey," he said. "You're back?"

"Just got in," said Kate. "How're things at home?"

He sighed softly.

"Your mom didn't get much sleep, and neither did Fred.

They're getting ready to go over to Amanda's house in a few minutes. Charlie and Sean are already there."

Kate slumped into the back of her chair. She had hoped… She didn't know what she had hoped. That the night would bring wiser counsel, maybe. But she already knew Marco was standing firm. And she understood why.

Kate had known from the beginning of this godforsaken case that Marco wasn't involved in Kelly Lawson's murder, and Amanda knew him even better than she did. She should have known that he was innocent.

"Are you still there?" asked Bert. For once, his voice didn't calm her down. Maybe it was all the coffee she'd had already.

"Yes," she said glumly. "I'm here. Will you be taking Mom and Fred over?"

"Yes," he said. "I'll check in with Amanda, see how she's doing. I'll stick around if they need the help."

"Thank you, Bert," she said, her heart overflowing suddenly. She could always count on him.

"What did you find out in Brandon?" he changed the subject.

Kate leaned her head back and stared at the ceiling. It could use a coat of paint. The whole place could use a coat of paint.

"It looks like arson, but we won't have a definitive answer for a while. It was still too hot to go inside. And we can't find Calder Bragg. He managed to save his truck and now he's gone. And he quit his job yesterday."

"Whoa," said Bert thoughtfully. "Sounds like he's had enough."

"Yeah," said Kate. "That's what I was thinking, too."

"But you know, he might be a danger to himself…"

Kate nodded and straightened in her chair. "I put a BOLO out on his truck. Just for a safety check."

"All right," said Bert. "This is the hardest part of any investigation, isn't it? The waiting?"

Yes, it was. The waiting. She had done everything she could think of. Now she had to sit back and wait to see what came of all the feelers she had out.

"I'd better go," she said. "I've still got a bunch of Brandon dealerships to call."

"All right, sweetheart," said Bert softly. "I'll call you later."

* * *

Forty-five minutes later, Kate had only managed to talk to two dealerships. One young woman wouldn't do anything without her boss's permission and he was in a meeting. Another man couldn't seem to grasp what she was asking him for and kept making her repeat herself.

Rob McKell had popped his head in a while back to say good morning and then had gone to his office with his own list. She could hear Charlotte in the duty room, talking pleasantly but firmly to someone at the other end. Tattersall's low, calm rumble reached her and she could picture his voice as low sound waves hitting her chest and bouncing back. Trepalli had taken his list to the break room where it was quieter.

O'Hara suddenly appeared at her door, startling her.

"Sorry, ma'am," he said. "I have someone from Vancouver PD who wants to talk to you."

Kate's eyebrows rose. Well, that didn't take long.

"Transfer them," she said.

A moment later, her desk phone rang and she picked up the handset.

"Chief Williams."

"Chief," came a woman's voice. "This is Police Constable Emery from the VPD. You asked us to check on a Christopher Adamos?"

"That's right," said Kate. "He's wanted for questioning in a murder case here in Mendenhall. We think he's still in our area but we wanted to cross our t's." She wanted to mention the possibility of interviewing whoever was at his house, but Emery started speaking again.

"Good thing you did, ma'am," said Constable Emery. "His truck is parked in his driveway. We can bring him in for questioning, but you'll have to contact the Major Crime Section and bring them up to speed."

* * *

"Holy crap," said Rob.

Kate couldn't stop nodding. She sat on one of the unused desks in the middle of the room. She had just finished telling them all what Constable Emery had told her.

"How long has he been back home?" asked Trepalli, clearly confused.

Kate knew how he felt. There was no way Adamos could have set fire to Bragg's house last night and been in Vancouver by this morning. Unless he had used a timing device?

"So Adamos didn't set the fire," said O'Hara.

"Doesn't look like it," said McKell. He looked crestfallen. He had been so sure that Adamos was still in the area. So had she.

She felt as if the ground had just shifted beneath her feet and she was struggling to regain her balance.

"We don't know that it was arson," warned Trepalli.

"What are the chances that it wasn't?" retorted Charlotte.

The phone rang and O'Hara swiveled on his stool to answer. Kate nodded everyone out of the duty room and into the break room so they could talk without interrupting him. Before they could resume, the storm door opened and Kyle Holmes walked in, pushing two boys who couldn't be older than ten or eleven in front of him.

"Keep going," he said gruffly when they faltered. The two boys turned frightened faces up to him but he shooed them forward, toward the duty room. He glanced into the break room as he walked by and gave them a wink.

"Probably shoplifting," said Tattersall.

Kate sighed. Holmes was of the "scare them straight" school of policing. She'd seen this little song and dance before. He would sit them down at one of the desks, open up a file on his computer, and start taking down their information. Then, when he figured they'd had enough, he would call their parents in to pick them up. He would never file charges, of course, but the whole event would be traumatizing for the kids. Kate suspected that his methods, while harsh, probably worked.

Still, she kind of felt sorry for the kids.

"So." McKell picked up where they had left off. "I guess we can cancel the BOLO for his truck." He still looked disgruntled, as if

Christopher Adamos had set out to discomfit him.

"Yes," agreed Kate. "I spoke with a detective at the Major Crimes unit of VPD and explained the case to him. He'll interview Adamos this afternoon."

"What about Adamos' phone?" asked McKell. "If we can get hold of it, we can see for ourselves if he harassed Lawson and we can see the texts he may have sent her."

Kate nodded. "I've already asked, but they can't do anything without a warrant. And we can't get a warrant until we have reason to believe he was harassing her."

"Well, that's a catch-22," muttered Tattersall, crossing his arms over his chest. He leaned against the lunch counter, his long, skinny legs crossed at the ankles. His pants always looked a little short on him.

"Not necessarily," said Kate. She stood up from the love seat and walked over to the window overlooking the parking lot. "Once we get Lawson's records, if we see that Adamos called her or texted her, we can obtain a warrant for his phone."

"Excuse me," muttered Charlotte. "I have a bureaucrat to frighten." She got up from the couch and left the break room.

Kate almost felt sorry for the bureaucrat in question. Before she could continue, her cell phone rang. She pulled it out of her pocket and looked at the screen. It was Bert. For a moment, she debated declining the call but then she realized he wouldn't call unless it was urgent.

"Excuse me," she told the others. "I'll be right back."

She walked out of the break room and out of the detachment, letting the door slam behind her. The sunlight blinded her for a moment and she fumbled trying to slide the icon over. Finally she got it.

"Hi, Bert," she said. "Everything okay?"

"More than okay," said Bert and there was no disguising the excitement in his voice. "My students found your truck!"

CHAPTER 26

To her surprise, the 2002 Chevy Silverado hadn't been sold to North End Motors in Winnipeg—it had been bought from them.

Kate sat at her desk, looking out the window, and tried to figure out what the hell it all meant.

The 2002 Chevy Silverado had been bought from North End Motors in Winnipeg on Saturday. Almost a week ago. While only a few years old, it had been pretty banged up and the dealer had been happy to take five thousand dollars cash for it. The buyer—a Kyle Carruthers—had taken the bill of sale and returned a few hours later with insurance papers and a plate from a pickup he said he was getting rid of. The dealer had recorded them.

Bert's student, eager to impress his superiors, had checked both. The insurance papers were fake and the plate had been stolen from a 2012 Toyota 4Runner in Winnipeg. The owner was away on business and hadn't reported the plate missing until two days ago.

Then the student checked into Kyle Carruthers and his address in Winnipeg. It didn't exist. Neither did Kyle Carruthers.

"Hey," said Bert, standing in her doorway. She'd been so busy frowning at the window she hadn't heard him come in.

"Hey, yourself," she said. "How are things at Amanda's?" Amanda and Marco's, she reminded herself.

"Your mother and sister and Camilla and Tina could probably run the world if they wanted to," he said, plopping down into one of her visitor chairs.

In spite of everything, Kate smiled. "What are they up to?"

"They got the tent company to come in right away and take the tent down. In the meantime, they got all the men organized to take down the decorations, put the flowers in boxes to donate to the seniors' home, and stack all the tables and chairs. They split the list of invitees into four and assigned them to four of the cousins to call and let people know the wedding is off. Rose and Camilla are dealing with the cake, the wine and champagne, and whatever else is left to do. Your mom is dealing with Amanda, keeping her busy with donating food to the Salvation Army and anyone else she can think of."

He looked at Kate, his eyes wide with admiration. "Those women could organize a military campaign."

Well, that was certainly true of Mom and Rose. And apparently Camilla and Tina, too. She sighed.

"How's Amanda?"

Bert shrugged. The light in his copper-penny eyes dimmed a little.

"You can tell she's been crying, but she's dealing." He glanced toward the open door and lowered his voice. "How's Marco?"

Kate hesitated. "I'm not sure," she said truthfully. "I think maybe he's angry."

Bert nodded after a moment. "Yes. I would be, too."

A flood of conflicting emotions swept through Kate, stealing her voice. She thought again about Amanda's accusation that she wasn't allowing Bert to move on. Was that what she was doing...?

"Coffee?" she said finally, getting to her feet.

Bert got up and followed her into the duty room.

Holmes had finished with the two kids, and their parents had come and fetched them. Tattersall and Trepalli were still on the phone, since Kate wanted to be sure they hadn't missed yet another 2002 or 2003 white-and-gray Chevy Silverado. Charlotte, O'Hara, and McKell were all on the phone, too.

She glanced inside McKell's office as they walked by. He caught her gaze and nodded in agreement when she pointed to the break room.

The three of them sat in the break room with their coffees and tossed around theories and ideas while the business of the detachment swirled around them.

After a while, Kate got up from the love seat, where she seemed to have taken root, and poured herself another cup of coffee. She was drinking way too much of the stuff. It was definitely affecting her sleep. She turned to the other two, pot in hand, but they both shook their heads no. Their deep male voices droned on behind her as she stirred sugar into the coffee.

Was it just a coincidence that there happened to be two white-and-gray 2002 or 2003 Chevy Silverados in the area? It could be. Of course it could be. Even if she didn't like coincidences. Not in an investigation.

But what else could it be? Christopher Adamos was well and truly in Vancouver. He was there with his truck. Was it possible he had never been in Brandon? Calder Bragg said he had seen him on Thursday, a week ago. A couple of days before the truck was bought in Winnipeg. Three days before Kelly Lawson was killed. Could Bragg have been mistaken about who he saw? After all, he didn't know him.

And it wasn't as if Adamos had introduced himself to Bragg. He'd just told Bragg to stay away from his girlfriend. He could have been anybody. But Bragg had said the man who accosted him was short and scrawny. And according to the constable she had spoken to in Vancouver, Adamos was both.

She needed those damned phone records.

Trepalli walked into the break room, empty cup in hand. McKell and Bert kept talking as he came up to Kate and poured himself a cup.

"My list is done," he said. "No luck. And Tattersall is almost done, too."

Kate nodded. She didn't think they would find another similar truck anywhere on that list. That would be just too much of a co-incidence.

"What about O'Hara and Charlotte?"

"O'Hara has been getting a lot of calls, so I don't know how far he's gotten. Charlotte's been dealing with B.C. Mobile."

It might be time for Kate to address the B.C. Mobile situation herself.

Next to her, she felt Trepalli's attention shift to the drone in the background.

"What if someone knew about Adamos' truck?" he asked in a lull in the conversation.

McKell and Bert both turned to look at him. Trepalli glanced at Kate, his color high.

"What do you mean?" she asked encouragingly.

He glanced at the other two, then looked at her.

"What if someone knew the type of truck Adamos drove and bought a similar truck?"

Kate stared up at him, not seeing him. She felt as if a small bomb had gone off in her brain. All the small, confusing pieces of the investigation flew up into the air only to fall back in a different configuration.

What if someone had decided to frame Christopher Adamos?

CHAPTER 27

All the dealerships in Brandon and Winnipeg had been contacted, with only the one hit at North End Motors. The detectives in Vancouver were waiting on her to provide a warrant for Adamos' cell phone before pulling him in for questioning. The BOLO on Calder Bragg was still out, with no success so far.

As for the Chevy Silverado from North End Motors, she had no idea what could have happened to it, but she put out a new BOLO for it, with the stolen license plate.

The student had asked the dealership to provide a photo and it showed a white 2002 Chevy Silverado with a gray stripe along the bottom.

"Looks like it's been rode rough, as my grandpa used to say," said Bert with a twang in his voice. He was looking over her shoulder at the computer screen.

Kate had to agree. There were dents on the driver side door and rust marks on the bumpers. Had that color combination been popular in 2002?

She attached the photo to the BOLO.

She wracked her brain for what else she could be doing, but could think of nothing. Her eyes were burning from staring at the screen.

"Okay, enough," said Bert firmly. "You've done everything you can for now. When's the last time you ate?"

Kate blinked up at him, her mind having trouble adjusting to the new topic.

"I had toast in Brandon this morning." But now that she thought about it, her stomach felt vast and hollow.

"Let's go," said Bert, taking her hand and forcing her up. "We'll go see Amanda and your family and eat something there. They have enough food to feed all of Mendenhall."

Kate complied with his fussing, but only because she couldn't think of anything else to do. Bert was right. The waiting was always the hardest part.

He let go of her hand as they entered the duty room. Marco sat at the duty desk, typing something into the computer, while Charlotte sat at her desk, staring at her screen, arms crossed over her chest. She glanced up as Kate approached.

"He's got another half hour before the deadline I gave him elapses," she said grimly. "After that, I'm calling the president of B.C. Mobile."

"I can call—" Kate started, only to be interrupted by Bert.

"After," he said. "You can call after you've eaten something."

Kate blushed but Charlotte smiled sweetly, her pique evidently forgotten.

"Don't worry, Chief," she said. "I'll call you as soon as I get it."

Kate nodded. O'Hara and McKell were evidently both out for lunch, but when she and Bert walked by the break room, she saw O'Hara sitting at the small table, eating a thick sandwich. She waved her phone at him and he nodded, still chewing.

The day was still beautiful, but storm clouds were building in the west. Mom had been right to worry about the weather for the wedding. Of course, it was a moot point now. A fresh wind kicked up dust in the parking lot, reminding Kate that Fall was just around the corner.

"We should go camping while the weather is still nice," said Bert, getting into her Edge.

Kate looked at him, aghast. "When did I ever give you the impression that I liked camping?"

He laughed and patted her knee before putting on his seatbelt. "Don't worry. You'll love it."

Her mind froze for a moment at the thought of sleeping on the ground and dealing with bugs in her food. And what about bears? There were bears everywhere.

"This may be an insurmountable obstacle," she warned, starting the car. "We may have to break up." She backed out of her space and turned toward the main drag.

"I have faith in us," said Bert. His hand reached out to stroke her cheek. "We're made of stern stuff."

Kate's thoughts immediately went to Marco and Amanda and she fell quiet. She had believed they were made of stern stuff, too.

The tent rental truck was just pulling away when they arrived at the house. Amanda's Tercel was nowhere to be seen. They parked behind the black pickup, which meant Charlie and Sean were still there. Only one of the white rental cars was parked in the driveway. Some of the Trepalli clan had left.

Kate and Bert automatically followed the driveway to the back of the house and Kate stopped to stare.

The backyard looked bereft. Without the tent, chairs, and folding tables, all that remained were paper napkins strewn across the flattened grass, the large folding table borrowed from Julianne for the cake, and empty cans of pop and plastic glasses rolling around in the wind.

It looked like what was left after the circus left town.

Kate swallowed and looked at Bert. He blinked and reached out to take her hand.

"Hello, dear."

Kate looked up at the deck and found Mom looking down at her. Mom looked tired. She wore a long-sleeved shirt over a pair of linen pants. She had shown Kate the lovely dress she had planned to wear for the wedding. Now she wouldn't get to wear it. Five days her mother had been here and Kate had barely been able to spare her any time.

"Not exactly the trip you had expected, eh, Mom?" she asked

softly.

Mom smiled down at her sadly.

"No. But these things happen."

"How are you, Hetty?" said Bert. "Where is everybody?"

"I'm fine, dear," said Mom automatically. "Everyone's inside, setting lunch out."

"What about Amanda?" asked Kate. "Her car's not here."

Mom nodded. "She and Sean went for a ride. I think they wanted some brother-sister time."

Kate sighed, wondering if it would be better for Amanda if everyone cleared out and left her to grieve on her own.

"Kate?" called Rose. A moment later she came into view. She wore jeans and one of Amanda's old shirts with the sleeves rolled up. She had dark circles under her eyes, too.

"Hi," said Kate. "We hear there's food to be had."

"For you, your police officers, and the rest of Mendenhall, too. Come on up."

Well, Rose wasn't kidding. Kate walked in, followed by Bert, then Mom. Then Kate stopped, flabbergasted. No wonder Amanda didn't want to be here.

The kitchen looked like a fierce wind had gotten in, rummaged around for a while, then left. There were dirty dishes in the sink and on the counter. A pitcher of juice sat in a puddle on the counter by the fridge. A long pan filled with what looked like puff pastry balls sat on the stove top. Empty plastic containers took up the rest of the space on the counters, with a wild variety of lids strewn among them.

Camilla and Tina stood at the sink, washing dishes, while one of the Trepalli cousins, a drying cloth over her shoulder, unloaded the dishwasher and looked for where the dishes were supposed to go.

Then Kate looked right, to the table Amanda used when setting out the meals before bringing them into the dining room when her restaurant was open. It was covered in stacks of plates and napkins, large plastic bins with what appeared to be skewers of meat, small tubs of sauces piled one on top of another, baking sheets covered in tin foil or plastic wrap.

From what had once been the living room but was now the part-time restaurant's dining room came the low voices of men and the higher voices of a couple of women. Before she could make out what was being said, Fred appeared in the doorway, leading half a dozen of Marco's cousins through the kitchen and out the door to the deck. Every one of them carried a green plastic garbage bag. Every head in the kitchen swiveled to follow their progress.

"Now you understand why I was on the deck," said Mom behind her.

At the kitchen sink, Camilla waved a soapy, gloved hand at her and Kate waved back.

From the front of the house came the sound of heavy feet climbing the stairs from the basement. Kate and Bert crowded into the doorway between the kitchen and the dining room in time to see Charlie, and Henry and Paul, Marco's dad and uncle, emerge from the basement. Each man carried a huge metal tray piled with plastic-covered food. They brought each tray to a table in the dining room and turned to go back downstairs.

"Holy..." said Bert in wonder. "How many refrigerators does she have down there?"

"Four," said Rose. "And they're all full."

Kate did a slow turn to take in the dining room and kitchen.

Daunted. That was how she felt.

"All that food..." she murmured.

Tina flicked a drying cloth over her shoulder and came to join them.

"We're donating some to the Salvation Army," she said. She waved at the dining room and kitchen. "And we're preparing donation packages for the Salvation Army in Brandon as well as the women's shelter there. The neighbors are getting some, too."

"As for the rest," called Camilla from the sink, "we're just going to have to sacrifice ourselves and eat it."

Kate grinned. "All right, then. Where do you want me?"

"Could you help Justine with putting away the dishes?" said Tina, pointing to the cousin at the dishwasher. "The sooner we empty it, the sooner we can fill it again."

"I'll go help bring the stuff up from downstairs," said Bert, heading toward the front of the house.

"And you can go supervise from the deck," said Rose to Mom, guiding her toward the door. "There are enough bodies in here. Would you like some punch?" she asked.

Mom smiled. "That would be lovely, dear."

In fifteen minutes, the dishes were done and put away. Bert had brought boxes up from the basement and Camilla, Rose, and Tina got busy parceling out the food for different agencies.

One of the cousins, who had been sitting at a corner table in the dining room, wrote up labels with a felt marker. Now she affixed a label with Amanda's name and phone number on it to every tray and plastic container.

Kate doubted that every food container would come back to the girl, but enough would. And Kate could buy her more. It was more important to make sure the food got to where it wouldn't be wasted. And out of Amanda's sight.

They filled the boxes, wrote where each was going on top, and piled them on the table in the kitchen. Then everyone grabbed a plate and filled it from the trays that remained in the dining room. Someone had filled a metal tub full of ice and placed pop cans in the ice. They all sat at the tables on the deck, bringing chairs out from the dining room as needed.

Kate had some chips with homemade salsa and guacamole, a mini wrap kept closed with a fancy toothpick, and some cheese and grapes. Bert spent a lot of time talking with Henry, Charlie, and Paul. Everyone looked a little bedraggled, but at least the backyard was clean again.

"I'm glad Amanda and Marco won't have to deal with all this," said Mom, waving a hand toward the lawn and the house.

Fred nodded and set his skewer of meat down. "Me, too," he said. "It's bad enough their hearts are broken without having to deal with logistics."

Kate and Rose glanced at each other. Kate had always suspected Fred was a romantic.

"They're young," said Mom equably. She dabbed at her lips

with a napkin. "They have time to figure it out." She gave Fred a sweet smile that was so intimate Kate looked away.

"Where did John go?" asked Rose, looking around. She pushed her thick brown hair away from her face with the back of her hand.

"Doing a final walkabout of the grounds," said Fred, nodding toward the lawn. Sure enough, John was walking slowly around the yard, stooping occasionally to pick up the odd bit of debris that had been missed.

"Making sure his daughter comes home to a clean place," murmured Mom.

Tears suddenly pricked Kate's eyes, and she lost her appetite.

Amanda and Marco were made for each other. It was heartbreaking that they had lost sight of that.

Bert wound his way around the tables and chairs and stopped a few feet from her.

"Charlie and Henry are going to drop off the boxes of food to the Sally Ann in Mendenhall," he said. "Paul and I are going to take the Brandon boxes," he said. "If you're ready, you could drive me back to my car and I'll swing back here and pick him up."

Kate glanced at Rose and Camilla. "Sorry, ladies. I do have to get back."

Charlie joined Bert. "I'll leave the pickup for Mom and Fred, if they need it. Henry and I will take one of their rentals."

Kate cocked her head at him. "Will you be able to fit all the boxes in the rental?"

"No worries," he said airily. "There's only a few boxes. We can always come back here if we have to leave some behind. It's not far to the Sally Ann. Right?"

This was Mendenhall. Nothing was far.

She stood up. "In that case, I will abandon you to finish up." She leaned down and kissed Mom on the cheek. "I'll see you at dinnertime," she said.

"If you can," said Mom calmly.

At that moment, Kate's phone dinged with a text message. She pulled it out of her pocket. It was from Charlotte.

RECORDS ARE HERE. YOU'D BETTER COME.

CHAPTER 28

There were days Kate wished for a bigger detachment building. That wasn't true—every day she wished for a bigger building. Somewhere with more room to spread out. Maybe an evidence lockup that was bigger than the closet they now used. Somewhere to put a big work table. A place to put a big white board so they could see all their timelines and evidence at a glance, away from the public.

But they didn't have a bigger detachment, so Charlotte had pulled out the huge roll of newsprint that lived in the storage room and taped the paper to the wall by the door inside the break room.

She was busy writing on the makeshift white board, transcribing information from a printout, when Kate walked in.

Camilla and Tina had made up a tray of dessert bars, cupcakes, and tarts, and Kate set it on the kitchen counter, seeing as Charlotte had moved the small table up to where she was working.

Kate dusted off her hands and walked over to where Charlotte had written down dates and times in one column, in black. The next two columns consisted of more numbers, one in green marker, the other in blue. Above the green column, she had written ADAMOS, and above the blue, LAWSON.

Kate stopped next to her.

"The column in black lists the dates and times that Adamos

called Lawson. The numbers in brackets are the length of the calls."

Kate studied the list, if she could call it that, as Charlotte kept adding to the other two columns. There were two calls in all. The first call was on August 13 and lasted for almost five minutes. The last one on August 26, the day Lawson died.

"The column in green are times and dates of text messages Adamos sent to Lawson. The one in blue are the messages she sent to him." She finished writing and placed caps back on the green and blue markers, which she then set down on the table. She waved the pages she held toward the wall.

"He started by calling her on the 13th," she said. "She must not have recognized the number because she took the call and they spoke for a while." She pointed to the next line. "He may have called after that, but there's no record since she didn't pick up except for the day she died. That last conversation lasted a good ten minutes."

"By then," said Kate musingly, "Lawson had moved out. Did he even know where she was staying?"

Charlotte shrugged. She was staring at the wall, eyes narrowed.

"I don't know. But he switched to texts when she presumably wouldn't return his calls." She pointed to the column in green. "Every day, at least a dozen texts." Then she pointed to blue column. "She only responded twice. We can assume she was responding because her text went out shortly after his text arrived."

Kate wondered if that was true. The man was harrying Lawson to the tune of a dozen texts a day. Whatever text she sent him could easily look like a response to one of his texts, even if it wasn't, simply because he sent so many.

"He was stalking her," said Trepalli from the doorway.

Kate and Charlotte looked around in surprise. Trepalli leaned against the door opening, his arms crossed over his chest. Behind him, through the storm door window, the sky was a solid gray with thunderheads advancing toward them.

"Yes," said Kate. "That's what it looks like."

Charlotte lifted a finger in the air.

"I forgot to tell you. B.C. Mobile also traced his phone's route, from tower to tower. He left Brandon on August 28, the day after her body was found, and drove directly to Vancouver. That's a twenty-four-hour drive and he did it in one shot."

Trepalli's dark eyebrows rose.

"Sounds like he was running."

It certainly did. Kate turned to Charlotte. "Can you send me the email?" She had to get a search warrant and send both the warrant and the list of calls—plus their analysis—to the detective in Vancouver.

"It's on the group drive," said Charlotte. "We need a warrant for his phone."

Kate nodded. "Yes, we do. Marco, can you take care of that?"

But Trepalli's gaze rested on the tray of desserts and his expression had gone bleak. Kate suddenly realized that she had been incredibly insensitive in bringing the desserts destined for his wedding reception to the detachment.

Holy cow, she was an idiot.

"Marco..." she began apologetically.

He tore his gaze away and looked at her. "No problem, ma'am. I'll get on it right away." He looked ten years older than he had moments before. He turned on his heel and went back to the duty room.

Charlotte looked at Kate questioningly and Kate sighed.

"I can be so dense sometimes."

Charlotte looked around the break room, clearly wondering what she had missed. She spotted the desserts and her face changed. She gave Kate a half smile.

"Yes, Chief. I guess you can be dense sometimes."

"Not helping, Charlotte," muttered Kate. She left the break room and headed for her office, nodding to O'Hara sitting at the duty desk. Trepalli was already on the phone. McKell was out. She seemed to remember he was giving a talk to a neighborhood watch group this afternoon.

When she got to her office, she sank down in her chair, feeling the weight of exhaustion like a heavy blanket over her head. They were getting close to something; she could feel it. She just didn't know what that something was.

The sky outside her window was getting darker. Should she go back to Amanda's and get Mom and Fred home? No. No, if she did that, Mom would believe that Kate thought her frail. And Fred would believe she didn't think he could look after Mom.

The wind rattled her window, letting in fresh air through the cracks with a whiff of ozone. In winter, she had to put plastic over the window.

She hoped Bert and Paul wouldn't get caught in the storm on their way back from Brandon.

Pulling up her keyboard, she keyed in the password for the group drive and scrolled down the subdirectories until she found one titled B.C. MOBILE. There she found the list of phone calls and text messages.

She spent the next hour crafting a message to accompany the list, explaining what their thinking was. Hopefully the VPD detective would be able to obtain Adamos' phone, and hopefully, Adamos wouldn't have erased the incriminating texts.

Then she wrote a bullet list of what they knew so far in the case and what questions she would really, really like Adamos to answer.

As she was finishing up her note, a soft ding announced a new email. She switched screens and blinked at the name in bold at the top of her screen. Herbert Ahuja. Who...? Then she remembered. He was the VPD detective who had agreed to help them. The man she'd been writing to. She opened his message.

CHIEF, I DID SOME DIGGING AROUND ON CHRISTOPHER ADAMOS AND FOUND THERE'S A PEACE BOND OUT FOR HIM. IT'S FROM WILLIAMS LAKE. HE IS TO STAY AWAY FROM KELLY LAWSON—AT LEAST THREE HUNDRED FEET—AND HE IS TO HAVE NO CONTACT WITH HER, BY PHONE, EMAIL, TEXT, LETTERS, OR ANY OTHER MEANS. IF YOU CAN GET ME THAT SEARCH WARRANT, WE CAN GET HIS PHONE AND SEE IF HE RESPECTED THE PEACE BOND. IF HE DIDN'T, WE'LL HAVE REASON TO HOLD HIM. THAT SHOULD GIVE YOU A BIT MORE TIME.

A peace bond. Well, the jerk had clearly not respected it. She could send Ahuja the list B.C. Mobile had sent them, but she would rather send him everything in the same email. Less chance of losing a piece.

As if the gods were listening, another ding announced a new message. This one was from the local Justice of the Peace. He was sending her the search warrant.

Hallelujah.

She responded to Ahuja with her analysis of the phone calls and list of text dates, the list from B.C. Mobile, as well as their map showing where and when Adamos had been on his drive to Vancouver, her summary of the case, the list of questions, and the warrant, and hit SEND. Then she glanced at the time. Almost three o'clock, which made it one o'clock in Vancouver.

Wouldn't it be nice if Ahuja could pick up Adamos this afternoon?

She sighed. The VPD was a very busy police department. Ahuja probably had his hands full with his own cases. If he came through with this in a timely manner, she would have to find a way to thank him.

Voices rose in the duty room and boot heels sounded on the linoleum floor. Kate looked up from her computer just as Trepalli appeared in her doorway. He was wearing his summer jacket, which was pocked with raindrops. Raindrops covered his thick black hair like dew. He slicked a hand over his hair to dislodge the water and wiped his hand on his pants.

"I have the warrant," he said, laying the sheet of paper folded in three on her desk. "The JP said he'd email it to you."

"He did," said Kate. "And I've already sent it on to the VPD. Good job, constable."

He smiled and shrugged.

"What else should we be doing?" he asked.

Kate blew a breath out on a gust of irritation.

"We wait. We need Vancouver to interview Adamos and we need to find that damned truck!"

Her tone was sharper than she had intended but Trepalli only nodded.

"In that case," he said, "I'm going to go grab a bite to eat."

Kate nodded, too, and watched him turn and leave. Technically, the boy wasn't even supposed to be here. She wanted to send him home, but suspected he would much rather keep his mind occupied with the case. Just as Amanda would much rather be busy dismantling a wedding and dealing with the onslaught of family.

It occurred to her suddenly that it was odd to have both the Trepallis and the Williamses working together with Amanda, while Marco stood apart from everyone. Of course, she didn't know how much—or how little—contact he'd had with his family since calling off the wedding. Maybe he was in constant contact.

She shook her head and warned herself to mind her own business.

She stood up to go get a coffee, then changed her mind and walked to the window instead. It had gotten colder outside. She could tell by how the cold air came off the window. The wind blew sheets of rain across the parking lot, which was almost full with her car, Trepalli's and Charlotte's, and the disused patrol car. She suddenly remembered that the new one was coming in soon. Hadn't McKell told her that? When was that? It felt like a year ago now, but it was the day her family arrived in town.

She rubbed her bare arms against the chill. Was Bert still on the road? These rain storms could be ugly on the open highway, with nothing to break the wind sweeping across the prairie.

Where the hell was Calder Bragg? She would have thought the BOLO would have resulted in a hit before now. His shiny red Ford Lariat shouldn't be that hard to find.

Unless he was hiding.

Her hands stopped rubbing her arms and she stared unseeingly out the window.

Unless he was hiding.

She rummaged around all the puzzle pieces in her mind and looked for the ones with Calder Bragg's name on them. Then she thought about Kelly Lawson and her unfortunate history with men.

Had Kelly switched out one bad man for a worse one? Doc Kijawa had said Lawson's most recent injuries were three years old.

That was during Adamos' tenure. But abusers built up to physical abuse. They often started with verbal abuse. Psychological abuse. They separated the woman from her friends and family. Then the physical abuse began.

Except for the ligature mark around Kelly's neck, there had been no sign of physical abuse on her.

Cars drove by, throwing up spray as they rolled through the forming puddles.

On impulse, she went back to her computer and pulled up the B.C. Mobile file. It had included a list of cell towers that had pinged Adamos' cell phone as he drove by. She hit print and went into the duty room. It was so dark outside that someone had turned the light on in the duty room.

"Do we have a map of Canada?" she asked.

O'Hara and Charlotte both turned to look at her.

"Yes," said Charlotte. "Hang on." She went over to one of the four sets of four-drawer file cabinets against the wall behind her and pulled open a drawer. After rummaging around for a moment, she pulled out a folded map.

"Bring some tape," said Kate. "And those markers of yours." She went over to the printer, grabbed the sheets, and followed Charlotte to the break room. She heard the thump of big feet on the linoleum floor, and a moment later, O'Hara stood in the doorway, close enough to grab the phone if it rang, but still able to watch them work.

Kate folded the map so that it showed only the southern part of the country starting with Manitoba. She and Charlotte taped it high on the wall next to Charlotte's makeshift whiteboard.

"Okay," she said, when they were ready. "I'll read out the towns. You circle them and mark down the date and time."

"Ready," said Charlotte, green marker in one hand and ball-point pen in the other.

"Regina," said Kate. "August 28, nine thirty-five in the morning."

Charlotte circled the city and wrote down the time and date.

"Moose Jaw, same day, eleven o'clock." A pause to let the girl write. "Medicine Hat, same day, three thirty in the afternoon." She kept going until she reached Vancouver. "Nine in the morning."

O'Hara came back to the break room—she hadn't even noticed he had left—and handed Charlotte a yellow highlighter. She used it to trace Adamos' trajectory from Brandon—at almost five on Tuesday morning—to Vancouver the next morning. He might have stopped to nap along the way, but never for longer than an hour.

"If he killed her," said O'Hara, "why didn't he leave right after? On Sunday night? Why wait until Tuesday?"

Kate stared at the map grimly, arms crossed over her chest. She was such a fool.

"He left as soon as he heard about the murder on the news," she said. "The information didn't get out until Monday, late."

O'Hara was staring at her, his gray eyes disturbingly pale in his waxen face.

"You're thinking he didn't kill her."

Kate nodded.

"Then who did?" asked Charlotte.

"Her husband, Calder Bragg."

CHAPTER 29

Someone would have seen him by now if he'd been on the highway," said Bert.

That was true. If Calder Bragg was heading back to B.C., he would most likely be driving the Trans-Canada Highway. Some eagle-eyed cop would have seen him by now.

They were standing at the edge of Kate's yard, overlooking the cliff that eventually fell away to downtown Mendenhall. It was the time of day when evening waited impatiently in the wings, but the sun wasn't quite ready to relinquish the horizon. The grass was still wet from the rain, and mosquitoes droned around them, barely put off by the bug dope they had slathered on. And the blackflies didn't even seem to notice the bug dope.

Kate glanced over her shoulder. The lights were on in the kitchen as Mom, Rose, and Henry Trepalli worked on Mom's special chicken marinade. Camilla and Tina worked at the other counter on a couple of salads. John was cutting up a long loaf of French bread. Sean and Charlie were busy setting up the picnic table as well as the table on her deck. And the dining room table was already set.

Because the rest of the Trepalli clan were about to descend on them for dinner. They were bringing wine and beer, and dessert.

"Who are all these people and what are they doing here?" she whispered to the universe.

Bert put an arm around her shoulders.

"Two more days," he said, "and they'll all be gone."

Feeling like a traitor to her family, Kate shook off the feeling of impending doom. "Do you think Marco and Amanda will come?" she asked.

Bert shrugged.

"Don't know. But I think it's great how the two families have come together."

Kate thought it was great, too, if a little weird. In an alternate universe, the two families would have been at war, each blaming the other for the failed wedding. But apparently shared grief could act like cement, binding two families together in common action for their children.

She turned back to the cliff. The sight of her town far below usually soothed her, but not this time. Not while Calder Bragg was still at large.

Calder Bragg wasn't suicidal. He hadn't been found yet because he didn't want to be found. She had sent constables to his former place of work to interview his boss and coworkers. None were particularly close to him. They didn't know of any friends who might shelter him.

She couldn't believe she had felt sorry for the man.

And yet, she'd had her suspicions at the very beginning. So had Boychuk. They'd both been surprised at his odd reaction to news of his wife's murder. It had bothered her but she had finally chalked it up to different people reacting differently to grief.

She had been thrown off by the discovery of Christopher Adamos' abusive relationship with Lawson. It had felt so right—he had abused her until she finally left him in Williams Lake, where she had obtained a peace bond against him. Then he had followed her to Vancouver and she had convinced Bragg to move to Brandon, hoping to shake Adamos off, no doubt.

Calder Bragg had told her about Adamos coming to see him in a 2002 or 2003 Chevy Silverado, white with a gray stripe running along the bottom.

And then Jane Hurst's farmhand Frank Alford had spotted a white pickup with a gray stripe at the bottom. An older Chevy, he had thought. And he didn't think it had Manitoba plates.

Bragg had fed her just enough information to let her jump to the wrong conclusion. And she'd fallen for it.

"You okay?" asked Bert.

She sighed. "Yes. Maybe. I'm trying to figure out how Bragg did the whole truck thing," she admitted.

"Do you believe him when he said that Adamos had come to his house?"

Kate waved away a couple of blackflies. Down below, a few streetlights were coming on. The rain had stopped an hour ago but she could smell it on the wind. There would be more before the night was done.

Did she believe it? Yes. Yes, she thought she did.

"I think that's what gave him the idea," she said slowly. "When he saw Adamos' truck—" She stopped at the sudden rise in noise from the house.

"I think the rest of the Trepalli clan has arrived," said Bert, turning around to look at the house.

Kate followed his gaze and saw people spilling out of her kitchen and onto the damp deck. Paul, Tina's husband, had commandeered the barbecue and was placing chicken thighs on the grill. There was laughter. There was loud talking. A few people caught sight of her and Bert at the bottom of the garden and waved. Kate and Bert waved back.

They were all so nice. So willing to make this work.

Bert took her hand.

"Come on. Let's go play nice."

Fine. She could play nice.

"Do you see Amanda or Marco?" she asked.

"Nope," said Bert, pulling her forward. "I can't imagine either one of them feels like being around all these people."

"I know how they feel," she muttered. Then she saw Mom bringing a bowl of marinade to Paul at the barbecue and she felt like an ungrateful witch.

Instead of showing them around or even spending any real time with them, she had immersed herself in a case. It was a murder case, true. She couldn't imagine sitting this one out just because she was on vacation—especially as she hadn't even left town. She had good reasons but she still felt like a heel.

Her family had made the effort to fly here for the wedding. The least she could do was be welcoming for the rest of the time they were here. And maybe apologize.

Charlie approached, carrying a stack of paper napkins.

"We'd better eat soon," he said, glancing at the sky. "We're in for a doozie, I think."

Kate looked up, too. She agreed with her brother. If the storm ever decided to break, it would be a doozie. Manitoba knew how to throw a good storm.

"All right," she said. "The seats on the picnic table are still damp. We should put down towels."

Just then, Bert's phone rang and he stepped away to answer it.

"I'll go get the towels," she told Charlie.

He immediately handed her the napkins.

"First, can you put one by each plate? Maybe under each plate?"

Kate nodded and took the napkins from him. It was definitely getting windier, and the temperature was cooling. Maybe they should just move everything inside.

Bert came back and put a hand on her arm.

"My summer student has found the truck," he said, a thread of excitement in his voice.

"You found Calder Bragg?" she said in surprise.

"No, no." He shook his head. "She found the Chevy Silverado in an impound lot."

"An impound lot," repeated Kate. "That was good thinking."

He nodded. "I think that kid's got a future in law enforcement. She checked the serial number and it matches the one from the truck that North End Motors sold. Only the truck no longer has a Manitoba plate. It has a B.C. one."

Son of a bitch.

"How did he have time to arrange it all?" she asked, more to herself than to Bert. Bragg—if it was Bragg, and she was sure it was—had stolen Manitoba plates to drive the truck off the dealership lot. He would have had to steal B.C. plates, too, if he wanted to be mistaken for Adamos.

They were both standing by the picnic table, ignoring the bustle on the deck that was beginning to spill over onto the lawn.

"When did Adamos go see Bragg?" asked Bert.

Kate thought back to the interview she had done with Bragg by phone.

"It was Thursday," she said. "A week ago, Thursday." Today was Friday, so a little over a week ago.

"He could have gone online to search for a Chevy Silverado of the same vintage," said Bert. "This is farm country. There are lots of old trucks around. Say he found one. You said the truck was white, right?"

Kate nodded. "With a gray stripe."

"Trucks of that vintage are pretty common," he pointed out. "North End Motors had one, after all. If they didn't, all he would have needed is a private space and a can of spray paint." He shrugged. "He got lucky."

"But then he was stuck with two vehicles in Winnipeg," Kate pointed out. "He wouldn't want to drive the Chevy to his place."

Bert thought for a moment and Kate realized she was crumpling the paper napkins. She walked over to the picnic table and began placing one under each plate. Bert followed her, still lost in thought.

Just as she finished with the last plate, he came back to her.

"It's easy," he said. "He puts the truck in long-term parking and comes back to Brandon in his own vehicle. Then, on Sunday, he drives back to Winnipeg and leaves his own vehicle in a paid parking lot, walks over or cabs it to the other parking lot and picks up the Chevy. He comes back to Brandon and kills Lawson. Then he dumps her body at the farm and drives back to Winnipeg. He leaves the truck somewhere far from where he parked his own vehicle, and cabs it to his truck. Then he drives home."

They stared at each other for long moments, Bert waiting for her to poke holes in this theory. But it made sense.

It made sense. Kelly Lawson would never have opened her hotel door to Christopher Adamos. But she would have opened it to her husband, especially if he was talking reconciliation. Or maybe Bragg called her from the hotel parking lot and asked her to meet him so they could go somewhere and talk.

She would have gone with him. His call might have been a relief to her. He wouldn't have killed her in the parking lot—too much risk. But he could have driven her somewhere out of the way and strangled her.

She sighed.

"I still can't figure out why he would have dumped her body in the Hurst's canola field," she said. "We've found nothing to say that he knew Marco."

Bert shrugged.

"You can ask him when you find him."

"We need to fingerprint that Chevy," Kate pointed out.

"I've ordered it towed in. We'll print it, but if Bragg's not in the system, then we'll have nothing to compare the prints against."

Kate smiled grimly.

"We have something." Bragg had given her one of Kelly Lawson's pay slips from Williams Lake. His prints would be on it. "You get me those prints. I have something to compare them against."

"It's ready!" called Paul from the barbecue. "Come and get it before all hell breaks loose!"

* * *

They almost made it to dessert before the drops started falling. After that, the house became crowded and all the younger Trepallis—and Sean—ended up sitting on the floor, leaving the dining room chairs, kitchen counter stools, love seat, and recliners for their elders.

After a while, Kate opened a few windows to let some air in. Even though it was stuffy and crowded, everyone seemed to be having a good time, loudly, despite the undercurrent of sadness.

Camilla and Rose sat together at the kitchen counter, their shoulders pressed together, their heads leaning toward each other. Kate wondered if they were strategizing on how to get their kids back together.

She stood up from the dining room table and went to open the front door. The wind was blowing the other way, so there was little risk of getting water on the floor. Bert looked up from his seat on the far side of her dysfunctional fireplace but she just smiled at him reassuringly.

A gust of wind puffed through the house the moment she opened the door and she stood in the doorway, cooling down and looking out at her neighbors' houses across the way.

Tomorrow, the kids would have gotten married. Instead, they were spending the night nursing their hurts, apart, away from their families, their friends...

She sighed and turned away from the night. As she did, she saw Charlie looking around the living room. When he caught her eye, he raised a phone in the air. Her phone. He came toward her and handed it to her.

"It's work," he said. "Sounds serious." He walked away, leaving her relatively alone in the entrance.

"Yes, St-Ives?" she said into the phone.

"Chief," he said—it always came out sounding like "sheef"— "we have the fingerprints from Winnipeg. They said you have an exemplar of Bragg's prints?"

"Yes. It's Kelly Lawson's pay stub. Bragg handed it to me. It's on a shelf in the evidence lockup, in a plastic bag."

"Very well," he said. "Fallon was on the fingerprint course last, but that was six months ago. He needs the practice."

"Tell him to be careful," said Kate.

"Will do. Goodnight, Chief."

She stood there, looking down at her phone, wishing she could leave and go to the detachment.

"News?" asked Bert, appearing beside her.

"The prints are in," she said, slipping the phone into her jeans pocket. "He needed to know where the exemplar was."

Bert nodded and looked around the room. "I think the younger ones are planning to try out Mendenhall's nightlife, such as it is," he said, nodding to the group of younger Trepallis huddling in the kitchen. Sean stood between two lovely young women, one of them Trepalli's sister, the other a cousin. Both of them had linked arms with him. His color was high.

At the counter, Rose and Camilla were talking with Tina and John. Someone emerged from Kate's room—now Mom and Fred's—with a bunch of jackets and sweaters.

"It's breaking up," she breathed in relief.

Bert gave her a knowing look. "You're planning to go to the detachment, aren't you?"

She grinned at him. She really had no shame.

CHAPTER 30

The prints matched.

First, Fallon had matched them, then Kate had taken a look. They matched.

"Holy cow," she murmured.

"Yes," said St-Ives to someone on the phone. "I am sending officers now."

She looked up from the end of the counter where she had set both sets of prints side by side to compare them. The log book lay on Charlotte's desk.

"It's a match?" asked Bert, sitting on the corner of Charlotte's desk.

St-Ives got on the radio and sent Black and Fredrickson to the scene of a disturbance at Joe's Bar. Kate hoped that wasn't where Sean had gone with the Trepalli kids.

"Yes, it's a match," she told Bert, setting aside the magnifying glass. She turned and leaned back against the end of the counter.

"You look surprised," said Bert.

Kate shrugged. "Maybe I am. Maybe I was hoping we were wrong."

St-Ives swiveled on the stool to face them.

"Yes," he said, "I agree. Adamos makes a much more likely suspect."

Kate nodded. He did. But he didn't kill Lawson. Calder Bragg did.

The storm door opened and they all turned to see who had walked in. McKell appeared in the duty desk opening, looking surprised to see them all. He was dressed in jeans and a sweatshirt.

"What's going on?" he asked, entering the duty room.

Kate told him while St-Ives answered another call. Friday and Saturday nights were always busy for the detachment.

McKell listened and then nodded. "I've been thinking about Bragg. Since no one's seen him anywhere on the road, I'm betting he's holed up in the area."

Bert nodded. "But where?"

"He doesn't have a cottage or another property anywhere in the province," said Kate. "We checked."

St-Ives finished with the radio and turned back to the conversation.

"He wouldn't stay in Brandon," he said. "Too much risk of being recognized. The same with Mendenhall. The town is too small and we've been looking for him. Any small town would be too risky."

"That leaves Winnipeg," said McKell. They all turned to look at Bert.

"We have the BOLO out for his vehicle," he said. "We can change it to an alert-and-apprehend order."

Kate nodded. "Please. We'll change it for the province, and for Saskatchewan, Alberta, and B.C., too, just in case." She looked at McKell. "We need a warrant for his arrest."

He nodded slowly. "And we may as well get one for his phone, too."

"Good thinking," she said. She glanced at the clock. Well past ten. Well, there was no help for it. "We'll have to wake the JP," she told St-Ives.

Bert slid off Charlotte's desk and pulled out his phone. He walked out of the duty room toward the front parking lot just as the duty phone rang again. It was still raining out, but if he stood under the overhang, he would stay dry.

Kate and McKell retreated to the break room, so as not to interrupt St-Ives any more than they already had. At this time of night, the ghosts of old meals and burned coffee filled the room.

The sound of the rain drumming down on the pavement and the cars acted like a cocoon and Kate sank down into the love seat, feeling absurdly comforted to be at the detachment, in spite of everything.

"Why are you here?" she asked McKell.

He shrugged and poured himself a cup of coffee.

"You usually check in at the detachment at this time of night. I knew you'd be busy with your family. I should have known better." He gave her the raised eyebrow.

Kate blushed at being caught out.

"I'm only here because of the fingerprints," she protested.

The eyebrow rose even higher.

"You didn't trust St-Ives to do the comparison?"

"Of course, I did," said Kate, now uncomfortable. "I just like to be sure."

"You're a control freak, you mean," said McKell. His lips twitched in laughter and she seriously thought about throwing something at him.

Bert came back in and saw them.

"Okay, I've updated the BOLO. We'll download his photo from Motor Vehicles and attach it to the BOLO. As soon as you get the arrest warrant, we'll add that to it, too."

"Thank you," said Kate. "I'd better get St-Ives to do the same."

"He's busy with the phone," said McKell. "I'll get the warrants and update the BOLO. You go home. You've only got one more day with your family."

"Nag, nag, nag," muttered Kate, standing up. "Tell St-Ives to call me if anything comes up."

* * *

If anything, the rain got worse as the night wore on. Kate lay in bed, huddling under the blanket and cuddling against Bert, and watched the flicker of distant lightning through the fabric of the spare bedroom's curtains. They billowed out with the wind, but she couldn't bear the thought of closing the window. She loved the scent of wet earth and fresh air swirling through the bedroom.

The thunder, while still far away, seemed to be coming closer. She hoped her constables weren't having to get out of the patrol cars too often. She used to hate patrolling during storms.

At least the rain and lightning would discourage partygoers. She glanced at the bedside clock. Almost two thirty. On a regular Friday night, things would have started calming down by now.

Below the sound of the wind, Bert's soft snoring sounded a counterpoint. The man could sleep through anything, but if she whispered his name, he was suddenly awake and concerned.

Smiling softly, Kate eased out of bed and reached for her housecoat. She might as well get up if she couldn't sleep.

Opening the door carefully, she slipped out and padded bare-foot to the kitchen. She turned on the light from the hood vent. It was just enough to let her navigate the room without stumbling into anything.

She poured water into the kettle as quietly as she could, then stood by the dining room's French doors, staring past her ghostly reflection to the night beyond while the water heated up.

"Can't sleep?" whispered Mom behind her.

Kate's eyes refocused and she saw the second ghost in the door. She turned with a smile.

"I love a good storm."

Mom smiled, too. "I remember."

Kate walked over to Mom and placed an arm around her waist. "Tea?"

"Scotch?" countered Mom.

Kate's eyebrows rose. "Is that Fred a bad influence?"

Mom's grin lit up the room.

"If so, don't tell him."

Kate laughed and went to unplug the kettle. Two minutes later, they were sitting at the kitchen countertop, sipping Kate's Glen-livet. They both took a moment to properly appreciate the golden liquid evaporating on their tongues.

"Now," said Mom, setting her tumbler down. "What's really bothering you? Is it this case? Or Amanda and Marco?"

A heartfelt sigh escaped Kate before she could hold it back.

"Both. But mostly the case. We found that poor woman on Monday morning," she said glumly. "Here we are on Saturday morning and we're still no closer to catching her murderer."

"I wonder if that's true," mused Mom. She sipped and set the tumbler down again. "I thought you said her husband killed her."

Kate nodded.

"Yes, it's become clear that he did kill her. We wasted so much time looking for the boyfriend she ran away from that now we can't find the real killer."

They sat in silence for a minute. The house felt cool and Kate rested her bare feet on the stool's rung rather than on the cold floor. Mom had had the good sense to wear her housecoat and her slippers. Her hair was down, a cloud of fine angel hair all around her face.

"Where could he have gone?" asked Mom. "You've got police everywhere looking for him, don't you?"

"We do," said Kate. "And we still can't find him. It's starting to look like he went to ground." She didn't understand it. She could understand that he'd stuck around after the murder because he was planning to pin it on Adamos, but at some point, he realized they were circling closer and closer to him.

"He set fire to his own house," she murmured.

"Is that where he killed his wife?" asked Mom.

The moment suddenly felt surreal to Kate. What was she doing sitting in her kitchen, drinking scotch and discussing murder with her elderly mother?

"It could be," Kate admitted. "We don't know for sure." There was so much they didn't know for sure. Had he called Lawson and invited her back home?

"Probably not," she finally said. "He wouldn't have risked having the neighbors see her car. Or her. I think he lured her out of the hotel she was staying at. Then he drove her to the field and killed her. Or killed her before and dumped her in the field."

"That poor girl," said Mom. She reached for the bottle and added another inch to her glass and Kate's. "What I don't understand is the connection to Marco."

"Me, neither," said Kate, taking a sip of the Glenlivet. "As far as we know, Calder Bragg never met Marco, never intersected with him." So why try to implicate Trepalli in Lawson's death?

Mom sighed softly and looked out the window above the kitchen sink. The incidental glow from the streetlights showed the wild thrashing of the trees.

"If I was going to make a run for it," she said, "this is exactly the kind of night I'd choose."

Kate stopped, her glass halfway to her lips.

This was exactly the kind of night she'd choose, too. Everybody wanted to hunker down in this kind of weather. Even cops. And if cops were out patrolling, the rain made it very difficult to pick out make and model of cars, let alone license plates. And he had a history of switching out license plates.

He might not even be in Canada anymore. It would be simple enough to take the 75 South to North Dakota. From there, he could go anywhere. She knew the BOLO had been sent to the border crossing at Emerson, but what if he had crossed before the BOLO had been issued?

She would ask O'Hara to check with the feds in the morning to see if Bragg even owned a passport.

A door at the end of the hallway opened and Bert came padding into the kitchen, wearing only his pyjama bottoms, his rusty hair awry. Kate had time to appreciate the solidity of his frame, the muscles moving easily beneath skin gone golden from the sun, the sprinkling of gray curly hairs on his chest. He wasn't very tall but he was exactly right for her.

He stopped the moment he saw Mom.

"Oh, sorry, Hetty," he said. "I thought Kate was alone." He looked at Kate and held up his hand with her phone in it. "It's St-Ives."

Kate set her tumbler down and slid off the stool.

"Thanks," she said automatically, taking the phone from him. She glanced at the clock on the stove. Almost three fifteen.

"I'm here," she said into the phone.

"Chief," said St-Ives. "Winnipeg called. One of their patrol units spotted a red Ford Lariat driving down Portage Avenue, going west. They didn't get close enough to read the license plate number. One driver."

"Why didn't they stop him and verify?" asked Kate in frustration.

"They didn't have the updated BOLO," said St-Ives. "The driver has now left city limits. I've sent Jones and Fallon to intercept the driver at Portage La Prairie. And I've got Fredrickson and Black at Mendenhall town limits in case the driver gets past them."

Kate nodded to herself. All right. It might not be their man, but they had to stop the truck and make sure.

"I'll be there in fifteen," she said and hung up. Then she stood staring down at the phone for a few moments, sorting through her thoughts.

"Katie?" said Bert.

She looked up at him.

"A truck matching Bragg's was spotted in Winnipeg. They let him get away but the driver is heading this way." She turned to her mother. "Sorry, Mom. I have to go."

"I know, dear," said Mom. "Be careful."

Kate headed for the hallway, Bert right behind her. "I'm coming with you," he said.

Fine. He had no jurisdiction in Mendenhall but he was a peace officer. And she appreciated his presence.

Ten minutes later, they were both dressed, Kate in her uniform and Bert in his jeans and sweatshirt. He had brought a jacket with him but it wasn't waterproof. Kate dug through the front closet until she found her large black umbrella.

Mom stood in the entrance watching them lace on boots and get ready. Finally Kate gave her a hug and a kiss.

"Go back to bed," she said. "You've still got hours before morning."

Mom tilted her head and gave her a look. "You honestly think I'll be sleeping after this? Just make sure to call me when it's over."

"Will do," promised Kate.

Bert leaned over and gave Mom a kiss.

"Don't worry, Hetty," he said. "I'll keep her safe."

Mom patted him on the arm and then they left. Kate wanted to grouse at him for saying something like that to her mother. He couldn't keep her safe, for pity's sake. She was a cop.

Hood over her head, she ran around to the back of the Edge and pulled out the portable cherry lights. She slid into the driver's seat and clipped them to the visor. She was already soaking wet. Bert grabbed the cord ends and loosely draped them around the radio's volume knob until they needed to be plugged in.

She drove as fast as she dared on the wet pavement, and less than five minutes later, she pulled into her regular parking spot at the detachment. To her surprise, Trepalli's Mustang was parked in visitor parking. At least McKell had gone home.

"Did you call him?" asked Bert as they ran for the door.

"I did not," said Kate. But someone clearly had.

"I guess it involves him," said Bert, holding the door open for her. She went inside and he shook the umbrella out before standing it in the corner and following her into the duty room.

St-Ives and Trepalli were bent over a map that had been laid on Charlotte's desk. They had pushed her monitor out of the way to make room.

"Update?" asked Kate when they both looked up at her. Marco was in uniform. He hadn't shaved and there were dark circles under his bloodshot eyes. Had he been awakened? Or had he even gone to bed?

"None," said St-Ives. "Jones and Fallon are still outside Portage, and Fredrickson and Black are still at the entrance to Mendenhall. No sign of Bragg yet."

Both men were looking up at her with identical serious expressions. Kate blinked. Two handsome men with black hair, one about twenty years older than the other. Except for the fact that St-Ives had gray eyes and Marco blue, they could have been father and son.

"What time did Winnipeg spot him?" asked Kate.

"It was three oh five," reported St-Ives promptly.

She glanced up at the clock above the duty desk. Three thirty-five. It took about an hour to get to Portage La Prairie from Winnipeg. Bragg—if it was Bragg—should be passing by Jones and Fallon within the half hour.

"Tell Fredrickson and Black to be ready to set up a roadblock on the west highway. Cones, flares, sawhorses, the works. When I give the word, they're to place the patrol car across both lanes, lights flashing." She pointed a finger at St-Ives. "They are to stay safe! Use the glow sticks to wave down the traffic." Once a couple of transport trucks were blocking the lanes, there'd be no getting by them.

She looked at St-Ives and Trepalli, aware that Bert was at her back. A traffic stop in the middle of the Trans-Canada, in the middle of the night, in the middle of a storm...

"I'm going to Portage," she said suddenly. She took off her wet cap and slapped it against her leg.

"I'm coming with you," said Trepalli, straightening. "I know where Jones and Fallon have hidden themselves."

Kate shook her head. "No. If you insist on coming to work, I'd like you to stay with St-Ives and provide support. All our constables are on stakeout. If something happens here, you'll be the only one who can help."

Trepalli opened his mouth to argue, clearly unhappy with her decision. She raised a hand.

"Marco, you know I'm right."

His mouth remained open for a few seconds, then he snapped it shut.

"Yes, ma'am," he said.

Kate looked at St-Ives.

"If you need to reach me, use the phone, not the radio. We don't know if he has a scanner or not."

"Yes, ma'am," said St-Ives.

Kate turned around to leave and caught Bert giving Trepalli a sympathetic smile.

CHAPTER 31

With no buildings to interrupt the wind, the storm on the highway felt much worse than in town. Or maybe it was actually getting worse.

Kate finally turned up the heat when her wet uniform leached the warmth from her skin.

She started out fast but slowed down after she fishtailed and Bert grabbed for the dashboard. It was hard enough to see through the windshield wipers going at full speed. The rain sounded like stones hitting the roof of the Edge.

The Trans-Canada Highway was a four-lane divided highway. Bert kept an eye on the two lanes heading west, toward Mendenhall, while Kate kept an eye on her side of the road.

There was very little traffic at this hour, and most of it was transport trucks going well over the speed limit. She took to flicking on the cherry lights as she approached them, forcing the drivers to slow down as she passed them.

"You're enjoying this," said Bert accusingly as they passed yet another transport truck that had been forced to slow down at her approach.

Kate shrugged. "They're going too fast for the condition of the road."

"So are you," Bert pointed out. He hadn't let go of the dashboard.

"I'm driving perfectly safely," she said primly. "You're just a sissy."

He snorted and they carried on in silence for the rest of the way.

When they approached the outskirts of Portage, Bert put Kate's phone on speaker and called Brendan Jones.

"Chief," said Jones, picking up.

"Any sign of him, constable?" asked Kate, keeping her gaze on the road.

"Not yet," he replied. "Where are you?"

"We're approaching the MacGregor exit," said Kate. "We'll pull over there and be ready to stop him if he manages to get by you."

"Sounds good," said Jones. He always sounded like he was commenting on the price of hog futures. Calm. A little bored. "We'll keep you posted."

The sign for the exit for MacGregor came up and Bert suddenly said, "Right here."

Kate peered through the pelting raindrops and finally saw it. A service road that paralleled the highway. She slowed drastically and took the entrance carefully. A light standard lit the way. The service road allowed farmers to access their fields. She did a three-point turn on the narrow gravel road and ended up with the car's nose facing the highway, but far enough from the highway and the light that she wouldn't be immediately visible. A short, paved section connected the two lanes heading east with the two lanes heading west, intended to allow emergency and service vehicles to cross over. On the other side was another service road, with another light standard lighting the entrance to that service road. They were the only lights for miles.

Now all they had to do was wait. She shut off her lights and put the car in park. She wanted to look like the car had been abandoned. Even with the light, Bragg would have trouble seeing it from the other side of the highway in this monsoon rain.

Bert handed her her phone but kept watching the approach from Portage. Kate scrolled though her telephone directory and tapped the icon for Fredrickson.

One ring, two.

"Chief," said Fredrickson. "What's happening?"

"Nothing so far." She told him where she was and that Jones and Fallon hadn't seen any sign of Bragg yet. "Keep your eyes open," she warned. "It's very hard to see through this and he should be coming out of Portage any minute now."

"Yes, ma'am," said Fredrickson, and she thought she heard laughter in his voice. Well, maybe she didn't need to treat him like a rookie. She glanced at Bert but it was too dark to see his expression.

"Just be careful," she said. "He's already killed once."

"Yes, ma'am," said Fredrickson, all trace of laughter gone from his voice.

"You're ready to set up the barricade?"

"We are. We'll be hard to miss."

"Good."

She hung up and placed the phone in the cup holder. She and Bert sat in silence, listening to the rain pelt down on the hood and roof of the Edge and watching the transport trucks going east and west.

"Pickup," said Bert and Kate squinted at the darkness. Yes, there was a pickup driving through the rain, heading west. As it passed their vantage point, however, Kate sighed.

"Not a king cab."

This was going to be even harder than she had imagined. They could see a vehicle coming from a ways away but couldn't tell what color the vehicle was until it drove by the light standard.

"Relax," said Bert, squeezing her knee. "There are three points of contact. He won't get by all of us."

Kate placed a hand over his on her knee but kept her gaze on the opposite side of the highway. She loved how he said "us," as if he were an honorary member of the Mendenhall force.

"Thanks for doing this with me," she said.

She saw him nod out of the corner of her eye.

"Nowhere I'd rather be," he said. "Besides, I promised your mother."

They were quiet then. It was enough to be together, even if it was on a stakeout. The rain increased and the smell of it filled the car, filtered by air vents. Then the lightning started, soon followed by rolls of thunder. She shivered reflexively and turned up the heat.

Five minutes later, her phone rang and she almost jumped out of her skin. She scrambled to pick it up, dropped it, and Bert had to fish it out from between the console and his seat.

"Constable," she said, reading Fallon's name on her screen.

"He just blew by us," said Fallon loudly to be heard over the sound of a speeding engine and rumbling thunder. "He's driving like a maniac!"

"All right," said Kate. "Follow him but don't try to catch up. Fredrickson and Black are setting up a barricade. We'll box him in."

"We're right behind him," said Fallon.

She hung up and turned to Bert.

"You ready?"

"Ready," he said.

"Anywhere he can turn off before he reaches us?"

"Only more service roads like this one," said Bert. "It would be pointless for him to take one. They don't go anywhere."

She nodded and put the Edge in gear. There was no traffic coming toward her so she crossed the east-bound highway and entered the connector strip. No traffic coming from Portage, either. She entered the west-bound lanes and pulled up far enough from the light standard so as not to be immediately visible.

A few minutes for Bragg to reach her position, then maybe fifteen—at the speed he was going—to reach Fredrickson and Black.

"Call Fredrickson," she said. "Tell him he's got fifteen minutes, maybe twenty and that he should set up now."

Bert picked up her phone and, in a moment, was relaying her message to Fredrickson.

When he hung up, she asked him to phone St-Ives and put him on speaker phone.

"Chief," said St-Ives after the first ring, "what's happening?"

She explained briefly, pausing for a moment when lights appeared in her rearview mirror. But they were too high and wide to be a pickup. Transport truck. As it passed her, she asked St-Ives to send Trepalli to join Fredrickson and Black with the decommissioned patrol car. They could park it across both lanes of the highway with the lights on.

"DC McKell is here," said St-Ives. "He can help, too."

Kate didn't ask what McKell was doing there. There wasn't any time.

"Get a move on," she ordered St-Ives. "You don't have much time."

"Trepalli is already on his way," said St-Ives. "The DC is following in his car."

At that moment, a pair of headlights appeared in her rearview mirror that were the right height and width. She slipped the phone into the cup holder without hanging up.

"Ready with the lights?" she asked, her gaze fixed on the rearview mirror.

"Ready," said Bert.

Unfortunately, she didn't have a megaphone in her private vehicle, but the cherry lights were unmistakeable.

"Pickup," said Bert, raising his voice to be heard over the drumming of the rain.

She wanted to put her car in drive to be ready to pull out behind Bragg's pickup, but her rear lights would alert the oncoming driver.

"Say when."

They waited, Kate watching the rearview mirror, Bert the side mirror. She squinted as the truck's headlights dazzled her eyes but didn't dare switch to night view. Then the truck came abreast of the light standard. It was shiny red.

"Go!" she told Bert and immediately stepped on the brake, put the Edge in gear, and pulled out behind the pickup truck.

Please let it be Bragg, she found herself thinking, even as the bright red and blue lights attached to the sun visor began alternating in the unmistakeable police signal to pull over.

The red truck made no move to slow down and Kate stepped on the gas so as not to get too far from him.

"Watch the spray!" called Bert and she slowed down, barely avoiding the spray from his back wheels.

"Son of a bitch," she whispered, her attention focused on the slick road and the truck pulling steadily away from her.

"He's fishtailing!" said Bert.

Yes, he was. Fallon was right; Bragg—if it was Bragg—was driving like a maniac. She slowed down even more, allowing the distance between them to grow, but staying close enough to see his taillights. She didn't want to cause an accident. Or be in one.

At this rate, he would get to the roadblock before they were fully set up. Next to her, Bert twisted in his seat and looked behind. She didn't dare take her gaze off the front, but the reflection from her rearview mirror strobed red and blue.

"That'll be Fallon and Jones," said Bert, turning back to the front.

Good. With two cars behind him and a barricade ahead of him, Bragg would have no choice but to stop. She glanced to either side of the highway. Ditches. Wide ones, but still too dangerous for a speeding truck to take.

Bragg suddenly pulled into the left lane to pass a slow transport truck.

"It's working," said Bert, and Kate saw what he meant. Up ahead, half a dozen transport trucks, four in the right-hand lane, two in the left, were slowing down, forcing Bragg to slow down, too. Between the two rows of trucks, the familiar strobing lights of a patrol car pierced the rainy night and reflected off the panels of the trucks.

Good boys.

Behind her, Fallon and Jones drew nearer. Her speed dropped to seventy, then fifty as she kept her distance from the transport trucks. Forty, thirty, twenty. Then the first truck up ahead came to a stop, its brake lights flashing brightly in the rain. Soon all the others were slowing to a stop, the combination of so many air brakes piercing the noise of the rain.

Bragg, having no choice, slowed to a stop, too. Kate pulled up behind him and parked diagonally. The patrol car pulled up next to her.

Kate pulled up her hood—why, she didn't know—and turned to Bert.

"You have to stay here," she said. Without waiting for his response, she slid out into the rain, slamming the door behind her. She heard two car doors behind her but was busy pulling her Glock out of its holster. She pulled the slide back and approached the driver's side door. Two shapes suddenly flanked her and she glanced over to her right. Jones. She nodded him over to the passenger side of the pickup and she and Fallon stopped a few feet behind the driver's door.

Kate looked at Fallon. "Megaphone," she said. There was no way her voice would be heard over the rain.

Fallon ran back to the patrol car and pulled the megaphone from the trunk. He ran back and she nodded at him to proceed. He looked as sodden as she felt.

"Driver of the red truck!" shouted Fallon into the megaphone in his best police intimidation voice. "Stop your engine, roll down your window, and drop the keys to the ground!" His voice rolled out of the megaphone like the voice of doom. He repeated it once more before the window began to roll down.

Suddenly Bert's voice came through the rumbling thunder.

"Stay in your truck!" he shouted and she looked around to see him waving a flashlight at a truck driver who was getting out of his cab to see what was going on. The beam landed on the man's face. "Stay inside!" shouted Bert. "Police!"

The man scrambled back inside and slammed the door shut.

She caught a glimpse of two figures running between the lines of transport trucks and was about to shout at them to go back when she realized it was McKell and Trepalli. They stopped in the shelter of one of the transport trucks, just in case Bragg had a weapon.

"Throw your keys out!" shouted Fallon.

Kate didn't hear them land but she saw the arc of their trajectory in the strobing lights.

"Put both hands outside the truck and open your door from the outside!" continued Fallon.

Kate inched closer, Glock held in both fists in front of her, ready to shoot the bastard if he tried anything.

Two hands appeared through the opening, one of them sliding down the side of the door, feeling for the door handle. Then the door opened slowly.

"Now come out with your hands in front of you!" ordered Fallon.

Kate became aware of pale faces looking down at them from the transport trucks. It was getting on toward dawn and the rain was beginning to let up.

A figure dressed in jeans and a black leather jacket and white baseball cap stepped down onto the step and then hopped to the pavement.

"Walk backward toward my voice," said Fallon, and waited until the figure had taken a few steps backward. "Now get to your knees and place your hands on your head."

The figure did as he was ordered and suddenly McKell and Trepalli came running around the front. Trepalli pulled out a pair of handcuffs and cuffed the man's hands behind his back. Then he and McKell pulled him up and turned him around.

Kate breathed a sigh of relief and slid the Glock back in her holster.

It was Calder Bragg.

CHAPTER 32

"Tell me you got the warrant," said Kate in a low voice to McKell as they all trooped into the detachment.

He leaned closer to her. "Yes," he said. "And one for his phone, truck, and any other possessions, too, but you owe the JP a bottle of the good scotch."

Kate looked at him in alarm. Had he bribed...?

"For waking him up," added McKell, and she relaxed. Technically, they didn't need an arrest warrant, but it didn't hurt to have one and it looked good in court. It proved that a JP thought their evidence was strong enough to issue a warrant.

St-Ives stood in the doorway to the duty room, arms crossed, legs apart, looking like the wrath of God. They all stopped and looked at him uncertainly. Even Bragg, looking like a wet dog between Fallon and Jones, cringed back a little at the sight.

"Did it not occur to any of you to phone in and let me know what was happening?" he demanded, his French accent very pronounced.

Kate stepped forward.

"Sorry, Emile," she said placatingly. "Things got very busy there for a bit." She placed a hand on his arm and gently moved him out of the doorway so that Fallon and Jones could lead Bragg in.

Bragg was still in his black leather jacket, but the white tee-shirt underneath was soaking wet, as were his jeans. His hat was gone—where, Kate had no idea. The guy's blue eyes were blood-shot. There was a look of confusion on his face, as if he had no idea what was going on, and he was shivering.

He had no reason to be confused. McKell had explained quite clearly back at the barricade when he formally arrested Bragg on suspicion of murdering Kelly Lawson. She had wanted to arrest him herself but it was best to avoid giving defence counsel any reason to claim she had a conflict of interest, given her connection to Trepalli.

"Take him to the shower," said Kate. "Let him warm up. We'll find something for him to change into." She waved at Trepalli, who was carrying a medium-sized suitcase that they had pulled from Bragg's truck.

She had left Fredrickson and Black behind to finish pulling the barricade and supervise the tow truck that would bring Bragg's truck to the compound behind the detachment.

Bert came up to her and she handed him her keys. There was no point in him sticking around now that Bragg was in custody. And it was pointless to have one more person dripping on the floors.

"You come home soon and change," he said.

"Yes, Mom," she smiled. He gave her a peck on the cheek and left, giving McKell and Trepalli a wave.

Fallon and Jones led Bragg to the back where the bathroom and changing room were. Marco set Bragg's suitcase on Charlotte's desk and opened it. He rummaged through it and found a pair of jeans, a tee-shirt, a sweatshirt, and socks. Then he closed the lid and walked to the changing room with the clothes.

Kate stood next to Charlotte's desk and looked down at her-self. She felt as if she'd been in a cold shower.

"Yes," said McKell, watching her critically. "You do look like a drowned rat. We all do."

"Not I," said St-Ives, spreading his arms out to show off his nice, dry uniform.

Kate sighed, suddenly exhausted. It was five o'clock in the morning. In the background, she heard the sound of their one shower running. Billows of steam began to spill from the open door to the changing room.

She desperately wanted to change into dry clothes, but she would do it at home, after a hot shower.

"You might as well go," she told McKell. "Don't interview him now. Let him get some sleep."

"You should get some, too," pointed out McKell.

Kate smiled. "I'll go home soon. Take a shower. Change. Then I'll come back. I have to call the Crown prosecutor's office in Winnipeg and fill them in. There's the charge packet. We need to search his truck, get his phone records... You know, the whole shebang."

McKell frowned and crossed his arms over his chest. "I should be helping with all that."

Kate laughed. "Yes, I'm sure you're disappointed about missing out on the paperwork. You need to have your wits about you when you interview him. Come back around noon. Maybe by then we'll have more information. And Albertson will be here soon. I'll get him to help, too."

McKell looked like he wanted to argue but finally he nodded.

"I'll see you in a few hours," he said, and left.

The phone rang and St-Ives stepped up to the platform to answer it just as Trepalli returned from the back, hands empty.

"He keeps saying he doesn't understand why we think he killed his wife," he said grimly.

Kate shook her head. She really was too tired to deal with this tonight—this morning—but she would go in and talk to him before she left.

The smell of old coffee reached her, turning her stomach. Time for a fresh pot. Lord knew, she was going to need it today.

She headed for the break room, Trepalli right behind her.

St-Ives hung up and leaned through the opening.

"That was the tow company," he said. "They're on their way. Can you listen for the phone? I have to go unlock the gate."

Kate waved a hand over her head to show she had heard. It looked like St-Ives was going to get wet, after all. But when she passed by the door to the parking lot, she saw that the rain had lightened. Maybe the storm was finally over.

She busied herself emptying the old coffee and rinsing out the pot, dumping the filter with its wet grounds, and refilling the pot with fresh water. As she reached inside the cupboard on tiptoe for a fresh filter, she caught sight of Trepalli standing in the middle of the room, his hands in his pockets, looking down at the floor.

"You should go, Marco," she said gently. "There's nothing more for you to do here." That wasn't quite true, but the boy wasn't even on duty.

He looked up from studying the linoleum.

"She wants to meet with me today."

Kate came down on her heels, hand clutching the package of filters.

"Are you going to?"

He shrugged.

"Of course. I love her."

Kate wanted to ask him what Amanda wanted to talk to him about but she was afraid it would be about separating their assets. It looked like Rose had been right. It had been a mistake for them to buy that house together before they were married.

She sighed softly.

"Go home, Marco. You need sleep."

He nodded and looked away.

"Haven't been able to sleep in a while."

Kate thought her heart was going to break. She wanted to hug him and tell him everything was going to be all right. But she couldn't. She was his superior officer. And she didn't know that things were going to be all right.

He cleared his throat and removed his hands from his pockets.

"I would like to return to duty," he said. "Monday night is shift change."

Kate nodded. He had taken a few weeks off. One to get ready for the wedding and two more for their honeymoon. "Of course," she said. "I'll let Martins know."

"Thank you. Goodnight, Chief."

"Goodnight, Marco."

He turned and walked away. The back of his jacket was all wet in a large V down his back. He went out the storm door and let it slam shut behind him. A moment later, she heard his car engine start up and saw the sweep of his headlights as he backed out of visitor parking.

The door to the compound opened and she heard St-Ives tromp down the hallway toward the break room. She turned back to the coffee pot and set about making fresh coffee.

"The pickup is in the compound," said St-Ives from the doorway. "I'll put the keys in the key lockup."

Kate nodded. "Fresh coffee in a few minutes," she said.

"Good."

She finished and went back into the duty room. She was cold and clammy.

Jones and Fallon came out of the changing room, escorting Bragg between them to the other side of the duty room, where the cells were. Bragg looked at her as he walked by. His blue eyes were huge. He had a blond stubble on his face. His cheeks were ruddy, probably from the hot shower, and he was dressed in warm, dry clothes. They hadn't given him his shoes, however, probably because they had laces. Or because they were still wet.

Fallon and Jones were still wet and probably just as miserable as she was. When they had disappeared into the back, Kate turned to St-Ives.

"I know it's close to shift end, but let them go get changed if they don't have a change of clothes here."

St-Ives nodded.

Kate stared at the door through which they had disappeared and finally leaned in to St-Ives, even though there was no one else in the room.

"Keep an eye on Bragg," she ordered. "Suicide watch."

His eyebrows climbed up his forehead, but he just nodded.

"And ask O'Hara to get in touch with the duty Crown counsel this morning. Maybe around nine o'clock. He can provide them with the primary grounds to support remanding Bragg into custody."

"Will do," he said. "I can start the charge packet, if you like."

At that moment, Fredrickson and Black returned, slamming the storm door behind them. Kate made a mental note to adjust the spring on the door.

"Everything go okay?" she asked as they entered the duty room.

"Yes, ma'am," said Fredrickson. The front of his uniform pants was all wet, as was his ball cap. She suspected the rain had made it into his jacket. He looked even taller and skinnier than normal. Carlos Black looked pretty much the same. Even his godawful little mustache looked wilted.

"Do you have a change of uniform here?" she asked them.

"I do," said Fredrickson.

Black blushed and shook his head. Kate sighed. She always had a change of uniform at work, and a change of civilian clothes, too. It had come in handy more times than she could count. But she didn't want to change at work. She wanted to go home and have a hot shower.

"Go get changed," she told Fredrickson, "then take Carlos home so he can get changed."

"I can just wait until shift end," protested Carlos.

Kate glanced at the clock. It was a little past five thirty. She shook her head.

"You're not staying in wet clothes for an hour and a half," she said firmly.

Carlos nodded and went into the break room while Fredrickson went to get changed.

She caught St-Ives looking at her with a smile and she scowled at him before following Carlos into the break room to finally get her coffee. She sat in the love seat while Carlos sat at the tiny table, nursing a mug of black coffee. She was desperately grateful that he didn't want to talk.

When she heard St-Ives talking to Fallon and Jones, she stood up. Time to talk to Bragg.

"Chief?" said Carlos.

"Yes?"

"That was good work tonight."

She smiled down at him.

"Yes, it was, wasn't it? We did good." She walked out, still carrying her coffee, and entered the duty room in time to see Fallon disappearing into the change room.

"Let me guess," she told Jones, who was sitting at Charlotte's desk in front of Bragg's suitcase. "You don't have a change of clothes."

Jones looked down.

"No, ma'am," he muttered. He would have looked like a little boy caught with his hand in the cookie jar if not for the pouches under his bloodshot brown eyes and the faint stubble on his plump cheeks.

"Will you make that mistake again?" she asked tartly.

"No, ma'am," he repeated, risking a glance up at her.

Oh, for Pete's sake.

She went to the door to the lockup and paused before going in. She rapped noisily on the door frame.

"Are you decent?" she asked. There were two cells in lockup, each with its own toilet and small sink. There was no privacy.

"Yes," came Bragg's voice.

She went inside and stood in the open area in front of the cells, looking at him. He was sitting on the bunk of the right-hand cell. It had a plastic-covered foamy for a mattress, with a wool blanket folded at the foot. Not luxurious, but enough to meet a detainee's basic needs.

The ghost of past detainees lived on in lockup in the form of a faint smell of vomit.

He stood up as she entered and came to stand in front of the bars separating him from freedom.

"Chief Williams, what the hell?" He opened his arms, as if to encompass the lockup. "Why have you arrested me?"

In the dim light from the one lightbulb in the ceiling, she studied him. He looked a little confused, a little angry, a little fearful.

"Mr. Bragg," she said, suddenly so weary that the words slowed coming out. She took a deep breath. "Mr. Bragg," she repeated.

"As we've already told you, you are under arrest on suspicion of mrdering Kelly Lawson."

He stared at her as though she were an alien that had just landed in front of him.

"This is crazy," he said.

She raised a hand. "Please let me finish." He had been told all this on the highway, but she wanted to repeat it here, now that he was dry and warm. "You have the right to counsel. If you do not have a lawyer, we will provide you with the phone number for a lawyer referral service. Would you like to retain or consult with a lawyer now?"

He shook his head once. "I don't need a lawyer! I haven't done anything wrong."

Kate shrugged. "You have the right to change your mind at any time. Get a lawyer, Mr. Bragg. The charge against you is very serious."

"I haven't done anything!" he protested.

Kate studied him for a moment. He looked so sincere. So believable.

But those had been his fingerprints in the truck he had bought to implicate Adamos. Then another thought occurred to her.

It was still possible that Adamos had killed Kelly Lawson. Maybe all Bragg had done was try to implicate Adamos in her murder.

She couldn't think straight anymore. She needed to go home for a bit.

"Whatever. We will interview you in a few hours. You have the right to legal representation. Anything you say can be used in court as evidence. If you refuse to get a lawyer, then at least get some rest."

She turned her back on him and, ignoring his protests, walked out of the cell area.

CHAPTER 33

Fredrickson dropped her off at home before taking Carlos to his place to get changed. Kate stood on the sidewalk in front of her house and watched the patrol car head down the street. As far as she could tell, none of her neighbors were up this early. She took a deep breath of the cool morning air.

The rain had stopped and the clouds were clearing off. The sun wasn't up yet but it was on its way judging from the lightening in the sky and the pink tinges in the east. Already there was enough light to read a newspaper by.

Her Edge was parked in the driveway and the black pickup was parked behind Bert's green Honda. Everybody was home.

A massive shiver shook her and she set off across the lawn toward the front door. What did it matter if the grass was wet? She couldn't get any wetter.

The door opened as she approached the stoop and Mom stood there, a sweater pulled across her chest.

"Hello, sweetie," Mom said with a smile. She stepped back to let Kate in. When Mom went to wrap her arms around her, Kate stepped back.

"I'm all wet," she warned.

"I don't care," said Mom and proceeded to give her a hug. Kate hugged her back and then put her away firmly.

The aroma of coffee wafted through the house and Kate sniffed with appreciation.

"We're just getting breakfast ready," said Mom as Kate bent to remove her work boots. "If you're hungry."

Kate's stomach rumbled emptily and someone laughed. Kate looked up to see Fred leaning in the kitchen doorway.

"I think that answers your question, my dear."

Kate grinned and returned to her boots. They were damp and hard to remove.

"I have to take a shower first and get changed."

"That's fine," said Charlie, appearing next to Fred. "We'll wait on you."

"Where's Bert?" asked Kate, finally free of her footwear. Her socks weren't exactly sodden but they were definitely damp. And her feet were frozen.

"Getting dressed," said Mom. "He just had a shower, too."

There had better be hot water left, thought Kate, looking at the number of people in her house.

"Sean?" she asked. "Still sleeping?"

Charlie snorted. "He rolled in around four thirty, the hound dog."

Kate's eyebrows rose. "Really?"

"Yep. He went on and on about one of your constable's sisters."

"Oh, dear Lord," Kate blurted out, to everyone's laughter.

"All right," said Mom, taking her by the elbow. Then she stopped. "Your jacket."

Kate had forgotten she was still wearing it. The twill fabric of the jacket was soaked through. She shrugged it off, struggling a bit with the wet sleeves. Mom took it from her and pulled a hanger from the closet.

"We'll have to hang this somewhere to dry," she murmured.

Kate would have stuck it in the dryer but she was too tired to make the argument. She went down the hallway and into the spare bedroom. Bert was sitting on the bed, putting socks on. He stood up.

"All booked?"

She shook her head. "Not yet. I wanted to give him a chance to sleep first. Wouldn't want anybody accusing us of questioning him when he's too tired to know what's good for him. I did inform him of his rights. Twice."

"What did he say?"

She shrugged. "Oh, you know. You've got it all wrong. I didn't do anything wrong. The usual."

He smiled tightly. "Are you going to question him?"

"No. McKell is, in a few hours. So I have time to shower, change, and eat two breakfasts."

He laughed and kissed her cheek.

"I'll be next to the coffee pot."

Kate took a long, hot shower and dressed in jeans, a tee-shirt, and a warm sweatshirt. Then she pulled on her slippers and left her room.

The smell of bacon enticed her down the hallway to the kitchen where Bert and Charlie sat at the counter, drinking coffee, while Mom and Fred worked at the stove.

Mom looked over her shoulder at Kate's entrance. Her gaze swept Kate from head to toe.

"Almost ready," she said.

Bert poured coffee into a cup emblazoned with "COP GAMES 2011," added a bit of sugar, and handed it to her.

Charlie slid off the stool and said, "Sit."

She did, and watched contentedly as her family—Bert included—chatted and laughed while getting breakfast ready. Charlie took over the toaster and Bert pulled the orange juice and creamer out of the fridge and placed them on the dining room table.

She felt herself relaxing for the first time in days. Even so, a small voice nagged at her. Had she arrested the wrong man? She needed to talk to the Vancouver detective to see if he had learned anything in his interview with Adamos.

By the time breakfast was on the table, sunlight flooded the kitchen and dining room. Kate and Charlie talked about growing up in St. Lambert, on the south shore of Montreal, and all the trouble they had gotten into as kids. Then Mom and Fred chimed in with stories of their own childhoods—Mom growing up on a farm in New Brunswick, Fred coming from the Eastern Townships. Even Bert shared a few stories about growing up in Winnipeg along the Red River.

Kate had finished breakfast but was still gorging on beautifully ripe strawberries when Sean stumbled up the steps to the back deck. They all turned to look at him as he walked in through the kitchen door.

"Well," murmured Mom. "Look what the cat dragged in and didn't have the heart to eat."

They all laughed at poor Sean, who stood blinking in the sunlight, his face bristly with whiskers, his hair tousled, bags under his eyes, and his shirt buttoned crooked.

"Coffee," he muttered.

Kate put a hand on Mom's arm to keep her in her chair and got up to fetch a mug. Moments later, Sean sat at the table, nursing the coffee and wincing every time someone spoke or laughed too loud.

They were still sitting at the table, surrounded by the detritus of breakfast, when Rose and John arrived.

"Where's Amanda?" asked Mom, looking around.

"She left," said Rose, frowning.

Left? What was that supposed to mean?

Around the table, smiles slowly disappeared.

"She left a note," explained John. "Said she needed some alone time. She left us the keys to the car. She said she'll be back before we leave."

Mom turned to Kate. "Where could she have gone without her car?"

Kate shrugged and looked down at her coffee cup.

Marco had a car. And he had planned to talk to Amanda.

"When did she leave?" asked Bert.

"Sometime in the night," said Rose. "We never heard a thing."

Somewhere deep inside Kate, a little flame of hope flickered and caught.

CHAPTER 34

O'Hara was on the desk, duty log next to him, filling in the online version.

"I hear you had a busy night," he said, looking up as she walked by.

"We definitely did," agreed Kate.

Colin Parker sat at one of the common desks, pecking away at the computer keyboard. His hands were so big that she often found typos in his reports. At six feet four and with shoulders like a linebacker's, he looked like he perched rather than sat on the chair.

"Anything to report?" she asked O'Hara.

O'Hara shook his head.

"Fender bender. No injuries. Driver didn't see the pedestrian early enough and had to slam on the brakes. The guy behind him rammed him. We need a crosswalk at Main and Second."

Kate sighed. That was true. It had been true for the two years she'd been in Mendenhall. She'd finally made it a formal recommendation to City Hall, but still they hemmed and hawed.

Apparently, somebody would have to die to justify the cost of putting one in.

"Put it in the report," she said. "I'll try to make the case to the mayor. What about our guest?"

O'Hara leaned back against the stool's back.

"Mr. Bragg had breakfast, then slept for six hours. He's just finishing lunch. Abrams is in there with him."

Well. Nice to know being detained hadn't affected the man's appetite.

"Did you contact the duty Crown counsel?" she asked.

"Yes, ma'am," said O'Hara. "Jessica Llewellyn. She's expecting the charge packet whenever we finalize it. And the Brandon arson investigator called. The fire at Bragg's house? Definitely arson. Gasoline was the accelerant, starting in the crawl space."

She was about to answer when McKell came out of his office, surprising her. She hadn't seen his car in the parking lot. He wore a fresh uniform and polished boots and was freshly shaven. He didn't even have the decency to look tired.

"I just spoke with Detective Ahuja in Vancouver. They picked Adamos up this morning and interviewed him. He denied anything to do with Lawson's death. He said he left Brandon the day after he learned she was dead."

Of course he would deny it. That didn't mean he didn't kill her.

"They also checked his phone and downloaded his text messages." His blue eyes suddenly looked navy as he frowned.

The phone rang and O'Hara turned to answer it. Kate followed McKell into his office and closed the door. McKell had almost the same view from his office window as she did, but in summer it was obscured by a maple tree in full leaf. It cut down on the amount of light he got, but it provided shade and kept his office cooler than hers. Right now, sunlight cast dappled shadows over McKell and his desk.

She sat down in one of his comfortable visitor chairs.

"What do the texts say?" she asked.

McKell picked up a sheaf of papers stapled in one corner and handed it to her silently.

Kate started reading. After a few minutes, she looked up at him.

"Holy crap."

He nodded. "The bastard harassed her. She didn't respond,

mostly. If you read on, you'll see where he threatened to kill her husband if she didn't leave him."

Kate felt the blood drain from her face.

"When? When did he make the threat?"

"The same day he confronted Bragg."

So, that was why she left Bragg without even trying to explain. She was trying to protect him.

Kate shook her head in disbelief.

"Go to the end," said McKell, leaning back in his chair and linking his hands over his flat belly.

Kate flipped to the last page. It was just more of the same. Vitriol. Then she read more carefully.

TELL ME WHERE U R OR I SWEAR TO GOD I'LL KILL HIM!

U CAN'T HIDE FROM ME, U BITCH, U R MINE!

He didn't know where she was. Finally, she looked at the time and date stamp of the last dozen or so messages. They ran from Sunday, August 26, to Monday, August 27.

He'd been sending her text messages after she died.

"He didn't know she was dead," she said, looking up from the pages.

McKell nodded. "He stalked her, threatened her, and threatened her husband, but he didn't kill her."

Kate leaned back against the chair, a wave of relief threatening to swamp her.

"Thank God," she murmured. "I was starting to doubt myself."

McKell grinned, turning his severe face handsome.

"If you like that," he said, "you'll love this." He opened one of his desk drawers and pulled out a clear plastic evidence bag. There was a rolled-up belt in it.

"O'Hara caught it," he said with great satisfaction. "In the change room, where we'd hung Bragg's clothes up to dry."

Kate took the bag from him and studied the belt. At first she didn't understand what he was on about. Then she noticed the studs. A whole line of them at the top of the belt and another at the bottom.

"Holy..." she whispered.

"And it matches!" McKell was practically crowing. "And Winnipeg called. They searched the Silverado they impounded and found fresh scratch marks in the leather armrest." He raised an eyebrow. "How much do you want to bet the leather will match what's under Lawson's nails?"

Kate grinned.

"That would be a sucker bet," she objected.

* * *

Kate sat in her office for an hour, ordering her thoughts and making notes on a yellow pad. She needed McKell to guide the interview carefully—if there was to be one. Bragg had refused counsel but he might change his mind. It always amazed her how people waived their rights to counsel for fear asking for a lawyer would make them look guilty.

Not asking for one made them look stupid, as far as she was concerned.

She checked her phone again, in case she had missed the telltale buzz of an incoming text, but there wasn't one.

She'd texted Marco, letting him know they were going to interview Bragg if he wanted to watch. He might have been cleared of Lawson's murder, but it would still be unethical to let him sit in on the interview.

That was almost an hour ago, and he still hadn't responded.

Hmm.

Finally she stood up, gathered pen and pad, and walked out of her office. McKell walked out of his when he heard her. He was carrying a flat box.

"Are you sure you don't want to sit in?" he asked.

Kate shook her head.

"No. I'll watch and listen. If you need something, I'll bring it in. Otherwise, we won't interrupt you."

He nodded.

"I'll take those, too." He nodded to the pad and pen in her hands. She handed them over and they parted ways, McKell through the ident room to their tiny interview room and Kate to the break room to fetch two glasses of water.

When she walked out, she paused at the opening to the duty desk. O'Hara looked at her questioningly.

"The recording is set up?" she asked.

"Yes, ma'am," said O'Hara, nodding to his computer. Kate glanced at the monitor. It showed McKell in the interview room, placing the box on the corner of the table and the pad in front of the chair he would use. He flipped the pad over so Bragg wouldn't be able to read what was on it.

"Holmes will stay, just in case," he added.

Kate smiled. What he meant was that he wanted someone else to answer the phone so he could watch the interviews.

After interviewing the vet last spring, she had requisitioned—and obtained—a camera for the interview room. It felt a little like putting pearls on a pig, but she didn't care. A video recording was always better than a plain voice recording.

"All right," she said. "Bring him in."

She went to the interview room, handed McKell a glass of water and set one in front of Bragg's uncomfortable metal chair.

"Good luck," she told McKell and went back to the ident room, from where she would watch the interview.

No attempt had been made to hide the camera mounted in the corner of the interview room. The recording would capture both men, but anyone in the ident room would only see McKell's back through the one-way mirror.

She heard the tromp of heavy boots on the linoleum in the hallway, and a moment later, Holmes entered, leading Calder Bragg. Bragg looked at her as Holmes nodded him into the interview room. She didn't say anything. Let him see that the interview would be observed, as well as recorded. Inside, Holmes pulled back Bragg's chair and indicated that he should sit. Then Holmes left, closing the door behind him, and headed for the duty room, no doubt to replace O'Hara on the desk.

She wished she were the one doing the interview. She sensed a certain arrogance in Bragg. She suspected he would trip over it if it was just her in the room with him. But she couldn't. Shouldn't. She had too much inherent bias in the case.

Inside the interview room, McKell leaned over and glanced at Bragg's feet under the table. He was in his stocking feet.

"Your shoes are still wet?"

Bragg nodded. "It takes a while for leather to dry."

McKell reached over to the box mounted at the far end of the table by the wall and pressed the switch that would turn on the video and voice recordings. He recited the date and time before identifying himself.

"This is Mendenhall Deputy Chief of Police Rob McKell interviewing Calder Bragg. Mr. Bragg, I know you've been read your rights several times, but I will repeat them for the recording." His voice was calm. She wished she could see his face.

Calder Bragg's eyes had gotten wider as McKell began the routine that always preceded an interview. His mouth flattened and he looked pale.

As if he hadn't truly believed this was happening until now.

"Mr. Bragg, you are under arrest for the murder of your wife, Kelly Lawson. You have the right to remain silent. You have the right to legal counsel. If you don't have a lawyer, or can't afford one, we can provide you with the phone number for a lawyer referral service, including for a Legal Aid lawyer. Now that I have told you your rights, are you still willing to talk to me, or do you want to retain a lawyer now?"

He had kept his voice neutral, so as not to influence Bragg's decision. Bragg stared at McKell for a few moments, but she doubted he was actually seeing the DC. Was he considering his options?

Finally, he shrugged.

"Thank you, Chief McKell. But I didn't kill my wife. I don't need a lawyer."

McKell nodded. "That's Deputy Chief," he said mildly.

Kate studied Bragg through the glass. The man looked so damned sincere.

"You can change your mind at any time," continued McKell. "Let's get started. How did you and your wife get along?"

Whatever Bragg was expecting, that wasn't it.

He shrugged again.

"We got on fine. Some arguments, of course. But essentially, we were still newlyweds."

McKell nodded. He flipped over the yellow notepad and looked down at it. "But you hadn't known her long before you married."

Bragg looked surprised. "I knew what I needed to know."

"Did you know about Adamos? Her old boyfriend?"

Bragg's mouth tightened and he looked down at the table where his fists had suddenly clenched.

"She told me about him. Not his name, though." He shook his head and a look of bewilderment swept over his face. Kate thought it was genuine. "Why would she want to go back to him, after everything he'd done to her?"

McKell didn't answer. Instead, he came at it from another angle.

"The medical examiner set your wife's time of death at around six p.m. on Sunday, August 26. Can you tell me where you were at that point?"

Bragg's eyes closed as if in pain. Then he opened them and looked at McKell. "I was in Winnipeg," he said. "I went there at around lunch time and I stayed the night. I returned early the next day for work."

"Where did you stay in Winnipeg?"

"Some cheap motel on Portage Avenue. I probably still have the receipt in my wallet. You have the wallet."

Kate didn't doubt he did have a receipt. It would be easy enough to rent a room, park his Lariat in front of it, and then call a cab to take him to wherever he had stashed the Silverado.

"Why did you go to Winnipeg?" asked McKell.

Bragg sighed and leaned back.

"I needed to get away," he said.

"Tell me more about that," said McKell. "What did you do? Who did you see?"

"I went to a nearby bar for a drink. No, I don't remember the name. After a while I realized I didn't want to see other people so I went back to my room."

"Did you talk to anyone?"

Bragg shook his head. "Just the bartender, to ask for a drink. I doubt he remembers me. There were a lot of people there."

How convenient. He didn't remember the name of the bar or talk to anyone.

"When you were notified of your wife's murder," said McKell, "you informed us that you threw her out because you were sick of her lies. Can you tell me more about that?"

Bragg shrugged and looked down at the table.

"She told me it was over with her old boyfriend. That there was no one else. That she loved me." He glanced up at McKell. "She told me he used to beat her up and she still went back to him."

"Can you tell me how you know she went back to him?"

Bragg looked surprised.

"Isn't it obvious?"

Kate studied his face. His jaw was tight, the muscles bunched in the corners. He had no proof, but he truly believed Lawson had lied to him.

She looked around as Holmes returned to the ident room where she was observing. He handed her a cup of coffee and she nodded her thanks.

"Where did you go yesterday?" asked McKell. "After your house burned down?"

To Kate's surprise, Bragg's eyes filled with tears. He blinked them away and took a deep breath.

"It was just too much. You know?" He looked at McKell and then looked away. "I just started driving and kept driving. I ended up in Dauphin. Spent the night there. The next day I drove to Winnipeg. I was going to get good and drunk and spend the night there but, in the end, I just wanted to go home. To Brandon, I mean, since I didn't have a home anymore. I needed to deal with insurance and figure out where to go from here."

McKell shook his head slightly. "Mr. Bragg," he said patiently. "We looked through your suitcase when we pulled out dry clothes for you. We found insurance papers, birth certificates—for yourself and your wife—mortgage papers, and a few keepsakes. How did they escape the fire? People don't normally keep those items on their person."

Because he was planning to burn down his house, thought Kate. Anger seeped through her, pushing out any objectivity she might have had left.

That bastard.

"Now you're accusing me of burning down my own house?" Bragg looked shocked but Kate just didn't believe him any more. "Why would I do that?"

McKell shrugged and didn't answer the question. "Why were you on the highway last night? In the middle of a storm?"

Beside her, Holmes muttered, "Because he figured no one would be looking for him in the storm."

"I couldn't sleep," said Bragg, "so I decided to go back to Brandon." He shrugged again but Kate wasn't fooled. "I wasn't worried about the storm. I have a good truck. I can't tell you how surprised I was to be stopped at a barricade and arrested."

Kate cocked her head. Maybe looking at him from a different angle would help her see him more clearly.

But no.

"We'd been looking for you since the fire," said McKell. "Winnipeg and Brandon, too. We were worried that you might hurt yourself after the fire, on top of losing your wife. Then we found a truck that looked exactly like Christopher Adamos' truck. I believe you've met him, when he came to tell you your wife was leaving you. Do you know anything about the truck we found?"

Bragg's eyebrows rose in surprise.

"Of course not. Why not ask Adamos? He probably abandoned the truck in Winnipeg."

McKell was tense, Kate could tell. It was there in the bunching of his shoulders. She felt the same way and found herself leaning forward a little.

O'Hara joined her and Holmes in front of the one-way glass. He gave Holmes a look and the man sighed and left to staff the duty desk.

"I didn't say that we found the truck in Winnipeg," said McKell mildly.

Bragg looked uncomfortable but shrugged. "An assumption."

McKell nodded and looked down at the yellow pad again. His

fingers traced down the page until it stopped about halfway down.

"The plates on the truck—B.C. plates—came back stolen. We dusted the truck for fingerprints and found yours," he said softly. "Can you explain that?"

The slightly smug look on Bragg's face faded away, replaced by anger.

"I see you're determined to pin Kelly's death on me," he said with dignity. "I would like to speak to a lawyer now." His cheeks were flushed and he crossed his arms over his chest.

McKell nodded. "Of course," he said smoothly. "But I want to answer a question you had, first."

"What question?" asked Bragg.

"You asked why Kelly would have gone back to Adamos. She didn't."

This time, Kate didn't think Bragg's surprised look was feigned.

McKell pulled the sheaf of papers from under the yellow pad. "Here," he said, placing the stapled pages on the table in front of Bragg, who made no move to look at them.

"What is it?"

"A transcript of text messages between Christopher Adamos and your wife."

Bragg's finger reached out and drew the pages to him. He sat for a few minutes, reading page after page. Finally he looked up.

"I don't understand…"

"It's very simple, Mr. Bragg. Christopher Adamos is an abusive son of a bitch. When Kelly finally plucked up the courage to leave him, in Williams Lake, she had a peace bond against him, forcing him to stay away from her. Then she moved to Vancouver, where she met you. I think she was probably happy there. Then something happened. She might have seen Adamos, I don't know. Whatever it was, it spooked her enough that she persuaded you to take the job in Brandon. And that was fine, too, for a while, but Adamos found her again. Only this time, he was threatening you, the man she loved. She left you so Adamos wouldn't hurt you."

Bragg looked down at the transcript again, his hand brushing the page.

"Why didn't she tell me?" he whispered. His face was blotchy and the hand touching the pages trembled.

McKell shrugged.

"I don't know. My guess is she didn't want you involved because she knew what Adamos was capable of. The problem was she didn't know what you were capable of."

McKell placed the transcript on top of the pad, then placed both on top of the box. "Interview terminated at…" he glanced at his watch. "13:30 by Deputy Chief Rob McKell." He stood up and gathered the box and the yellow pad.

Wait for it, thought Kate. Wait.

Bragg looked haggard, as if he'd aged ten years in the last few minutes.

"I didn't know," he murmured. "I thought she was cheating on me."

"And for that she deserved to die, along with your unborn child?" asked McKell softly.

Bragg winced as if McKell had struck him.

"We'll get you a phone, Mr. Bragg, to contact your lawyer." Then he reached over and toggled off the recording switch.

O'Hara shook himself and opened the door to the interview room. He motioned Bragg up and led him back to his cell. McKell followed them out and stood next to Kate, watching O'Hara and Bragg disappear into the hallway.

"You didn't confront him about the belt," said Kate, still watching the door.

McKell sighed.

"We'll need to interview him again with his lawyer. We can bring up the belt then."

Kate nodded and accepted the yellow pad and the box. It contained Bragg's belt. They were sending it to the lab, where she was sure they would find epithelials that would match Lawson.

Then there was the substance under Kelly's nails, which the lab had identified as leather. That would match the leather seat on the bogus Silverado.

"My guess," said McKell, "is that when Adamos came to Bragg's house and demanded he let Kelly go, that was the last straw. He's probably the jealous type. Kelly was an attractive woman, she would have gotten lots of male attention. And Bragg couldn't handle it. So he decided to kill his wife and frame Mr. Adamos."

Kate nodded. "He probably found Trepalli's business card in his wife's purse at some point. He probably suspected her of having an affair with him. So Bragg decided to muddy the waters and leave the card in her hand. He didn't care who got blamed, as long as it wasn't him." She took a deep breath, trying to regain her calm.

McKell frowned. "Just how many murderers did he think we'd need?"

Kate nodded. "I'll bet he stalked Trepalli, found out who his friends were, decided to leave Kelly's body in the Hurst's canola field." She shook her head. What a waste. What a complete waste.

"We'll be getting his phone records, credit cards expenses— and anything else we can think of," said McKell, heading for the door. "Don't worry. The case is solid."

Yes, it was. They had enough to hold him until he could see a judge on Monday. By then, all the paperwork would be ready and they could hand the case over to the Crown with a bow on it.

She headed for her office. Holmes was still on the duty desk, talking on the phone, and she could hear O'Hara's voice from the cell area. She closed her office door behind her and leaned against it, suddenly awash in fatigue.

When they got the phone company records, she was willing to bet they would find proof of him calling Kelly at the hotel, probably on the room phone, since he would have known they would check her cell phone records. He probably persuaded her to meet him, probably in the parking lot of the hotel, where he would have been waiting in the Silverado.

Did he sweet-talk her? Tell her he was sorry? Offer to try again?

And Kelly went with him. She trusted him. He drove her somewhere nobody would see, then strangled her to death. He waited until it was dark, then he dumped her in a canola field like so much garbage, hoping to frame someone else for the murder.

In the end, he tried to frame both Adamos and Marco. Just in case.

She pushed away from the door and went to sit at her desk, setting the box and pad down. The day felt gloomier suddenly, even though the sun had been shining for the past few hours.

Bert was supervising the interview of the sales person who sold Bragg the truck in Winnipeg. He already had his students checking the parking lots in the area where Bragg abandoned the truck after killing Kelly. They would find where he parked his Lariat while he drove the Silverado back to Brandon. She had no idea what he had done with Kelly's clothes, but they had his. She stared at the box containing the belt that he had used to murder his wife. And child.

CHAPTER 35

Kate drove home three hours later. She had met with the JP and had Bragg held until the next court date—Wednesday, rather than Monday, as she had hoped. O'Hara was making arrangements to transport Bragg to remand in Winnipeg. In the meantime, McKell had been speaking to the Crown counsel and presenting the facts they had.

By Wednesday, they would have everything in place: the phone records, the parking lot where Bragg had left his Lariat, the epithelial match to Kelly Lawson from Bragg's belt, the match from the leather under Lawson's nails to the leather armrest in the Silverado... and hopefully a positive identification of Bragg by the salesperson at the Winnipeg lot where he had bought the Silverado.

For now, that was all she could do. Now she could spend her last evening with her family in peace and quiet.

But when she got home, they were all gone. She closed the front door and stood in the entrance listening to the silence. Where were they?

Then she heard a door open in the kitchen and Bert appeared from the deck in knee-length khaki shorts and a short-sleeved white shirt. He was barefoot.

"Hi," he said, walking over to kiss her. "How did it go?"

"Fine," she said. "We're shipping him over to you for remand."

"Did he lawyer up?"

Kate bent over and began unlacing her boots. "Yes. Doesn't matter. We've got the truck, the substance under her nails, and his belt—the murder weapon, we think. And pretty soon, we'll have his phone records."

It was hard to shake the sadness. Even the beautiful afternoon didn't help. The thought of Kelly Lawson finally escaping Adamos only to end up with an even worse monster...

"Hey," said Bert, drawing her up and putting his arms around her. "It's over. You got him."

Kate sighed. "Yes, we did. Thanks for your help." She pecked him on the cheek and stood back. "Where is everyone?"

"They're all at Marco and Amanda's place," he said. "They called both families and told them to show up for dinner for their last night here."

Kate's eyebrows rose.

"Well, that's a good sign. At least they're talking to each other."

Bert nodded.

"Go get changed. I was waiting on you."

Kate changed into red capris and a long white linen shirt and pulled out her fancy red sandals for the occasion. Maybe if she dressed cheerful, it would improve her mood.

Bert drove them in his Honda. The streets were slowly clearing of Saturday afternoon shoppers. It was getting on to dinnertime and too early for Saturday night revelries. The sun was well into its downward trajectory, sending long shadows across tree-lined streets. It was going to be a lovely evening.

The street in front of Amanda and Marco's house was crammed with cars and pickup trucks. Bert ended up parking on the next block over and they walked back, hand in hand.

The front door to the house was open, spilling sounds of laughter and talking out onto the front yard. By silent agreement, Kate and Bert walked up the driveway and around the back of the house.

Kate had expected the backyard to look forlorn without the tent and tables, but someone had moved half a dozen of the small tables that usually lived on the deck onto the lawn, with chairs to go with them. She saw Rose sitting with Camilla and Tina, and Mom and Fred, each with a glass of wine sitting in front of them. Charlie was on the deck, leaning on the railing, talking with Henry, Marco's dad. More bodies milled around the lawn and the deck.

"Isn't that Sean?" asked Bert, nodding to the deck.

Kate looked where he was pointing and saw Sean leaning on the deck railing, talking to a pretty girl who looked an awful lot like Marco.

"I thought you said he was shy," said Bert, watching Sean stroke the girl's bare arm.

Don't look, Kate told herself. Just don't look.

"Let's go find Amanda," she said instead, leading the way up the stairs. Once they were on the deck, Kate saw why tables had been moved to the lawn. Two long tables had been set against the wall of the house. They sagged under the weight of plastic-covered trays and plates. A few of the younger Trepallis were sneaking a taste of the contents. People greeted them as they went by and they waved back but went inside. The empty kitchen looked as if a wild wind had torn through but it smelled wonderful.

They heard voices coming from the other side of the wall and went through to the dining room. A few of the cousins—and maybe one of Marco's brothers?—were standing around the dining room, drinking beer and laughing. John and Paul, Marco's uncle, were coming around the tight corner of the stairwell from the basement with another long table with folding legs. They had to go out the front door to maneuver the table.

"How much food is there?" Bert blurted out.

John looked over his shoulder and grinned.

"Is there ever too much food?" he asked philosophically.

Two of the cousins went to help Paul and John and they managed to round the corner without damaging the walls.

At that moment, Marco and Amanda emerged from their spare bedroom and came toward them. Kate went to say something, then closed her mouth. Bert squeezed her hand and she glanced at him, but he was staring at Marco and Amanda.

There was something odd about them. They both had the same expression on their faces.

Amanda noticed them first.

"Oh good," she said. "You made it." She glanced at Marco and he nodded. He was dressed in jeans and a yellow shirt with the sleeves rolled up. Amanda wore a flowery summer dress with skinny straps and a fitted bodice and swirly skirt. They stood so close that their arms touched. They looked like everybody's idea of a perfect couple.

"Just leave the table here, Uncle Paul. Let's all go outside. Now that everyone's here, we have something to say."

Paul and John exchanged glances, as did Kate and Bert. The cousins looked uncomfortable, but everyone obediently trooped to the deck and spread out against the railing. The sun was beginning its long sweep down and cast shadows over the assembled.

Marco moved to the steps and called down to the people on the lawn.

"Could you come up here, please? Amanda and I have something to say."

He looked so serious that Kate's stomach began to flutter. What now?

Bert put his arm around her and snugged her up to his side.

Soon, everyone was gathered on the deck and staring at Amanda and Marco in trepidation. Two of the cousins had given up their seats for Mom and Fred. Rose stood next to John, and Charlie and Sean stood behind them.

Kate's stomach got ready to do a somersault.

"First," said Marco, "Amanda and I want to apologize for what we put you through this week. You all came here expecting a wedding, and instead, you got melodrama. We are so sorry. It really wasn't fair to you."

Camilla and Henry looked at each other, then looked back at Marco.

"We're all just sad that it didn't work out," said Henry. There were nods around the deck. Mom was looking intently at Amanda, and Kate turned to look at her, too. The girl's hands were clasped in front of her and there was a glow about her. Kate blinked in confusion.

"We decided it would only be fair to go see the marriage commissioner this morning and apologize to her, too," continued Marco.

"As it turned out," said Amanda, "she was still available." She turned to Marco, who fished something out of his pocket.

"So we got married," he said. He took Amanda's left hand and placed a wedding band on her finger, then handed her another band, which she placed on his finger.

They both turned to their assembled families and waited, trepidation warring with joy on the faces.

Kate turned to look at Bert, who was staring at the young couple in astonishment.

Into the silence, she said, "See? I told you they should have eloped!"

As if her words broke the paralysis, both sets of parents rushed forward and a great cheer rose up among the younger set.

CHAPTER 36

The following morning, Bert went to pick up Rose and John at Amanda and Marco's house while Charlie and Sean hooked the trailer onto the pickup truck and piled the suitcases inside the trailer to make enough room for everyone in the truck.

Kate watched them work for a bit, then went inside to check on Mom. She was wandering from room to room, making sure she hadn't forgotten anything, while Fred finished their packing.

"You have time for coffee," suggested Kate.

Mom looked around at her.

"That would be lovely, dear." She scanned the bathroom counter. "I was sure I had left my hairbrush here."

"It's packed away," called Fred from the bedroom.

Kate smiled and went to pour the coffee.

It had been a heck of a week. She had only managed to visit with her family in snippets here and there, and now they were leaving. None of them seemed to hold it against her, however.

According to Rose, the newlyweds had already left for their camping honeymoon. Kate had been smiling since last night. She had so hoped that they would reconcile.

The celebration had lasted well into the night, with toast after toast to the newlyweds. Then, as the party broke up, there had been goodbyes and promises to keep in touch. Sean had looked woebegone as he said goodbye to Maria, Marco's sister, but Kate suspected there would be a trip to Toronto in his near future.

And when they got home, Bert, Charlie, Sean, and John each took a corner of the picnic table and walked it over to Mrs. Buckley's backyard. Mom had bought a flower arrangement as a thank you for Kate's neighbor, but it was too late to bring it over. Kate promised to do it in the morning.

She finished fixing their coffees just as Mom entered the kitchen. Today she wore a pair of loose navy cotton pants and a striped navy-and-white top with three-quarter-length sleeves and a pair of white slip-on shoes that would be comfortable for the flight back. Her hair was up in its customary bun. She looked fresh and rested, as if she hadn't gone to bed way too late.

"Thank you, dear," she said, taking the stool next to Kate's.

They sipped in comfortable silence for a while. Finally Kate pushed her cup away.

"I'm sorry this visit was so... disjointed," she said. "I feel like I hardly got to see you. Any of you."

Mom took another sip before answering.

"Kate, never apologize for your dedication to your job. The work you do is important. We all understand that. And we're all very proud of you."

Kate felt herself blushing and shifted uncomfortably on her stool. "I could have delegated."

Mom laughed. "It's not in your nature, dear."

Kate grinned, in spite of herself. "How about we come down at Christmas?" she suggested. "It's usually pretty quiet at that time of year. We could spend a week and get a good visit in."

Mom looked at her and slowly arched an eyebrow. "Or you could spend two weeks and get a very good visit in."

"Sounds like a plan," Kate laughed.

At that moment, Bert returned with Rose and John. Fred emerged from Kate's bedroom with his and Mom's suitcases and Kate went to take one from him only to have him frown at her with mock severity.

"I'm not quite feeble yet, young lady."

The three of them went outside and Fred brought the suitcases to Charlie, who tossed them up to Sean inside the trailer. John and Bert brought the suitcases from Bert's car, and next thing Kate knew, the trailer was loaded, the door was locked, and they were all saying their goodbyes.

Charlie hugged her fiercely and whispered in her ear, "You've made a good life for yourself, sis. I'm happy for you."

To her surprise, tears sprang up in her eyes.

"Thanks, Charlie. Next time I'll come and check out St. John's."

"Absolutely," he said. "I'll even let you take the bed."

Rose cried as she hugged Kate, but they were tears of joy. Her baby was married and now she looked forward to grandchildren. John gave her a sound kiss on the cheek and a quick hug, and Sean tried to smile through his gloom as he hugged her.

"It's just a short flight from Halifax to Toronto," she said quietly as he released her. He nodded and smiled slightly.

She gave Fred a quick hug and a kiss, and then it was Mom's turn. They hugged long and hard and both had tears in their eyes when they finally let go.

Bert shook hands with the men but hugged Rose and Mom.

Then everybody got in the truck with Charlie behind the wheel, and the pickup slowly started rolling down the driveway, the trailer following behind. Kate and Bert followed behind and stopped on the sidewalk to watch her family leave.

Charlie rolled down the window and stuck a hand out to wave goodbye.

Kate and Bert waved back.

"By the way," she said as they stared at the receding trailer. "I told Mom we'd come down for Christmas."

Bert glanced at her. "Really?"

She turned to face him. "Yes. And I was thinking maybe we could see if Marco and Amanda's marriage commissioner could make time for us."

Bert's eyes lit up but his expression was uncertain.

"As in... to marry us?"

Kate nodded and smiled at the man she loved.

"Yes, but only if we elope."

Bert whooped with joy and swung her off her feet.

THE END

Dear Reader,

Thank you for reading *The Wronged Woman*. It is my sixth Mendenhall Mystery and I hope you enjoyed it. If you did, please consider leaving a review wherever you purchased the story, or on Goodreads.

Reviews are valuable, no matter what rating you give the story. Reviews make the book more visible in online stores and give potential readers a sense of whether or not they would like to read it themselves.

If you would like to join my mailing list to receive (very) occasional updates on my upcoming novels, short stories and writing news, please drop me a line at marcelle.dube@gmail.com.

You can find me on Facebook here: https://www.facebook.com/marcelle.dube.3 and on Twitter here: https://twitter.com/marcelledube?lang=en. And my web site is at www.marcellemdube.com. Come visit.

Thanks, and happy reading!

Marcelle

About Marcelle Dubé:

Marcelle Dubé grew up near Montreal. After trying out a number of different provinces—not to mention Belgium—she settled in the Yukon for 35 years before moving to Alberta. She finds that Albertans are the same as Yukoners in all the ways that count. She has a number of novels in print and ebook and her award-winning short fiction has appeared in magazines and anthologies. Learn more about her and her published work at www.marcellemdube.com.

BOOKS BY THE AUTHOR

Mendenhall Mysteries series:
The Shoeless Kid
The Tuxedoed Man
The Weeping Woman
The Untethered Woman
The Forsaken Man
The Wronged Woman

The A'lle Chronicles series:
Backli's Ford
Epidemic

Standalone novels:
Ghosts of Morocco
Identity Withheld
Jilimar
Kirwan's Son
Obeah
On Her Trail
Shelter

www.ingramcontent.com/pod-product-compliance
Lightning Source LLC
Chambersburg PA
CBHW021003260626
47169CB00006B/1911

* 9 7 8 1 9 8 7 9 3 7 3 0 5 *